Kingdom of
the Shades

A FIVE DIRECTIONS PRESS BOOK

Kingdom of the Shades

A NOVEL

C. P. LESLEY

TARKEI CHRONICLES 2

ISBN-13 978-0692264492
ISBN-10 0692264493

Published in the United States of America.

A Five Directions Press book

Cover images: pointe shoes © Hitdelight/Shutterstock; Reed Flute Cave, Guangxi, China © Bernt Rostad via Fotopedia, Creative Commons Attribution 3.0 Unported license. For terms, see http://creativecommons.org/licenses/by/3.0.

Book and cover design by Five Directions Press
Five Directions Press logo designed by Colleen Kelley

FIVE DIRECTIONS PRESS

Contents

❀   *i*   ❀

MORE BY C. P. LESLEY
Legends of the Five Directions
The Golden Lynx (1: West)
The Winged Horse (2: East)

The Not Exactly Scarlet Pimpernel

Tarkei Chronicles
Desert Flower

All my books are available in print, and most of them can also be found in Kindle and ePub formats. To stay up-to-date on my publishing plans for this and other novels, check my blog at blog.cplesley.com or my publisher's site (www.fivedirectionspress.com). I love to hear from readers, so if you have any questions about my books, please e-mail me. You can find current contact information on my blog.

Although much of *Kingdom of the Shades* stands alone, the action rests on the story developed in *Desert Flower*. As a result, I recommend reading that book first.

If you enjoy this book, please consider leaving a review at your favorite online bookseller and/or Internet book club. It will help other readers find it.

Bourrée

CHOLI WALKED THROUGH THE tunnels toward the girls' cave, thinking of what her teacher had told her. To her right, she saw a crack in the rock, an alcove just large enough to sit in. She went to it, crossed her legs under her, and placed her hands, palms up, on her knees. Anyone who saw her meditating would not interrupt her, and she needed solitude. The chatter of the girls' cave would distract her.

Choli closed her eyes, trying to picture her teacher as he had portrayed himself just now. A younger Danion— much younger, tall and slender and strong, but with hair as glossy black as Choli's own. He was a handsome man in middle age, with lean features and a clean, sharp-angled face, black eyes, and olive skin. The diamond-shaped ears of their shared heritage on him had a particular elegance, set off by the garnet earring he had retained from his years as a priest. These days, he had an extraordinary quality of stillness, as though nothing quite touched him; a gentle serenity and wisdom. Choli could hear, for life on the streets had taught her the importance of nuance, his shifts of mood and expression, but others often complained that Danion had no feelings.

Even so, she found it difficult to imagine him as he had appeared in the story he had told her: passionate and rebellious and proud; so attracted to his human wife that they had formed the spontaneous mental link that his people called the joining; so deeply in love that, uncounted years later, he could not tell Choli how she died. Pictures from the story tumbled together in her head. Danion embracing his sister, arguing with his father, teasing his Pannthu friend Thuja, kissing his wife just to see what it felt like, although Tarkei's rigid customs did not permit kissing.

It seemed incredible. She was not accustomed to thinking of him as a person, like anyone else, confused and uncertain and vulnerable. At thirteen, Choli wanted her mentor to have all the answers; for a moment, she resented his showing her other facets of himself. Yet it was flattering, too. Danion was a very private person; who else in the caves knew that he had once been married, let alone joined? He had treated her, briefly, as an adult, worthy of his confidence.

And was the story so out of character? Choli thought of everything she knew of Danion—pilot and diplomat, scientist and priest. In his way, he continued to chart his own course. How many people leave a comfortable home and travel halfway across the galaxy to lead a civil disobedience movement against a government known for its atrocities? Danion had; otherwise she would not have met him. And he had taken her in, a child of the streets. Not many people would do that, either. A few moments ago, he had called her his daughter, had told her she reminded him of Sasha, the dead wife he loved.

Choli dropped her head on her knees. Perhaps the Tarkei were right to view love as the greatest form of disorder. She had loved her mother, and her mother had died, abandoning her to a childhood of poverty and scorn. Danion loved Sasha, and Sasha died, leaving him in grief so profound he could not talk about it. Now she, Choli, loved Danion, the father she had never had, and he perhaps loved her. What would happen to them?

She thought of Danion's wife as he had described her: a human woman who danced on her toes, black-haired and gray-eyed, just tall enough for her head to reach his chin but strong—stronger than anyone would think to look at her—graceful and flexible and beautiful, resilient and warm. She imagined Sasha's partner—a big, blond, brown-eyed Russian named Slava, who had made Danion jealous for a while. What had they looked like, dancing together? She could not imagine.

Her thoughts returned to the joining. She and Danion came from the same species, although they had grown up on different planets. Once Choli's people, the Kazrati, had lived on Tarkei's giant moon, Orbfire. They had destroyed Orbfire's environment with their warfare, then taken their violent ways into space, leaving their Tarkei siblings to develop in a different direction. A century later, they reached Kazratan, and there they stayed. But her people and Danion's came from the same genetic stock. If he could conquer the odds, however high, and meet his soul mate, could she? And if she could, did she want to, knowing the price she might pay?

❋

In the cave Choli had left, Danion of Tarkei held a pink satin shoe up to the candle flame. With one finger he traced the Tarkei script, so familiar after sixty years that he did not need to see the writing to know what it said. "For thee, *kaleita*, may the stars always smile—Alessandra Sinclair." Sasha, his *kaleita*, his bond mate. Perhaps he should not have surrendered to the urge to tell Choli her story. What had he thought, that the child would accept the happy ending and go about her business, comforted?

Choli was not that kind of child. Of course, she asked what happened next. And Danion, while he had not answered, was left with the memories.

He rested his head on the rough wall behind him, the silky fabric warm in his palm. The shoe, worked over to a ballerina's exacting specifications, had a living quality to it, that mixture of hard and soft edges that gives life its savor and its challenge.

In this part of the story, though, most of the edges were hard. Danion, once priest of the suns, pressed his back against the stone and allowed himself to remember.

1. Penché

"FONDU AND STRETCH, AND side and stretch, and back and stretch, and side, relevé." Camille Delagardie, ballet mistress of the Xantera Ballet Company, perched on a stool, the tiny studio's one concession to comfort, and snapped her fingers in time to the music produced by the starship speakers. An elegant woman, with dark eyes and hair, highlighted by a dramatic white streak, and the aristocratic bearing of a classical dancer.

Alessandra Sinclair, prima ballerina, cast her an occasional glance as she bent and stretched. Camille was in her element. True, she had only two people to boss around today instead of her usual seventy, but those two—Alessandra and her partner, Viacheslav Zoshchenko, nicknamed Slava—were high on the list of Camille's favorite people to boss. For the next four weeks, they could expect to receive her full attention.

Not that Alessandra, known as Sasha throughout the allied planets, minded. Camille's autocratic style masked a warm heart and a formidable dedication to her art. These qualities of hers had made Sasha, and Slava as well, interplanetary stars. Sinclair and Zoshchenko, people said, as they had once said Nureyev and Fonteyn. On occasion, it happened, these inspired pairings of dancers. Here the credit belonged to Sasha's parents, who had seen the potential when Sasha and Slava were children. Her parents were dead now; they had lived long enough to see the partnership's initial flowering but not the acclaim that had greeted it in the last two years. And here they were, on their way to an off-season gala for the president of Chandar, one of Tarkei's newest allies.

"Double time. And up, and up, and up, and up, and balance, and hold, and hold. Other side," the human metronome said. Sasha spun at the barre. From here she could see herself in the mirror. She could be any dancer in any studio in the galaxy: long hair confined in a bun at the nape of her neck; eyes intently searching for flaws; long dancers' legs and a slim body clad in leotard, tights, and pointe shoes. Danion said she was beautiful, but as her husband he was prejudiced. She tried to move beautifully, at least.

They had finished this exercise. Sasha turned again, facing her partner's muscular back. Slava, close as a brother. For a while, they might have become closer, but that ended long before she met Danion.

"Frappé," Camille said. "Double front, double side, double back, double side. Same in relevé. Passé and hold; outside pirouette from fifth. Reverse. Cambré in all directions. Balance in fifth, hold, other side."

Yes, ma'am. The music resumed at a faster tempo, and Sasha had to concentrate on beating her feet front and back of the ankle, or back and front, depending on the direction. She repeated the series on pointe, pulled her right foot up to the level of her left knee, balanced, brought it down, turned 360 degrees, and reversed the whole combination.

Whew, the difficult part was over. Bending forward from the hips, she spared a thought for Danion, who should have been here, piloting the shuttle, but who at the last minute had received a call from his father, the prime minister of Tarkei. Prime Minister Jenat required his best pilot for a diplomatic mission of some urgency; and Danion, grumbling, had acquiesced. What was he doing at this moment?

In response to Camille's chanted commands, Sasha returned to an upright position, then arched backward. Again she returned to center and began to sweep her upper body toward the barre, then away. As she did, she touched the mental link that joined her to her husband, querying him. The link was thin, evidence of how much distance separated them from Tarkei, but she could hear him. He sat in the midst of dinner with his family—his lively sister, Iqara; her human husband, Geoffrey Anderson; and Jenat, austere as ever on the surface but unable to conceal the pleasure he felt at the return of his only son.

Don't forget to thank him for me, she said along the link. It was because of Jenat that they had a place to practice: most shuttles do not come equipped with studios, no matter how small. This one was particularly pleasant— wood paneling and a wall of mirrors, as well as the barre set into one wall. If they started in the far corner and chose their steps carefully, they almost had room for center practice.

I did, Danion said. You are well?

Missing you, she said. Otherwise, fine. And you?

The same.

Camille left her stool and walked around the studio, touching a shoulder here, a hip there, more as reminder than as correction.

Sasha balanced on pointe, feet tightly crossed in fifth position, arms in an open circle around her head. "Fingers," Camille said.

Sasha looked up. Sure enough, one palm tilted toward Slava's back, where the audience would be if they were performing. She corrected it and, in response to the music's signal, turned, left foot replacing the right in front, bent her knees and pointed the left foot to begin the routine on the other side.

Again, the frappés demanded her attention, but when she reached the cambrés, she allowed her thoughts to return to Danion. He had left only four days ago, and as she had told him, she missed him already: the glint in his dark eyes; the short black hair that was so much fun to run her fingers through; the laughter that bubbled along the link even when he appeared most serious.

She sighed. Weeks would pass before she saw him again, unless he could finish the diplomatic mission early. He had promised to come to Chandar and fly her home, if he could. Balancing on the other side, Sasha hoped he would make it.

Adagio. Her favorite section, even if the long, slow movements intended to build stamina and grace were, in their way, as difficult as the rapid-fire footwork. Sasha loved the challenge of holding herself just right, extending her leg as high as she could, finding that special place inside herself where she was truly centered.

She was in arabesque penché when the floor disappeared. Leaning forward, one hand on the barre, left leg forming a straight line with the right, balanced on the toes of one foot, she had no way to save herself even when it reappeared an instant later. She crashed, the waxed wood bruising her cheek. Slava rolled over her, and Camille tumbled into her other side.

Her last thought was that she could no longer sense Danion. Then the ceiling caved in.

In Tarkakhan, Tarkei's capital city, Danion stood to say goodbye, hands held palm upward in respect for his father. Jenat stretched out his own hands, but they never connected.

A force, inconceivably strong, ripped through Danion, toppling him with the power of a sandstorm in the desert. He dropped into a ball, arms wrapped around his head. His father's home flashed out of existence. Voices bombarded him with questions. They might have been speaking machine language, for all the sense they made.

A pair of hands touched his shoulders. He heard Geoff's voice, sharp with concern. "Come on, brother. You'll be fine. We can't help until you tell us what's happening."

From an impossible distance, Danion drew on his resources—the years of Tarkei training in emotional control—and pulled himself toward the present. The voices had become a babble of worry by the time his head broke through the force field and he could breathe.

Geoff's dark eyes looked into his. Iqara, the family doctor, touched a professional hand to his right ear. His father had not moved, but Danion could see the tremor in those outstretched hands.

"No," he said to Geoffrey, to the three of them. His voice shook, but he did not care. "I am not fine. Sasha is dead."

※

The babble resumed, louder. Danion lay on the floor. He felt numb.

He touched the place in his mind where the link had been. Not more than five minutes ago, Sasha would respond. Now an aching void had opened where the golden thread had stretched; even his tears were frozen, swallowed by the vacuum of space.

Geoff's voice broke through the blanket of pain. "Are you sure?"

"Yes," Danion said. He sounded like an automaton, something else he could not help. "Quite certain."

His family reacted, each face reflecting grief in its own way. Iqara wept the tears her brother could not. Geoff had no expression—always the case when his feelings ran deep. Jenat, normally the most controlled of the three, could have been a statue, so still had he become, except for his eyes, which had the stricken look of a wounded bear.

Danion lay on the floor, searching for the bond that was no longer there.

※

Three days later, the report reached the prime minister's office. The shuttle carrying Sasha, Slava, and Camille had vanished into a vortex in space. The government of Chandar sent its apologies. It knew the vortex existed, but somehow it had been omitted from the charts submitted to the allied planets during negotiations. Decades had passed since the last ship was swallowed, but no ship that entered the vortex returned.

Danion listened without a word as his father gave him the details. In the last three days, he had not spoken to anyone, had neither slept nor eaten. Some inner resistance to displaying his grief to the world had prompted him to bathe and comb his hair, so his grooming, as usual, was impeccable. Comfort had become something beyond his comprehension.

Bad as he had felt before, he felt worse now. He should be furious: what use was an apology to him? Instead, most of what he experienced was guilt. A pilot as skilled as he would not have fallen into a vortex, charted or not. He should have been there; he should have prevented it. Some part of him recognized this as absurd, a vain striving for control.

It did not help. Death with Sasha was preferable to decades alone.

"What will you do?" his father asked. Jenat was showing unusual patience; Danion had long since lost track of the moment when the report ended. His silence had become oppressive, he supposed.

A vision formed before his eyes. Rusty sands separated from a rusty sky by mountains of granite and obsidian. Silver birds gliding, sparks glittering through their wings as the three suns rose. A face, kind and concerned: Sendar, his mentor when he lived there, and the only person he knew who might understand how the loss of Sasha affected her surviving husband.

"The mountain," Danion said. "I shall go to the mountain."

His father frowned. "Not that again."

"I don't plan to rejoin the priesthood," Danion said. Jenat looked relieved. "It served its purpose when I was there, but much has changed since. I would like to visit for a time, though, while I learn to accustom myself to Sasha's death." He stopped, fighting for control, and saw his father's face twist in sympathy.

"It's bad, boy." Jenat always called him "boy" when he was feeling affectionate.

Danion shook his head. "You cannot imagine."

Jenat grimaced, and Danion winced. His father had also lost a wife unexpectedly and at a young age: Danion's own mother, killed in an assassination attempt against the prime minister eighteen years before.

"I'm sorry," Danion said. "I didn't mean it that way. Of course, you do know much of what it's like. More than I can imagine, perhaps. Maybe you feel responsible, as I do. It's only..." He stopped. Why go on? He had no real understanding of what his father had experienced, and hurting Jenat did nothing for himself.

"It's only that we were not joined. I know, boy." Jenat picked up the ceremonial pen stand that had been a gift from some unknown dignitary and stared at it as though it contained the secrets of the universe. "And Sendar was. I know that, too." The pen stand returned to the desk with a thump. Jenat rubbed his fingers. "You're right. I can't tell how that changes things. It was bad enough when your mother died." His mouth twisted again. "You're not the only one who feels responsible. I could have found another pilot."

From somewhere, Danion mustered a rueful half-smile. "It seems that neither of us has perfect foresight."

Jenat walked around the desk, sat on its edge, and flicked his son's garnet earring, symbol of the sanctuary with its promise of reconciliation. "Something to remember, boy, when you're on the mountain. And when you come home."

Danion stood. His hand brushed Jenat's shoulder. "Thank you, father."

Sendar was waiting for Danion when he landed the shuttle. Danion came down the steps, too exhausted even to appreciate the stark loveliness of the desert, the silence that had lured him here. The peace he remembered lay out there, far away.

"Father told you I was coming," he said to Sendar.

The older man flicked his ear in welcome. "Of course. He is concerned, as am I."

Danion brushed a hand through his hair. "Thank you." He should explain that it had brought him and Jenat closer, this shared experience of grief, but the explanation required more energy than he had. Sendar seemed to understand; he usually did.

"I'm glad to see you," Danion said. It was true. Sendar's lean face, covered in lines and wrinkles, skin dried by the desert heat, looked as healthy and as spry as ever.

A lively mummy, Sasha had once called him. For a moment, Danion felt tears gather, but they did not fall. The years of Tarkei training ran deep.

Sendar watched, black eyes bright in his leathery face. Danion swung his bag over his shoulder and extended a hand toward his mentor.

"I feel nothing," he said, his voice flat even in his own ears. "I might as well be dead. As she is."

Sendar took the outstretched hand in his. "Come, Danion. I will show you your room. There is not much I can tell you that time will not say for itself, but you will have someone to talk to."

Danion sat in the window seat of a stone cell, not unlike the one he had occupied when he lived here. Marginally more comfortable, because these were guest quarters, but bare of furniture and ornamentation. From his window he saw the small mountain where he used to attempt meditation every morning at suns' rise. He had loved it there, so quiet and so beautiful, his own cherished hideaway.

He had first met Sasha there. Two years ago, in another life.

At his request, the computer was playing Ravel's *Pavane for a Dead Child*. Danion leaned his head against the rough stone of the window. From the garden below, faint scents rose. Except for the music and occasional birdsong, there was no noise at all.

No demands, no need to keep up appearances, no interaction with others unless he chose it—these elements of life on the mountain, taken for granted during his days as a priest, offered a lifeline. Here, wrapped in his cocoon, he could face reality at his own pace.

2. Chassé

FOR THREE MONTHS, DANION stayed in the sanctuary. Occasionally Sendar stopped by, listened if he wanted to talk, and went on, hands folded in his sleeves, the picture of serenity. The agony of the bond's dissolution faded into a chronic ache, like a sore tooth, then transformed itself into a scar, the kind that gave off sharp twinges under certain conditions in case he had forgotten it was there. The bandage of silence, once essential, became tight, then uncomfortable. Danion realized it was time to go home. Time to put his life back together, if he could. He said goodbye to Sendar, not without regret but secure in the understanding that he could return if he needed to.

Late that afternoon, he stood at the entrance to his house in Tarkakhan. He pressed his hand against the lock, and the gate in the adobe wall swung open. The garden, filled with flowers of numerous planets, beckoned him in. Against the far wall, he saw the bank of azaleas that had, on one memorable day, reminded Sasha of her ravaged home planet. The scar shot out a bolt of pain. Danion flinched.

Basalt pebbles crunched under his feet as he walked down the path. The house, an adobe triangle trimmed in red wood, welcomed him. The bank of windows on the shady side, where the living room and his study were, stood open; the sunny side had only slits.

The furniture on the porch was not as he had left it. Someone had aligned it in perfect order.

Danion cast his mind back three months. He did not remember contacting the estate agent and asking her to look after the house; he had not intended to stay away for long.

Could he have called and forgotten it? The ten days between the moment he had experienced Sasha's death and his departure for the mountain were hazy; it was possible. Or perhaps his father had done it, after whatever Jenat considered an appropriate amount of time had passed. Danion shrugged one shoulder at the door and went inside.

In the hallway, he froze. The door to the living room stood open; he could see right through the room to the outside wall, beyond the floor-to-ceiling windows. Against the far window stood a slender form cast in flowing draperies, its stance rigid.

Not the estate agent. Definitely not his father. And, alas, not Sasha, who had carried herself as if a ballerina's perfect posture were the most natural thing in the universe.

"Danion," the apparition said in a frigid voice. "I see you have returned."

He was hallucinating. To give the mirage time to disappear, Danion walked toward the living room. At the threshold, he stopped and placed his bag on the floor.

The image remained. As he reached the doorway, she moved away from the window, revealing her features.

Smooth black hair drawn back from a marble face, green eyes chill in the light.

Face, voice, rigid posture—not an illusion but cold reality. Extremely cold, in this case. And it belonged to the one person he least wished to encounter at this or any other time.

"Reilu," he said, omitting the *-chan* that Tarkei normally attached to women's names and nicknames. "What are you doing here?"

Her lips tightened at the insult, but she gave no other sign of having heard. "I live here," she said. "I am your wife."

Caught between amazement and anger, Danion stared at her. Insanity was rarer on Tarkei than the joining; he had not had to cope with it before.

"I thought you married my cousin," he said at last. Of the responses he might have made, this was the weakest. Reilu tended to have that effect on him.

She came to stand before him, her pose radiating sweet reasonableness, a pose he disliked even more than he distrusted it. "That would be impossible, Danion. I am married to you. You wanted to set me aside, but you see how foolish that was. Your joining did not last two years."

"When did you arrive?" Another inessential point. Danion, struggling with a brain turned to mush, felt like an unwary animal who has stumbled over a vithra's nest. This was his house, not hers. Did she recognize that basic detail?

"As soon as I heard." Reilu put a hand on his arm, and he jerked it away.

"Get out of my house," he said in the chilliest, most level tone he could manage.

As if he had not spoken, she turned and walked toward the sofa. "Come and have some tea, Danion."

He stood watching her, a guest in his own home. Reilu sat in the center of the symmetrically aligned sofa, her face expressionless as ever. On the coffee table in front of her, he saw a teapot and two cups.

Her presumption infuriated him. But Danion, raised on Tarkei, where order ranked above emotion and even above honesty, could not bring himself to pick Reilu up and throw her out.

Which was the only way he was going to get rid of her. Even Jenat had failed to make an impression on that marble countenance, and his father's wake was littered with snubbed and intimidated souls.

Sasha's face flashed before his eyes. The scar burned, raw with pain, more intense because the shock of the initial cut no longer shielded him. Danion said the most wounding thing he could think of. "Do you understand, Reilu, that I loved Sasha? That I always will?"

With steady hands, she poured a red-gold stream into the cup in front of her. "Are you human, Danion, to think it makes a difference? There is no divorce on Tarkei. While she lived, you could pretend, and everyone would support you. But she is gone, and you belong to me."

She held one of the cups out to him. "As I said you would."

Danion picked up his bag. "Stay in the other room," he said. "Don't come near me. Don't speak to me, until you are ready to leave. If you so much as enter a room when I am in it, I will leave it. If necessary, I will renew my oath of celibacy. Do I make myself clear?"

The marble did not crack, but the lips curved in the smug smile of da Vinci's *Giaconda*. Danion did not wait to hear what she would say.

Upstairs, he threw the bag into a corner and collapsed onto the unmade bed, an arm over his face. His head ached, and the empty place where the bond had lain throbbed with mingled pain and rage. Danion cursed his father for having put him in this position in the first place and tried to disentangle his options. He hoped Reilu would leave him alone long enough to think; he had little faith that she would observe his restrictions—unless they served whatever purpose had brought her here.

By the laws of Tarkei, Reilu was within her rights, although what impelled her to exercise them eluded him. In obedience to an ancient tradition, their parents had signed the contract binding Reilu and Danion eight years ago and imposed it on their reluctant offspring (at least, Danion had been reluctant; he no longer felt capable of comment on what Reilu might have thought). The marriage did not require their consent and could not be broken, except under one condition, so rare as not to be worth considering. To escape it—and Reilu, for whom he felt a profound antipathy—Danion had joined the priesthood three months after the wedding. True, that had not been his only reason, but it had certainly contributed the largest share.

Six years later, he met Sasha, and that one incontestable circumstance became reality. He touched Sasha by accident, and the link formed. Formed and persisted, despite his efforts to break it. Accustomed to the rhythms of the mountain and wary of sacrificing his future for a legend, he had actually wanted to break it—odd as that now seemed—but his attempts had been like preventing flowers from blooming in prepared and watered beds. The bond strengthened and widened, and before long he would no more have broken it than have cut off his arm. No marriage contract could stand in the face of the joining, which linked two compatible souls.

Even then, Reilu had resisted. It had taken Jenat three months to get her out of his house, and apparently not even Jenat could talk her into accepting another husband. Now she was back, and Danion had to decide how to respond.

He could return to the mountain. He could master his dislike and live with her, knowing she could not replace Sasha in his heart. Or he could let her stay but exclude her from his life, acknowledging the façade she craved while denying her the reality to which she seemed oblivious.

Feeling the tightness in his stomach, Danion acknowledged that he could not accept her. It would be a betrayal of Sasha so profound that he would never feel comfortable with himself again. He had walked out on Reilu once and could do so a second time—would, if she made any attempt to cross the line he had drawn. Yet his departure had made no impression on her before, and he had no reason to think that repetition would lead to a different outcome. Danion, tired of fighting this inexorable force, decided to wait and see.

Geoffrey told him he was crazy, repeating it until Danion put both hands over his ears and slumped into his chair, overwhelmed with grief.

Iqara said, "Leave him be, Geoff," and flicked one of the covering hands in comfort.

His father said, "I hope you know what you're doing, boy, but you have my sympathy. I'm sure you haven't forgotten how the wretched woman glued herself to my doorstep."

Danion, old enough to conquer his resentment, did not remind his father how the wretched woman acquired the right to glue herself to either of their doorsteps and thanked Jenat for his sympathy. At least his father's understanding meant that the Tarkei government gave him plenty of work. His responsibilities as a pilot expanded to include diplomatic missions. A bit of ingenuity could stretch these out for months—just mastering the protocol required by different species ate up vast amounts of time.

The list of allied planets continued to grow, and conflicts surfaced with impressive regularity. Danion had plenty of opportunity to develop his skills, and he hardly ever had to go home. Even so, Reilu remained. Whatever her reasons for insisting on the marriage, they did not include spending time with Danion.

Four years passed in this way. Until one day, his father summoned Danion to his office. Not an unusual occurrence, these days. Just back from an off-planet session, Danion appeared not long after suns' rise. Selassa's rich red beams interlaced with the bright white light of her child star, Kana, in the first tier of windows, while the brilliant gold of Father Danar cast its aura around them.

"Sit," his father said. Danion, curious, sat. In his rebellious twenties, he had often endured such curtness from Jenat, but that had dissipated after his marriage to Sasha.

Examining his father more closely, Danion realized that this curtness was different—the result of distraction, not irritation, suppressed or otherwise. He waited for an explanation.

It came with surprising slowness. Few events had the capacity to rattle his father. Jenat invariably knew his own mind and seldom cared whether others agreed with him. Yet here he sat, doodling on an electronic touch pad like a reluctant schoolboy and avoiding his son's gaze.

"I don't know what you're going to do with this, boy," he said after a long pause. In the mingled light of the three suns, he looked old: the skin of his face less taut, the muscles less well-defined, the lines more visible. "You have a right to hear it, though. I had someone investigate your wife's death."

Danion stilled in his chair. Through a tight throat, he said, "Sasha?" A whisper of sound, but his father, intent on his own story, did not notice.

"I didn't tell you when I set up the investigation," Jenat said. "In part, I felt responsible for what happened to her, and in part, I thought you would blame yourself more than you did already. Or perhaps I feared you would blame me."

Such a concession, from a man who rarely shared his feelings with anyone, let alone his fears. Danion leaned forward, eyes intent on his father's face.

"It wasn't a coincidence, that you were asked to pilot that particular mission." Jenat added a curve to the doodle before him and stared at the result.

"The one that prevented me from taking Sasha to Chandar?"

"Yes. It was the other side that insisted I call you home. They were nervous, they said, that the Kazrati would interfere with the negotiations. They agreed to the talks only if Tarkei supplied its best pilot, someone with a record of evading Kazrati patrols." Another line on the doodle. Jenat still had not raised his head.

"Me," Danion said, although it was obvious. The aftermath had been so devastating that he remembered the mission with difficulty, but the demand had not been unreasonable. The Kazrati had a flexible and ever-changing definition of their own space, and he thought that the other side had had cause for concern. He said so.

"Of course, of course," Jenat said, waving a dismissive hand. "So we all thought. Not unreasonable and, it seemed at the time, a small price to pay for a successful outcome." He looked at Danion, extending both hands in apology. "I did not know, my son."

Danion realized he had copied his father's gesture only after the fact. "None of us did, father. No one ever does. How many 'if onlys' do you think I've had?"

Jenat did not answer.

"But something made you suspicious?" Danion asked. "What happened?"

Jenat returned to the doodle. "Nothing. Nothing real. Only I wondered at the convenience of it. The insistence that the talks could take place only then, and only if you were present. At first, I told myself it was foolishness, an old man's refusal to accept the order of the universe." He raised his head again, and Danion saw the strain in that normally implacable face.

"I loved my daughter," Jenat said.

Danion swallowed past a lump in his throat larger than a desert rock. His father didn't admit to loving anyone.

Jenat went on. "It was like seeing your mother reborn, so vivid and alive, so brave and beautiful and intelligent. I thought my grief was making me see plots where none existed. I resisted, but in the end, I had to know. So I hired someone to find out why only you could pilot that ship."

Danion felt as though their positions were reversed, as though he, for once, was in control and his father was not, except that the sentences reached him through a fog thick as cotton wool. His voice shook, and the words he wanted slid away. "And?"

His father's response came from far away. "Someone planned it, Danion. Someone wanted you out of the way, so they could substitute another pilot."

Somehow, he choked out the question. "A less-skilled pilot?"

"No," Jenat said. "A Kazrati pilot."

Sasha, in the hands of a Kazrati pilot. The world closed in, until Danion felt nothing but the weight of it bearing him down.

A hand touched his chin, and he opened his eyes to find his father's, narrowed in concern, not more than a foot from his face.

"Don't go off on me yet, boy. I'm not done." Jenat's bracing tone did not relieve the crushing weight that sat on his son's chest, but Danion tried to respond to the challenge. He pulled himself upright in his seat and gave his father his full attention.

"That's better." Jenat sounded gruff. "I can't prove whether she knew the new pilot was Kazrati, or whether she was duped, but the rest is quite clear."

"She?" Danion said.

A thought crossed his mind, so horrible that he dismissed it as evidence of his own prejudices. "You found out who gave the orders, then?"

Jenat dropped the touch pad into his desk drawer. In five words, he confirmed his son's worst nightmare. "I did," he said. "It was Reilu."

❉

Danion walked in Tarkakhan's central park for hours before he dared go home. The desire to wring Reilu's neck was so strong he didn't recognize himself. The mere thought of what she had done made his hands clench like claws. What universe did she live in, that she could callously send three people to their deaths and wreck the lives of half-a-dozen others, rather than accept that the man she regarded as her husband did not want her? How did one talk to such a person? And how had the rest of them failed to grasp the extent of her obsession before Sasha and Slava and Camille, and Danion himself, paid the price for their blindness?

Danar had set by the time he left the park. In his distraught state, Selassa's scarlet glow took on the hue of human blood. Hands clasped behind his back, Danion walked to his house, determined to rid himself of Reilu once and for all.

He found her in the garden, where she had long since reduced the colorful riot of plants to neat rows distinguished by species. She looked up as he came in. Perhaps she expected a visitor, for Danion had learned her routine early and avoided coming home at a moment when he would be forced to walk past her to enter the house.

She greeted him calmly, as though four years had not passed since he had spoken to her.

For an instant, Danion pitied her. Her total self-absorption left no room for reality to intrude.

"I know what you did," he said. To his surprise, and not a little pride, he kept his voice level. "How you arranged Sasha's death. My father has the evidence. To protect the family, he will withhold it, but only if you leave my house this afternoon and trouble none of us again."

Reilu dragged a plant from between the symmetrical rows.

"That's my altanai!" Despite what he had learned of her, Danion was shocked. Altanai, the most unusual of Tarkei's flowers, were rarely seen in nature. It had been his gift to Sasha, a memento of an incomparable performance.

Reilu looked at the plant that dangled from her fingers. "Oh, so it is. My apologies, Danion. It was in the way."

Then he understood, with a sickness that knotted his insides. The altanai was both rare and precious, a symbol of the link that bound him to Sasha. That had freed him from Reilu. Reilu had confessed to getting it—and Sasha—out of her way.

For the first time in his life, Danion lost his temper. The world took on the hue of Orbfire, crimson moon in a maroon sky. Thanks to some residue of self-control (or was it self-preservation?), he managed to keep himself from physically assaulting his tormentor, but by the time he had finished telling her—and half of Tarkakhan—what he thought of her, even Reilu appeared chastened.

Danion threw her belongings in the street and waited for her to leave. When she could procrastinate no longer, she edged down the path, shoulders bent. Then, suns be praised, she was gone.

Tarkei gates do not slam; they are too well balanced for that. Nonetheless, Danion managed a very satisfactory thunk.

❀

Life without Reilu was an improvement. After a few months of wondering when, and how, she would wriggle back into his life, Danion discovered that he could go home without fear of encountering her. His house recovered from its rigid exercise in symmetry; his garden grew out of its unfriendly rows. Iqara called in a dozen favors and found him another altanai.

The years passed. Jenat remained prime minister, although his formidable capacity for work diminished. Increasingly, Danion took on his father's responsibilities—aware of being groomed as successor, whether he liked it or not. Another family tradition fulfilled. Sometimes he wondered if this was the life he wanted, but he no longer knew the answer. After forty years, even the question faded into memory.

He did not forget Sasha. At moments—when the altanai bloomed in its multicolored glory, when he watched the suns rise, when he heard Ravel or Fauré, when he came across a holograph of her caught in some exquisite pose—she appeared so clearly in his mind that he thought he need only turn his head to see her. The pointe shoes she had signed remained a treasured possession; occasionally, in his stroll about his reclaimed house, he would stand before them, thinking of the day she had given them to him and the events surrounding that gift. At times like those, he could almost feel her soft skin pressed against his own, the long hair tangling in his fingers, her voice husky in his ears.

He did not forget her, but as the years slid by, the memories, like the shoes, acquired the patina of old, beloved objects. The pain ebbed. Once, long ago, he had loved, and the woman he loved had died. He remembered the love, and the death, through a haze of what had happened since. The intensity of the emotions, of all emotions, lessened. It was natural. He was ninety-four. Not a great age for Tarkei, but midway through his life. One cannot hold on forever to the passions of youth.

Life placed several landmarks that year. Geoffrey accepted a teaching position that required him to spend half his time off-planet. Iqara was elected full member of the Tarkei Academy of Sciences; when not visiting Geoff, she too was preoccupied. Their children, long since grown, had their own concerns. Thuja acquired a new ship and crew. And Jenat proposed a mission more significant than any before it, as well as more dangerous.

On Kazratan, the home of their ancient enemy, a resistance movement had emerged. Jenat wanted its members to know that Tarkei supported their cause. Wanted it enough to risk his son, still the only pilot he trusted to land on Kazratan without alerting its government. Would Danion agree to help the Kazrati find a better way of life?

Danion studied his father, wondering what Jenat had in mind. The proposal seemed out of character for someone whose main flaw in life had been overprotecting his children. Still healthy at 135, his father had lost the leonine stockiness so typical of his midlife self and now resembled an elderly prophet. Behind such a man, the tribes of Israel (to borrow Geoff's example) might have marched.

"Very well," Danion said, less as confirmation than as test. What was his father planning?

But Jenat gave no clue. "Good," he said. "I will make the arrangements."

Still puzzled, Danion left a week later.

The situation he found on Kazratan did not enlighten him. His father's information proved to be correct, and Danion succeeded in making contact with the resistance movement. With the priesthood, the Academy of Sciences, his piloting, his diplomatic experience, and his government work, he had so much to offer them that they soon elected him leader, listening eagerly, even avidly, to every statement he made. Most of them were young, as might be expected, with the heartbreaking naïveté so common among would-be revolutionaries. Danion came to care for them, to listen to their stories. Gladly he taught them what he knew, emphasizing the value of pacifism, of civil disobedience, of learning new values that could change not only the surface politics of Kazratan but the underlying culture of violence.

A young girl, found half-starving in the streets, reminded him so much of Sasha that he adopted the child as his daughter. Choli, a solemn thirteen-year-old with short dark hair like a doll's and warm brown eyes, embraced the entire community with her ready sympathy. Danion could not imagine how her sensitivity had survived life in the streets, but he treasured it. On the day she found Sasha's shoes, he told her the story of his marriage, although he had shared it with no one else.

Somewhat to his own surprise, he enjoyed life as a resistance leader. It appealed to the part of him that loved piloting, that had stood up to his father and tradition, that had refused to give in and accept Reilu because his forebears had decreed that he should. The part that loved Sasha, if that could be restricted to one part. It had received little enough expression in the last sixty years.

Spirit voices surrounded her, speaking a language she did not understand but vaguely recognized as one she had heard before. White light hurt her eyes, brilliant light that shone through her closed lids, causing pain even though she could not open them. If she had the strength to move, she would have turned her head. Instead, she seemed to be floating in a sea of light, the spirit voices bearing her up.

Slowly, the images crystallized. She could not see, but she could hear. The words took shape in her head. She struggled to separate them, to wrest the meaning from them, but at the instant they became clear, sensation left her, and she sank back into darkness.

And so it went, for how long she did not know. Wherever she was, time did not exist. She floated from the tunnel of darkness to the sea of light and back, spirit voices rising and falling around her.

Sasha Sinclair lay between soft clean sheets, listening to words that she almost understood. Her head ached; her whole body ached, as if someone had taken a bat and broken every bone she had. Her skin felt scorched; the sheets weighed her down, sticking to the curled paper that had once been epidermis.

❋

The brilliant light faded into a warm and welcome darkness, but the words evoked memories of terror and grief. Once she could hear them, she identified them as Kazrati. They sounded familiar because they came from the same source as Tarkei. Twisted by centuries apart, they remained recognizable, as certain words in Latin or German can be understood by a speaker of English.

The voices—which were not, after all, spirit voices—withdrew, accompanied by footsteps. Sasha forced her eyes open.

Hospitals look the same on any planet. In the bed on her left, Camille lay, flat on her back, stretched under another set of sheets. She could have been a corpse, if Sasha had not seen her chest rise.

Sasha turned her head in the other direction. Slava's eyes met hers. She wet her lips, not sure if she remembered how to talk.

"Where are we?" he whispered. "Can you tell?" Like Camille, and Sasha herself, he lay flat on the bed, his broken bones held in place with wires and pullies. Only his head moved, and that with difficulty. Again, like Sasha herself.

"Yes," she whispered back. In such a place as this, surely someone would be listening. It might be best if the listener did not learn too much. So she gave him an answer comprehensible only to Slava. "We're in the Kingdom of the Shades."

For a moment, he looked blank. Sasha lay still, hoping he would not ask again. Then he said, "*Bozhe moi*. You are certain?"

Sasha thought of the words she had heard. "Absolutely," she said. "The Kingdom of the Shades."

3. Attitude

THE SOUP GLOWED VIRULENTLY orange in the murky light that crept through the restaurant windows. Danion, regarding the dish with controlled distaste, vacillated between a scientist's curiosity and simple disgust. Where was his Pannthu friend, Thuja, when he needed her? He had watched her eat even more revolting concoctions than this.

"It looks good," Tamir said.

Danion viewed the boy with something close to astonishment. Tamir, a lively sixteen-year-old, waxed enthusiastic about many things that left Danion cold, but this surpassed them all.

"Would you like mine?" Danion asked. Tamir had suggested this restaurant; after one glance at the cutlery, Danion had decided he preferred hunger to whatever virus the china spoons contained.

"Oh, please," the boy said. "My mother made it just like that."

Danion passed him the bowl, making a mental resolution not to eat anything Tamir recommended. It would be unkind to be glad that the boy's mother was dead, but he felt thankful that he would never encounter her food.

"Aren't you going to eat anything?" the child on his other side said.

Danion gave Choli a half-smile, watching her vivid face crinkle in delight. Her hair, cut in a straight line at chin length, swung from side to side. Two months after her unofficial adoption, she was beginning to accept that she was safe, that Danion was her family and would not leave her. The knowledge gave her a kind of glow, softening her blunt features and allowing her sweet nature to shine through. A few more years, and she would be quite a charmer.

"I think not," he said.

Choli put her own spoon down. "Then you won't mind if I don't either?" Danion shook his head. She shot a glance at Tamir and whispered, "It's pretty awful, isn't it?"

"Quite," Danion said. He did not want to offend Tamir either.

The waitress, sulky as a Terran grizzly on a bad day, was slouching past at that moment. She glared at them as though they had insulted her and stalked off. As she passed a large holovid projector set into the bar, she jabbed one of the buttons and continued on her way.

Danion opened his mouth to demand that she turn off the set. There were no other customers in the small dining room (he understood why), and she had obviously done it only to pay him back. But before he had a chance to complain, music filled the room. Danion saw the picture on the floor and changed his mind.

Surrounded by tables and chairs, a human man, about thirty years old, well-muscled but with an extraordinary grace, stood alone in the middle of the floor, right arm curved above his blond head. Brown eyes gazed into the palm of his hand; his left foot pointed behind him. He wore pale green trousers tied at knee and ankles, an open shirt secured across his chest, and dance slippers.

Danion's hand clenched around the china spoon. Slava Zoshchenko. A man he had not seen in sixty years. Sasha's partner.

Slava knelt, right leg extended, profile to the audience. From the side of what must be a stage, a human ballerina clad in filmy dark green trousers, tied around her ankles, and a short green top that left her midriff bare advanced on pointe across the floor. Beneath the light green veil, her dark hair formed a cap that ended at her ears.

Danion heard the spoon crack between his fingers. He dropped it on the table. Choli touched his hand, her eyes wide with concern.

The ballerina placed her hand on Slava's shoulder, balancing on pointe, left leg stretched behind her, arm aligned to his. Danion was close enough to see her knee tremble as she found her balance.

When she had it, she let go of her partner's shoulder, lowering the supporting heel and bending the knee. Then she brought the back foot down and shimmied in a circle around him. Slava rose to his feet as she passed him, touching a hand to her waist. She leaned back, head against his shoulder, leg extended in front of her, then slipped across the stage, eluding him.

Danion stared at her, mesmerized. Should he leave? *Could* he? So much time had passed. He had almost forgotten how lovely she was, how beautifully she moved. More than anything, he wanted to reach out and catch her as she came by, to find her miraculously whole in his arms.

He could not. If he touched her, she would dissolve like the ghost she was. Struggling against the lump in his throat, Danion reminded himself that his wife was dead, that this was a holographic projection of an old performance by two people he had once known and, in Sasha's case, loved. The knowledge did not help.

Sasha took Slava's hand, her back to the audience, and jumped, landing on her left foot. On pointe, she drew the right leg up to her knee and extended it to the side. Slava walked her around in a circle, holding her arm above her head, positioned her, and let her stay there for a moment before she brought her leg down and circled him again. They repeated the series of steps once more.

Danion frowned at the stage. Something was wrong. Not that anyone here would notice, but obvious to him. Sasha's jumps were lower than usual, her balance uncertain. Her extended leg cleared 90 degrees but came nowhere close to its normal 135.

Slava caught her around the waist as she came out of a spin, and she again raised her leg to the side before twisting on pointe to touch his shoulder, poised in arabesque. She bent her knee and repeated the turns.

Danion's sense of wrongness grew. Sasha's balance was legendary; the critics raved about it. In the two years he had known her, as in the performances he had seen in her thoughts, she had never failed to release her partner's shoulder, to show the audience that perfect alignment—which was, after all, what they paid to see. It was part of her signature, along with the fouettés that had sent more than one reporter into ecstasy. She had not done it here, though, nor earlier, when Slava assisted her promenade.

She must be injured. Projected onto the center of the floor, the picture was clear enough that he could see lines of strain in her face. And was that a scar near her left ear, at the edge of the short hair?

Which should not be short, come to that. The day they met in the desert, Sasha's hair had tumbled past her waist. She had not cut it in the time they spent together; nor had she worn it short before. Her brother had shown him pictures of Sasha at five, and even then the black pigtails brushed her shoulders.

Danion leaned forward, focused on the dancers. Sasha was moving backward now, arms extended in a horizontal vee toward Slava, who followed her, hand over his heart. Danion resisted the impulse to do the same.

Somewhere deep in his thoughts, an infinitesimal spider began to weave its golden thread.

Choli broke into his reverie, saying, "This is wonderful." Then, with excitement, "A ballerina. She's a ballerina!"

Danion turned his head toward her. She remembered the story he'd told her the day she found Sasha's shoes.

"Yes," he said. "A ballerina, but not any ballerina. That is Sasha."

Choli's mouth dropped open. "Sasha?" She twisted on her stool—the better to see the ballerina, he assumed, although at this moment the stage was empty. "Your Sasha?"

"My Sasha," Danion said.

"Who's Sasha?" Tamir asked.

Slava returned alone, repeated the pose he had adopted before Sasha's entrance, and initiated a series of jumps. Danion, on the alert for incongruities, noticed that Slava, too, was moderating his steps. Under normal circumstances, Slava's jumps, like Sasha's balance, defied belief. These, although good enough to impress people unfamiliar with him, were nowhere near his usual caliber.

"Is that Slava?" Choli asked.

Danion nodded, too intent on the performance to talk.

"Sasha?" Tamir said. "Slava? Who are these people? What's a ballerina? What are you talking about?" Slurps of disgusting soup punctuated his questions, and Danion admonished him with a glance. The boy blushed. His table manners improved.

"Yes," Danion said. "That is Slava."

Slava left the stage, returning with Sasha and another green veil, about six feet long, which they held between them. While Slava watched, Sasha, holding her part of the veil at chest height, rose onto pointe and turned into arabesque, three times altogether. Each time, Danion held his breath; she seemed uncertain of her ankles, although she completed each repetition successfully.

Was it his imagination, or was Slava also concerned? Sasha wound the veil about her waist, turning toward him. Slava supported her, whispering something in her ear. Sasha nodded and moved away, unwinding herself again.

The thread twisted, a sparkling current aflow among his thoughts. Danion straightened, elbow on the filthy table, wondering. An old hurt, so familiar he had long since forgotten how life felt without it, ebbed away.

Tamir repeated his questions. "Explain it to him," Danion told Choli.

In the breathing space this brought him, he focused on the broadcast. Connected by the veil, Sasha and Slava continued to dance. Sasha made a series of turns in arabesque, leg straight out behind her. With each rotation, she had to raise the veil above her head to avoid catching herself in it. After three sets of turns, Slava took it away. He left the stage while she turned alone.

More changes in the choreography. It had taken him a while, but Danion had identified the piece they were dancing: the grand pas de deux from *La Bayadère*, Nikia and Solor in the Kingdom of the Shades. They had planned to perform it at the gala on Chandar, the engagement they had not lived to fulfill. He remembered watching them rehearse it, over and over, as they rehearsed everything. Those pirouettes used to end on one foot, not two.

The infinitesimal spider's infinitely thin thread doubled and tripled and wound back on itself. Danion felt a flash of pain in his toes, an ache in his head. Both vanished before the clatter of china hitting the floor told him that his hand, reaching for his wife's dancing image, had swept the pieces of spoon from the table.

Choli brought him back to the present. "Are you all right? You look as though you've seen a ghost."

"She is a ghost." His throat had tightened, and his voice sounded strange. It bothered Choli, he saw. He flicked a finger against her ear. "Do not fear, little bird. I have survived worse." She smiled at him, as though to reassure him, although concern showed in her eyes.

Sasha and Slava were back. He supported her in arabesque and lifted her as she jumped, beating her feet together. They held hands as he pulled her across the floor, her head turned away from him, resisting. Slava lifted her, face to the ceiling as though she were not merely a ghost but a corpse, then flipped her over and onto his shoulder. He walked about the stage, presenting her to the audience at various angles, then lowered her to the floor, so rapidly that she fell off pointe. She compensated by dropping her back foot and arching her arms in a Nikia-like pose, but Danion noticed her sharp intake of breath and the flash of fear as her heel hit the floor, as well as Slava's muttering in her ear as he pulled her into position.

Definitely injured, Danion decided. Under normal circumstances, Slava treated Sasha as though she came equipped with anti-gravs, tossing her in the air and swooping her one-handed over his head. That the Russian could come close to dropping her shocked Danion more than anything he had seen so far.

Watching them interact, Danion recognized another element that had disturbed him, visible only as it dissipated. In this pas de deux, Nikia, a temple dancer betrayed (like so many ballet heroines) by her lover, Solor, appears to him in a dream. She is a ghost, one of many who inhabit the Kingdom of the Shades, and when Solor first appears, she is distant and cold. She blames him for her death, or at least he thinks she blames him—it is his dream, not hers. He seeks her and at last wins her forgiveness.

All this Sasha had explained to Danion when he first watched them rehearse. He had seen his wife create Nikia, seen the classical purity of the opening—each step clear as a classroom exercise—transform into a subtle hurt that yielded at last to acceptance. To a Tarkei, Sasha's Nikia reassured by its understatement, but here she seemed not so much wary as frozen—an automaton instead of a ghost.

Could her image be embedded in an android, then? A computer simulacrum?

But an android would not waver in its balance, and an artificial creation would replicate the original as it had appeared in life.

Then there was the bond. He felt it, for the first time in sixty-one years. Every time it twisted, Sasha's dancing became more fluid, more like the person he remembered. Tiny details that Danion had learned to take for granted drew his eye: the balance held a split second beyond the music, the plié that bent a half-inch more than those around it, the subtle shift of the head that locked his wife's eyes with Slava's.

Across the line between life and death, Sasha stretched on pointe. From fingertips to arched foot, the pose expressed longing for a love eternally denied her. Slava responded, and the mechanical quality so foreign to their dancing melted away. The tips of her fingers brushed her partner's shoulder. Slava turned, but she was gone, a wraith in the mist. He sought her, but she remained elusive, confined to the world of dreams.

The music shifted, and so did the mood. Sasha spun round an imaginary circle. In this crowded setting, the movement sent her through various pieces of furniture—

cutting her off at the waist, then reassembling her. Danion noticed how each time her image fractured, his hands clenched, as though the real person were under assault.

At the same time, he was there, with her, filled with the fierce and vivid joy of flying through space, moving freely and fast yet with complete control. As she would have said, transcendence.

Raucous laughter broke into his reverie. A motley group pushed its way past the outer door—the crew of a trading ship, on leave and certain to cause trouble. One of them chucked the surly waitress under the chin, slipping an unseen object into her pocket and saying, "How yer doing, darlin?"

Danion bit his tongue to hide his disbelief. Choli, focused on Sasha, ignored the newcomers, but Tamir was laughing so hard that, if not stopped, he would draw the thugs' attention by falling off his chair. Danion touched the boy's arm and told him to hush.

One crew member imitated the dancers, to his companions' great delight. With a predictable lack of success, he attempted to grab the holographic Sasha around the waist and waltz with her. Watching him fall flat on his face added to the others' amusement. Obviously, they had started their drinking elsewhere.

"Turn it off!" A being larger than the rest—the leader, Danion assumed—punched the button and roared for beer. Slava and Sasha vanished.

Danion stood, gesturing to his companions. "Come."

"But I'm not finished," Tamir said.

"Bring it." Without waiting for an answer, Danion walked over to the waitress and gave her a handful of coins. She slipped them into her pocket, and Danion wondered how much of it the management would see. "Where did that broadcast originate?" he asked.

The surly expression did not lift, although he had tipped her far more than she deserved. "How would I know? It was the official channel." Her hands abrogated responsibility for the programming decisions of distant bureaucrats. She sniffed. "Pretty putrid stuff, if you ask me."

"Thank you," he said dryly, and strode from the room. Two sets of footsteps followed him into the street.

❋

In a theater in another part of the city, Sasha left the stage in a series of flying grands jetés. Guards and stage hands scurried out of her way. Slava ran after her. He reached the end of the corridor in time to hear the door of her dressing room slam.

"Get Camille!" he said to the Kazrati woman standing outside. "Now!" When he had seen her leave, he walked down the hall and knocked on the closed door. No one answered.

4. Pas d'Action

INSIDE THE DRESSING ROOM, Sasha cursed at the knotted ribbons on her pointe shoes. When at last she pulled them free, she ripped off the shoes and hurled them across the room.

She looked at her feet. Scarlet stained the pink tights. "Damn!" She smashed her hand against the nearest box, dropped to the floor, and burst into tears.

A click behind her told her the door had opened. "Oh, *ma belle*," said Camille's warm voice. "Now you cry?"

The familiar arms enfolded her, and for a few moments Sasha let the tears flow.

But the performance was less than half-over. She lifted her head, and Camille's sympathetic brown eyes met hers. Over the ballet mistress's slim shoulder, she could see long legs in green trousers: Slava.

"I can't do it," she said. "I thought I could, but it's a disaster, Camille. I feel like a robot. Not like Nikia at all."

Her voice kept breaking. She took a deep breath and wiped a hand over her wet cheeks. It came away streaked with black, and she shuddered.

"Those shoes are impossible," she added more calmly.

"Yes, I see," Camille said. "Well, that I can do something about. Slava, get Vestris. Ask her to come here. Next is *Ondine*, no? Then the abstract pieces?"

"Yes," Slava said. "But before I go, I want Sasha to hear that it was not a disaster. In the beginning, yes, she was too withdrawn even for Nikia. I, too, had trouble. I could not find my character. Then she changed. You did not see?"

Camille seemed about to object, then nodded. "You are right. The end, it was much better than the beginning. Think, *petite*. What came to pass?"

Sasha bit the tip of one finger, thinking. "I sensed..."

She stopped. She couldn't say that. "There was a moment when everything felt as it used to. Everything. I can still feel it, if I think about it. That hasn't been true since I came here."

Camille and Slava looked puzzled, for which she could not blame them. Then Slava's eyes lit up. "Ah, you found Solor."

She nodded. So did Camille.

"All will be well then. You will consider how to keep that image while I search for Vestris." With that, Slava left.

"Good," Camille said. "Now, *ma belle*, you will come with me. Your dancing, it is not a disaster, but your makeup! Even a clown does not look like this."

Sasha exchanged Nikia's green for a cotton robe and sat in front of the mirror. With a soft cloth and plenty of oil, she stripped off the hideous mask before reapplying the makeup from scratch.

Camille picked up one of the maltreated pointe shoes and bent it back and forth in her hands. "But how did you dance in these? It is a stone, this shoe."

"Worse than a stone." Sasha grimaced at her reflection. "I don't know what to do with them. I beat them and slammed the door on them and did whatever I could think of to soften the miserable things, but I couldn't roll through them if my life depended on it. Every time I went on pointe, I was sure I'd be stuck there for eternity."

A knock sounded at the door—Slava, since Kazrati did not knock. Typically, he treated it more as a signal than a request; in her mirror Sasha saw his reflected head, cut off from his body by the door.

"You have brought Vestris?" Camille asked. "Then show her in and go. You must both change costumes."

Their Kazrati guard edged her way around the door. Against the backdrop of the crowded dressing room, her neat military appearance, from cropped black hair to gleaming boots, seemed out of place. She stood at attention, her face wiped clean of emotion. "You require assistance?"

Camille wagged the shoe in the Kazrati's face. "These shoes, they are a catastrophe. Look at the feet of my Sasha. They bleed!"

Sasha thought of the many times her feet had bled in regular pointe shoes, but she saw no reason to mention that. The shoes were dreadful by any account.

Vestris, less experienced, looked suitably shocked. Camille pressed her advantage. "I cannot permit her to finish the performance in such instruments of torture. You must tell your superiors to release immediately the carton of shoes that they impounded. Otherwise, she cannot dance. You must also tell them, when this is over, to find for you a proper shoemaker who can learn to make the shoes correctly, or there will be no more performances."

In her mirror, Sasha saw the glare that her formidable dance mistress turned on the hapless Kazrati. No more than generations of ballet students could Vestris resist that scowl.

A frothy creation—green, gray, and blue, the colors of the waves—hung from a peg in one corner. "Excuse me," Sasha said, pushing past Vestris. She took the dress down and slipped it over her head.

"Perhaps they could release the tutus while they're at it," she said over her shoulder. "I can't imagine what good they are to the secret police, unless the officers dress up in them and parade around at night."

Vestris looked more shocked than ever at that irreverent suggestion, awakening in Sasha a momentary desire to laugh. To hide it, she picked up Nikia's costume and hung it on its peg, adjusting the folds with care.

A faint sensation, as elusive as scent, brushed her thoughts, and her hands stilled. There it was again, that fleeting touch she had experienced while dancing, as though Danion had reached out and run a finger over her face. The gold thread that linked them, thinned to invisibility since she arrived here, produced a soft tone like a plucked harpstring and hung shimmering in midair.

Quick, experienced fingers sealed the strip at her back. Looking over her shoulder, Sasha saw Vestris had gone. "Success?"

"I think so. Turn around." Sasha did. "It is well. You have a few extra minutes. The intermission will not end until they find the shoes, so sit down again and I will bind your feet."

Sasha sat. "We could change the order, you know. Put the flamenco and mazurka first, or drop *Ondine* altogether and substitute something else for *Apple Blossom*."

"But then why would they give us the shoes?" Camille looked astonished. "One must be firm with such people, my Sasha, or they will never cooperate."

"Camille, you are such an autocrat." Sasha, her spirits restored, kissed the ballet mistress's cheek to take any sting from her words. "What would we do without you? Have you had those shoes in reserve the whole time?"

Camille shrugged one elegant Parisian shoulder. "But of course, *ma belle*. The Kazrati, what do they know of ballet? Have you forgotten how much trouble I had with the costumes? I thought, suppose the shoes are not so good. So I asked Vestris to discover what happened to our supplies. Then the secret police would not release them, but now they will. It is fortunate, is it not, that your feet bled?"

"Unbelievable," Sasha said. "You are unbelievable."

Camille ran a comb through Sasha's hair, covering the scars and restoring the black-cap effect. "And since you have found your inspiration, my Sasha, how will you end this sure-to-be triumph of yours?"

Sasha looked around the crowded dressing room. An image, not her own, flashed through her thoughts: glittering velvet feathers, set against a background of black tulle. The thin gold thread sparkled and hummed, marking a distance immeasurable yet less than before. A wicked delight filled her.

"Odile," she said. "If they give us the tutus, that is. Odette's entrance and the pas d'action first, then Odile. You can program the music during the other dances, can't you?"

Camille's head snapped back. "Odette/Odile? Are you sure, *petite*? It is not too much?"

Sasha stretched. The bond's energy flowed through her until she felt light enough to dance into the dawn if necessary. She picked up the shoe Camille had dropped on the dressing table.

"Well, not in these things," she said. "But get me my shoes, and I'll dance Odile. We don't want these Kazrati to think we're a bunch of weaklings, do we?"

In the street, Tamir and Choli turned toward the cave entrance, but Danion headed in the other direction. "This way," he said. The two children exchanged puzzled glances, but they followed his lead. They skipped along, one on either side of him, as he headed toward the center of the city.

Tamir ran ahead. Good. Danion preferred to talk first with Choli, who knew about his marriage and might therefore be expected to understand. "That was Sasha dancing," he said. "With her partner, Slava."

Choli slipped her hand in his. "Yes, you said so." She watched him, head on one side like the little bird he called her. "Was it difficult, to see her again?"

Sometimes her perspicacity amazed him. She was only thirteen, after all. "Yes," he admitted. "Quite difficult, but a great pleasure nonetheless." The child's hand warm in his, Danion searched for words. "I think the performance is taking place here. That's what I want to find out."

At the edge of his mind, faint as a breath, the golden thread glittered. A tiny bubble of laughter, sparkling with sequins, brushed his thoughts and floated away.

Choli jerked to a stop, pulled herself together, and ran to catch up with him. "But how could that be? You said she was dead."

Danion turned to face her. Tamir waited halfway down the street, toes scuffing the pavement as he ate his sandwich. "I'm sorry," Choli said. "I didn't mean to hurt you."

"I'm not hurt," Danion said. Choli's years on the streets had bred an inordinate sensitivity to every shift in expression, especially his. "That was what I thought. And she may be. But that performance ... I don't think it's from the archives. Something strange is happening."

Choli bit her lip, as if trying to decide what to say next. Possibly wondering about his sanity. Danion, wondering himself, touched her cheek with his free hand and led her toward Tamir, who had finished his food and was tossing pebbles in the street. "Come," Danion told him, "and leave the stones to their fate."

"But where are we going?" Tamir seldom kept quiet for long.

"Here." Danion stopped in front of the window of an electronics store and pointed to the display, where twenty Sashas glided, supported by the hands of twenty Slavas, an unusually talented corps de ballet of clones.

The effect was disconcerting. Perhaps the store owner had the same reaction, for he soon turned off the duplicates and left one dancing pair.

"What are they doing?" Choli stood on tiptoe, hanging onto Danion's arm, her nose pressed against the glass.

Danion drew her away from the window. "That is one of her brother Tonio's pieces. Abstract, lovely to watch. It is called, I think, *Apple Blossom*. One of his less difficult pieces, technically speaking. It allows the dancers to rest between more complicated solos."

Leaning forward on tiptoe, Choli could have been a dancer herself. Sasha at thirteen must have looked much the same. "It's beautiful," the child said. "Much more beautiful than I imagined. How does she balance, standing on her toes like that? It can't all be the shoes."

"I don't know," Danion said. "You will have to ask her."

Tamir twisted his head. "Ask her? Choli said she was dead. I heard her just now."

"Tamir!" Choli, hands on her hips, glared at him. "Truly, you are the most heartless person alive."

She was right: Tamir had none of her sensitivity. Danion quelled his fear that Tamir might also be right, and himself a victim of delusion, and answered the boy. "Perhaps. That is what we have come to discover. If she is not, however, you will certainly have an opportunity to speak with her."

Even Choli paid attention to that. "You'd go and find her?"

"Suppose the secret police has her?" Tamir asked. The secret police had killed his parents, and he saw its hand everywhere.

"We would have to persuade the officers to part with her," Danion said.

Tamir regarded him with wide eyes, whether from shock or admiration, Danion could not tell. "You would fight the secret police?"

"For my wife?" Danion asked. "What do you think?"

Tamir's mouth dropped open. Danion ignored it, concentrating on the dancers.

❁

Apple Blossom ended. In a piece distinguished primarily by its prettiness, the transformation Danion had seen in *Bayadère* was less evident, but when Sasha abandoned her pointe shoes and returned in low-heeled black pumps and a long Spanish gown, the difference was clear. A black lace mantilla covered her short hair, a contrast to the rich burgundy of the gown, and she carried a fan in one hand, which she wielded with an insouciance that, to judge by their roars of approval, delighted the audience. Slava, his inescapable blondness set off by black tights and sequins, made up for his non-Spanish appearance with dash and flair.

They disappeared again, returning to perform a mazurka, then a tarantella in highly stylized balletic form. There was a break for political propaganda, and Danion fielded questions from the children while strolling along the crowded street, trying to avoid the attention of the electronics store owner. Then the dancers returned, and the pointe shoes as well, and for the first time that evening Danion saw a tutu, glistening white, layer upon layer of stiffened tulle reaching to mid-thigh, covered with long white feathers. Feathers adorned Sasha's headdress, too, enclosing the sleek black cap on either side. Odette, the Swan Queen, Sasha's favorite role.

Through the store window, he heard a haunting violin. His hands clenched into fists at his sides, and he held them behind his back. The golden thread flickered. It continued to strengthen, gradually but steadily.

He touched it, questioning, turning his head to one side or another, the way one repositions a transmitter to boost the signal. Was he imagining it? It seemed impossible that she could be alive, but more unlikely still to think he could bond with a ghost, even Sasha's ghost.

Choli divided her attention between him and the dancers, whereas Tamir, oblivious to emotional nuance, kept his eyes fixed on the window.

The swan glided across the stage, her arms rippling like wings. Choli turned back to the window, a child entranced. Sasha stepped out, testing her feet as they touched the ground, her humanity resurfacing after a day of bird life. Danion saw the physical strain that the difficult choreography placed on her—although he doubted anyone else would—but the unnatural, withdrawn quality he had noticed earlier was gone. Half-woman, half-bird, she stood in *attitude*, arms raised behind her, higher than normal human arms would go, with the sweep of a swan's wing.

Slava appeared, and the swan princess sprang back. Sasha as Odette whirled, her winged arms lifting. Danion could almost mark the moment that transformed her from swan to woman. Through the link, a feather brushed his ear. He shook his head, startled.

He still had no indication of where, or when, the performance had occurred, although he would have sworn those roars were in Kazrati. Hands clasped behind his back, Danion hoped, against everything he knew to be true, that it was happening here, now.

Odette fled across the stage, pursued by the enraptured Prince Siegfried. The music changed. Siegfried caught Odette by the hands. Only her feet moved, shivering with fear like a trapped animal's. Danion's stomach performed a series of cartwheels, echoing the quivering feet. The bond flicked his thoughts.

I have missed you, *kaleita*, he told her. How I have missed you. The feather stroked his ear again.

Odette's resistance yielded to acceptance, even a timid belief. She reached out, leaning forward, leg high behind her, and brushed her partner's cheek with her own. The force of the hidden sorcerer drew her away, the arms again became wings, and she left as she had entered, shimmering across the floor on pointe.

A harp sounded, and Odette's adagio with the prince began. Danion frowned at the screen. Why had he not noticed it before?

Whatever this was, it involved only Sasha and Slava. The rest of the company was missing. There were no other soloists, so it was not a gala, but neither was it a normal production. Nikia had danced unaccompanied by her fellow shades, and Odette lived on a lakeshore devoid of swans.

But there was no such performance. Not when he lived with her, not before he lived with her, not ever. Sasha's parents had built the company; she and her brother had jealously guarded its rights. Only once had such an engagement even been planned, but Sasha and Slava had died before they reached Chandar, not afterward. That timing he could not forget.

Odette spun, perfectly straight. Slava's hands supported her waist. She drew her right foot up the inside of her left leg, extended it to the front, bent forward, then fell backward. Slava caught her less than an arm's length from the floor.

Hearing Choli gasp, Danion suppressed a smile. *That* was the partnership he remembered, so inexplicably absent from *Bayadère*—the one where Sasha let herself fall, trusting Slava to catch her, and Slava was there, right where she needed him to be.

He no longer heard the audience, but when the pas de deux ended, renewed roars broke forth. Sasha, moving with the tragic fragility of a Victorian heroine, walked forward with Slava and curtseyed, arms swept behind her in broad, winglike curves. They left before the cheering ended, and the music changed again.

Danion froze. She wouldn't, would she? For a moment, he wanted to grab the children and run. There were limits to even his self-control. His feet, however, had other ideas. They clung to the pavement as if secured by magnets.

Choli was clapping. "It's wonderful. You told me, but oh, I couldn't begin to imagine!" Then, on a different note, "Is it over? You look so sad."

Somehow, Danion kept his voice level. "It is not over. Listen, Choli, you can hear the music."

The child turned her head as the display went dark. One spotlight flashed. Sasha and Slava stood in its circle, hand in hand. Slava looked the same, but Sasha's white feathers had become black velvet and tulle, and her exquisite fragility an elegant hauteur. She leaped, leg slightly bent in *attitude*, while Slava, as Siegfried, watched, unsure of her identity. Her obvious self-confidence drew him and confused him at the same time. Odette? Not Odette? Should he believe her face or her actions?

"She's so different." Choli poked Tamir in the ribs. "Tamir, look, she's like another person."

Tamir poked her back. "Look yourself."

Sasha pointed her foot and spun seven times across the stage, stopping in front of Slava, who held her steady. She stood there, on pointe, face to the ceiling, arms and bent leg swept behind her. The music shifted from triumphant to haunting, and Sasha tipped her head forward until she was looking straight into her partner's eyes.

Danion, momentarily blinded, felt someone—no, two someones—shaking his arms from either side. He pressed his hands against the hard surface in front of him. It was the store window.

At the edge of his vision, Choli's concerned face glimmered. He pushed against the glass, forcing himself to concentrate on the smooth surface, fighting the remembered sensation of Sasha's waist between his hands. Sixty-three years ago, she had danced Odile with him, a reluctant and inexperienced partner but the only one available. A moment that had changed his relationship to her forever.

Standing straight again, he touched Choli's shoulder. "I'm fine," he said. An absurd statement, but the best he could do. He doubted Choli believed him, but it reassured her enough that she turned back to the screen.

On the stage, Sasha had snapped her head to face them, Odile submerged in shock, gray eyes huge in her too-thin face. Slava, perfect partner, reacted, turning her on pointe so that the audience saw only her back. By the time she finished the turn, she had regained her composure. She imitated her own performance as Odette, tentatively at first. Then she found the characterization again, and the hesitancy gave way to a wicked enjoyment Danion remembered too well. Another hallmark of that long-ago day.

Poor Siegfried, as usual, didn't stand a chance. Danion watched in sympathy as the prince tumbled under the spell of Odile's beautiful black wings. She flirted outrageously; he responded to every shift in mood. She rejected him and he pined; she beckoned to him and he ran to sweep her up. When she had subjugated him completely, she whirled in triumph: thirty-two flawless fouettés. How she managed them, given the evidence of injury that Danion had seen and still saw, he could not imagine. He tipped his head in silent acknowledgment.

For you, Danion, a familiar voice said in his head. *They were for you.*

The window reflected his shock, his smile. Choli and Tamir were staring at him as though the sight of him smiling astonished them.

The bond flashed again, and for a second Sasha was there, with him—or was it memory?

It couldn't be. He experienced her exhaustion and the exhilaration mixed with it. *You should be exhilarated,* he said. *An extraordinary achievement under any circumstances, and especially these. Where are you?*

The golden thread hummed, but she did not answer. Danion suppressed his disappointment. She wasn't here; the whole thing existed only in his imagination, up to and including the revived bond. Blame it on nostalgia unleashed.

In his thoughts, a swan raised its wings against the sky and became a silver bird. Through its featherless membranes, the three suns of Tarkei shone, multicolored sparks against the sky. The bird became a pink skirt, and he heard his wife's voice say, Think with your heart.

Another unforgettable performance, more precious even than the day he met Odile.

The audience had gone wild, Choli and Tamir among them. "Did you see it, Danion? Did you see it?" they shouted, jumping up and down, as though he had not been standing there beside them from the beginning.

The music, drowned in roars, stopped. Sasha curtseyed, swept-back "wings" gracefully arrogant, head inclined the merest fraction—a star's acceptance of her due. Inside the store, the owner was cheering.

The music resumed, and Slava leaped in a great circle around the stage. More cheers. Then Sasha was back, exultant and predatory. Slava stepped out, raised her high above his head in an impossible lift, then lowered her to arabesque. She swept her head down, then up, and ended with arms like broken wings before his face—Odette's signature pose.

Across the link, Danion flicked her ear.

Why, thank you, beloved, she said.

By the three suns, she *was* there. He asked again, Where are you?

In the Kingdom of the Shades, she said. Where are you?

Here in the world, Danion said, in everyday life. Disappointment weighed him down. So she was dead after all, and he was hallucinating. In the Kingdom of the Shades. A ghost.

Fighting depression, he waited for a moment to see if the broadcast would mention the location and date of the performance. Wherever it had taken place, he would have liked to know, but the credits supplied no information.

The store owner switched the channel. Danion sighed. "Let us go," he told the children. They walked without speaking back to the caves.

✳

Inside, Danion dismissed Choli and Tamir. They ran off, eager to tell their friends about their day. No doubt they would have spread the tale throughout the caves by tonight.

He walked through winding tunnels, brushing past the few resistance members he met with a quick nod of acknowledgment. Some of them turned to watch him as he passed. No one demanded his attention, though. For that, he was grateful.

At last he reached the cave he called home. Beyond the cloth hanging that provided minimal privacy, he sank onto the scarlet pallet that, with a single wooden trunk, constituted his furniture. It reminded him of his cell in the sun priests' mountain sanctuary. A welcome contrast to his surroundings: the Kazrati preferred the ornate and monumental.

But that was beside the point. Danion rested his head against the stone wall and tried to work out what had happened to him.

He could feel the thread, faint but clear, connecting him to Sasha. If he concentrated, he could see a room, so tiny and crowded with makeup and costumes and pointe shoes that it was difficult to imagine that it could fit one person, let alone two. Sasha sat on the floor, head on her knees, wearing Odile's black tutu and her pink satin shoes, too tired to move. Beside her knelt Camille, motherly concern clear in the lined face, one hand stroking his wife's short hair. They were all alive, then, or none, but wherever they were, the three were together.

Camille, too, looked as though she had not yet recovered from a recent illness. What had happened to them?

Danion dropped his head into his hands and thought. None of the many legends that surrounded the joining mentioned an outcome like this. The bond arose spontaneously, through physical contact, but however far it lay outside conscious control, it was real. How could it regenerate if one partner was dead? And why would it regenerate after so many years and in such a peculiar way, changing Sasha's appearance and her dancing, making her look injured and lost? She had to be here, and alive.

A half-formed memory surfaced, triggered by Odette's tutu but not recognized at the time. He had seen the costume Nikia was to have worn for the gala. Improbable wear for even so improbable a creature as a ghost: a white tutu, like Odette's but without the feathers. Sasha had said white was traditional for human ghosts. Giselle had worn white as well—a satin bodice and a skirt of ankle-length white tulle.

Danion's hands trembled. He had better leave that path alone for now. Focus on Nikia. Only on Kazratan, and on Tarkei itself, did ghosts traditionally wear green. The green of spring, symbolizing the eternal cycle of life and death and the spirit world's place within that cycle.

He touched the link. She was not on Tarkei. Nothing he saw looked like his home planet. So she must be here, if she was alive.

Think with your heart, she had said. And what did his heart say?

Short hair, wrong costume, injuries, bond pointed to Sasha's continued existence. Moments of interaction, the shift in her dancing, her shock when he reacted to Odile's tipped head—it was difficult to write these off as an active imagination, especially the last.

Set against them were, if he were honest, only two factors, both undeniable. First, people do not return from the dead, whether after sixty years or sixty minutes; second, he loved Sasha so much that if he could hallucinate her presence, he would. Would have, any time these sixty years.

Which brought him full circle, didn't it? Because in fact, he had not done so until today.

In the shadows of the cave wall, Danion pictured his father's face. Had Jenat guessed that Sasha was here? It would explain his willingness to send Danion on this mission, which otherwise seemed so out of character. His father received daily intelligence reports filled with rumors; he might well have heard this one.

Jenat would not tell a person who had suffered as Danion had, "Your wife may be alive, but I can't say for sure." He would think, Suppose I raise false hopes. But he might put Danion in a position to find out.

Not conclusive, but one more piece of data pointing in the same direction. Danion watched the shadows, the golden thread humming in his mind.

5. Adagio

A SILVER HEAD POKED around Danion's curtain. "May I come in?"

The head belonged to Nirrtu, one of the few older members of the resistance movement. Older than Danion himself—by a good twenty years, Danion guessed, although out of courtesy he had refrained from asking. Nirrtu's lined face suggested a long and difficult life, and not always a pleasant one.

In contrast, Nirrtu himself seemed quite pleasant, as well as capable and intelligent and, a rarity in this company of youngsters, mature. Danion found his cynical observations a refreshing antidote to the youthful idealism that at times threatened to inundate him.

"Please." Danion indicated the other end of the scarlet pallet. Nirrtu, with an agility admirable in a man of his years, dropped into a cross-legged position that reminded Danion of Sendar, his mentor from the priests' sanctuary. In the dim light, he looked like an ancient gnome.

Like the Tarkei, the Kazrati wasted little time on preliminaries. Nirrtu voiced his concern right away. "Tamir came to me with a most peculiar story. Something about you having a wife who is a prisoner of the secret police. Here on Kazratan."

"Not exactly," Danion said. "Tamir tends to exaggerate."

"Ah." Nirrtu relaxed against the wall, uncrossing his legs and holding his knees. "I told him he must be mistaken. I can't imagine you having a wife. You seem very self-contained."

"Thank you, I think." Danion kept his voice dry. Nirrtu enjoyed needling people; it was one of his less appealing traits. "But in fact, I did have a wife. In that Tamir could not be mistaken, for I told him myself."

Nirrtu watched him, dark eyes intent. "In that case," the Kazrati said with unusual calm, "perhaps you should explain where the exaggeration occurred."

Danion hesitated. "That is the difficulty. I am not sure what I saw. Even the facts are not yet clear."

In his head, details tumbled over one another, mingled with memories and bright sparks of love. Sasha's shocked face, those remarkable spins, the Kazrati costume, scars and pain and the incongruities visible only to him—where should he start, to make it comprehensible? Each time he selected one incident, others jumped in front of them, demanding his attention. Amid them ran the gossamer thread, the clearest evidence but the least acceptable to anyone unfamiliar with the joining.

"You could begin at the beginning," Nirrtu suggested.

"It would take too long," Danion told him. "Especially if my suspicions are correct."

"Begin at the end, then. What happened? Tamir mentioned a video broadcast."

"Yes." Danion spread his hands. "You will think me insane, probably, but I will do my best. Sixty-three years ago,

I married a human woman, a dancer named Alessandra Sinclair. Sasha. Not just married. Bonded. Does the joining exist on Kazratan?"

"The joining," Nirrtu said, a thoughtful expression on his face. "I've heard of it. It's rare, though." His brow wrinkled. "I thought someone told me Tarkei didn't experience it. That it was a legend there."

"It does exist," Danion said. His listener's eyes widened. "You must believe that. Without it, my story makes no sense."

"*You* were joined? Yourself? To a human?"

"Oh yes," Danion said. "Of that there is no doubt. We lived together for two years. Then she was killed, or so I thought. She vanished in space, and I could no longer sense her. Until today, when I saw her dancing in the performance that Tamir described to you."

Nirrtu leaned forward, one hand supporting his chin. The pose reminded Danion of a statue he had once seen.

"Do you sense her now?" Nirrtu asked. "Do you know where she is?"

"Yes and no." The golden thread had thickened to the point where Danion could touch it at will; it lay quiescent in its old place, flickering like a candle flame when the wick is low.

"Danion, please." Nirrtu, not the most patient of listeners, spread his hands in obvious irritation. "Ambiguity does us no good."

"I can sense her," Danion said, "but the link is weak. Even at the best of times, it ebbs and flows, and I'm not sure why. At the moment, I need her to tell me where she is, and I haven't been able to communicate with her long enough to find out. If I had to, I could walk there, but depending on where she is, it might take a long time or prove hazardous to my health—or hers. For the link to regenerate completely, I must touch her."

If he only could. The need to hold Sasha, of necessity repressed for sixty years, surfaced with the vengeance typical of buried feelings. Danion rubbed his aching palms.

Nirrtu must have noticed, since for once he refrained from teasing. He sounded, in fact, quite serious. "She meant much to you, then, this wife?"

Danion let his breath go in a soundless whistle. "More than I can say. That is part of the problem. I wonder whether what I feel is real, or whether I'm deluding myself because I want so much for it to be true."

"And where does the secret police come in?" Nirrtu asked. "Or is that Tamir's invention? In all honesty, Danion, this whole business seems quite implausible."

Black velvet and tulle, sequins and toe shoes, makeup and tutus and hair that felt too short. It was a long time since Danion's world had included any of these things, but it did now. They floated on a cloud of exhilaration that did not emanate from him.

Yet Nirrtu's skepticism was understandable. How could a person who had not shared the thoughts of another imagine the impact of such an experience, let alone believe in it? And Nirrtu was not the trusting type.

Danion shrugged. "I understand. But the bond is real. Even in Kazrati legend, can the joining recur in the absence of one partner?"

"Not to my knowledge. Although I am not an expert on the joining, Danion."

"In any event," Danion said, "it was Tamir, not I, who suggested that she might be under the control of the secret police. If she is here, I suspect she is in government hands, because the only detail I managed to discover was that the program aired on the official channel. I did tell Tamir that, if the secret police had Sasha, I would free her, and so we must. You can see that for yourself, Nirrtu. Three people went missing at once, and wherever they are, they are together. Alone or as a group, they could become powerful hostages for our good behavior."

Nirrtu relaxed. "Finally, something that makes sense to me. You are right. So we must discover what you saw." He rubbed his upper lip. "I apologize in advance, Danion, but I must ask you a difficult question. How, exactly, did you lose your wife? Is it possible this broadcast was made here, but sixty years ago? I did not see such a program, it's true, but I do not take much interest in dance."

Danion watched the candle flame flicker, as the bond flickered in his mind. "That would explain the program but not the regeneration of the link."

Everything came down to that, and Nirrtu had admitted he did not believe in the joining. Danion held out his hands in silent apology for forcing the man to deal with a metaphysics for which he was unprepared. "In truth, I am no more familiar with dance than you, except for what I learned from watching Sasha rehearse and perform. When we met, I didn't know enough to identify her as a ballerina. But if you asked me, I could list the steps she performed, in order; I would need only to query her mind. She learned to speak Tarkei in the same fashion. That is how the link works."

He touched the golden thread. "At this moment, she is sitting in her dressing room, talking to Camille, who is her teacher and her friend, about the shoes she wore for the first part of the performance."

Nirrtu's eyebrows rose. "Yes," Danion said. "You don't believe me, but it is true. And I will answer your question. Sasha's ship was taken over by a Kazrati pilot, who flew it—we assume deliberately—into a vortex near the planet of Chandar."

Nirrtu leaned forward again, elbows resting on his knees. "Is that so? Then she is here. Was here, definitely, and may be here now. The vortex is not a secret. Everyone on Kazratan has heard of it. It is a passage in time and space."

It was Danion's turn to stare. "Do the Chandari know that?"

Nirrtu spread his hands. "You're asking me? But I would guess not. From their perspective, a ship would go into the vortex and not come out. This is where they land. Sometimes it's six years in the future, but it could be sixty or six hundred. There's no way to predict when a particular ship will emerge." His mouth quirked in a kind of self-mockery. "If there were, I'm sure the military would have found a use for it."

Danion dropped his head in his hands, overwhelmed by the possibility that his cherished dream had become reality. "Find out, Nirrtu, please." To his own ears, his voice sounded muffled.

The bond flickered. It was strengthening again, a golden web linking him to Sasha across the eternal night of space.

A hand touched his shoulder. "As soon as possible," Nirrtu said.

❀

Camille had left to check on Slava. After a while, Sasha pulled herself together enough to strip off Odile's lustrous black feathers and ease the pink satin from her aching feet.

Her big toe was bleeding again. Damn those wretched shoes.

She removed her tights, put on her underwear, and applied a second coat of medical sealant to her damaged toenails. Wrapping the cotton robe around her, she sat in front of the mirror to remove her makeup. Her own face emerged from behind the mask. Ugh, she looked dreadful.

An echo of someone else's dismay, filtered across a great distance, touched her thoughts, mingled with hurt and hope. Danion. But where was he?

A knock sounded at the door. "Come in," she called. A dark head, with one dramatic streak of gray down the right side, peered around the edge. Camille, back from checking on Slava. "Ah, *ma belle*," the ballet mistress said, "and how do you feel now?"

Sasha rubbed her forehead, which ached with fatigue and tension. "Well, I'm vertical, more or less. Beyond that, I don't think I'd go. I probably should have listened to you about Odette/Odile. It was worth it, though. Despite a rocky beginning, we can claim a spectacular end, don't you think?"

Camille edged around the door. "You made me proud, *petite*." For Camille, that was high praise. Already the ballet mistress was frowning. "But your tutus, you should hang them up." Sweeping Odile's tutu into her arms, she hung it on a nearby peg and smoothed the glittering sequins that edged the velvet feathers.

"Of course. I'll do it before I leave. Oh, thank you."

Camille collected another armful of costumes and arranged them one by one. "Your foot is still bleeding, I see."

"Occupational hazard. You know that. Just don't tell Vestris until she finds the shoemaker."

Camille smiled. "True. At least the military governors liked your performance. That should help. Perhaps they will give Vestris whatever she asks."

"I hope so, although I worry about Vestris," Sasha said. "I like her well enough, but I think she knows what works to her advantage, and it isn't necessarily us."

"*Naturellement.*" Through the mirror, she saw Camille bestow on her the look one gives a naïve youngster. "It is not a democracy, where we are. I am sure Vestris reports to her superiors, whether she likes us or not. But when we succeed, she and her partner succeed also. So they will help us as long as we do not ask them to break the rules."

"I suppose you're right." Sasha suppressed a sigh. She wanted to talk about Danion, but among the many topics that were not safe to mention, her husband topped the list. The walls, as they said in bad melodramas, had ears—and eyes. Danion had been persona non grata on Kazratan since he organized the relief of Xantera; and his connection with Tarkei's prime minister, not to mention his own skills as a pilot, had done nothing to endear him to the Kazrati authorities in the two years that followed.

Not two, three. She had spent ten weeks in the hospital and another six months in recovery before the mad dash to prepare this performance began. What must Danion have thought, with the bond so weak for almost three-quarters of a year?

Another knock interrupted this cascade of thoughts. "Come in, Slava," she said. Slava's sleek blond head inserted itself through the half-open entrance.

"You must do something about this, my dove." He squeezed through the door. "You endanger my abilities to perform. When I have starved myself enough to enter your doorway, I will no longer have strength to lift you."

"It's awful, isn't it? But if I move the stuff behind the door, there's nowhere else to put it. And I can't move the sink, whatever I do. Here." Sasha collected the few remaining costumes and hung them on their pegs.

Slava settled himself on a group of boxes cleared of clothing and watched as Camille picked up the discarded Kazrati toe shoe and, wielding the local equivalent of a penknife, peeled back the pink satin covering.

"You are turning surgeon?" he asked. "Or cobbler?"

Camille shook her head at him. "The shoes, they are a disaster. You know this already. The question is, what must improve? Here with my knife, I seek the source of the problem. Then I will know what to tell the shoemaker."

Ignoring her companions, Sasha pulled on a pair of pants and turned her back so she could fasten them under the robe. Then she damped a cloth in the small sink placed inconveniently behind the door and wiped it over her face and neck. Finally, she pulled a loose, round-necked tunic over her head and let the robe slip to the floor before pushing her arms through the sleeves.

"You look like a good Kazrati soldier," Slava told her. "Short hair and all."

She turned to find him grinning at her. "Don't remind me."

The grin became laughter. "Don't complain. It has reached the tips of your ears. Quite stylish. You should have seen yourself when they first did it. You looked like a lost sheep, all eyes and scars. Not so much as a stray curl."

"You are a bad tease, Slava." Camille stripped the satin from the shoe and held it up. The two dancers dropped their verbal sparring and stared at it.

"A wooden box? Are they out of their minds?" Sasha said.

"Well, at least I know where to begin," Camille said, "although what I must deal with, I shudder to think. You will excuse me while I seek Vestris. Do not tarry long, *mes enfants*."

Camille departed, shoes in hand, to find their Kazrati guards. Slava and Sasha trailed behind. They could not leave the theater alone, but they saw no reason to hurry. It was bad enough being prisoners under a kind of luxurious house arrest without going out of their way to make life easy for their captors.

"It was a good performance, I thought," Slava said. "Beginning halfway through Nikia and Solor."

"I agree," Sasha said, "although I can't be completely recovered, even now. I'm exhausted."

"Me too." He hesitated, then said, "In Black Swan, something happened, no? Or did I imagine it?"

Sasha glanced at him, then around the wings. She didn't see anyone, but she felt nervous. "No, it was real. It comes in bits and pieces, but at times I can sense him. Ever since that moment in *Bayadère*. Right then, in Black Swan, I'm not sure what happened. It felt as if a door opened, then shut again. It shocked him, I think."

A memory surfaced: a shuttle-craft cargo area and Danion's hands around her waist. The pose was the same. No wonder it had shocked him.

"It's not a coincidence, then," Slava said. It took her a moment to realize he was referring to the bond reforming, not to her husband's state of mind. Of course, he knew nothing of her dancing Black Swan with Danion. "We should keep our eyes open."

She nodded. "You can't imagine how glad I am. I'd begun to wonder if he was dead."

Slava's hand touched her waist. "I am happy for you, my dove. It has been difficult, no?" He forestalled any reply she might have made, saying more loudly than necessary, "Ah, there is Camille. Come, Sashenka, Vestris awaits."

Sasha waved at the Kazrati, who raised a hand in return. Together, the four left the theater. Vestris's partner, D'Toth, joined them on the street outside.

❧

The garden of their beautiful birdcage glowed in the clear evening. The silver gleam of Kazratan's sister planet blended with the pale gold and delicate blue of its two moons, casting overlapping shadows on the faces of the five who relaxed among the bushes and the soft chirping of a summer's night. Empty plates and glasses decorated shimmery tables, and in the mingled moon- and planet light they sparkled diamond bright. Vestris and D'Toth sat to one side, conversing quietly in Kazrati; the three humans clustered in the center, speaking more softly still in English, sprinkled with enough ballet terms to obscure their meaning—or at least lull their guards into disregarding their conversation. It had been a long day.

"This business with Solor," Slava said to Camille, "is more important than I thought. I don't pretend to understand it, because I never did, but whatever it is, it motivates Sasha, and we need to watch how it develops. It could make a big difference to our performances."

"I see," Camille said. "You find it growing stronger, *ma belle*? Your sense of the character?"

It was a relief to talk about it, even in this Aesopian way. "Yes," Sasha told them. "Quite definitely. It happened while I was dancing. Not just Solor and Nikia. Siegfried and Odette/Odile, especially. Even when I was thinking about them in my dressing room."

Camille nodded. "That is good. I have worried about you. The crash, it was severe, and you had the worst of the head injuries. And then you were so sad. I worried that perhaps you had lost—how do you say?—your spark."

"It's been only nine months or so," Sasha said. "But yes, I worried too. I hadn't expected it. I would have thought nothing could affect me that badly."

"Indeed, my dove, you broke my heart. Solor, Siegfried, Albrecht—I could not compete with any of them."

Sasha groaned in protest, but Slava laughed. He enjoyed teasing her.

"In any case," Camille said, "it is well to recapture what worked in the past. Such restraint, it does not benefit the performances. One must put it behind one and go on, do you not think? I am glad you are beginning to do so."

"Yes," Sasha said. "It's about time. Without emotion, I will never break free, and I'm sure that in the end that's what we want, isn't it?"

Slava's brown eyes gleamed like opals in the multicolored light. "But of course. We are Sinclair and Zoshchenko, are we not? It is not so long since we were known throughout the galaxy. If fate has decreed that we end our days here, let us at least refuse to languish in obscurity. That would not do."

Sasha stretched her arms over her head. Such dear friends, and how well they understood one another.

Her gesture attracted Vestris's and D'Toth's attention. With one fluid movement, Sasha rose. "I'm so tired. I can't bear to chatter another minute, even about dancing. Enjoy the garden, everyone. Good night."

Plate in hand, she sauntered into the house.

6. Relevé

SASHA SAT IN THE window seat of her room, listening to the chirps outside. Her departure had cleared the garden, and she could enjoy the soft light without fear of observation. Such a beautiful evening, and after the day she'd had, she needed it.

Leaning back against the window frame, she curled her feet under her and let the breeze play over her face. The hectic pace of this morning seemed as distant as the moons. How nervous she had been. Her first performance in almost a year, and she had felt far from ready. Less than two weeks preparation!

But the request was really a command, so it had meant fifteen days of hurried planning, costume fittings, the rush to find pointe shoes, and rehearsals—not to mention nonstop exercises to build her strength, still limited by her injuries. She had had little time to think, let alone feel. She had known it would show in her dancing, and it had, even if the audience, unfamiliar with ballet, had not detected it. It was a rare event in her life, the struggle to produce a character; hers usually appeared as if by instinct. Like her altered appearance, the change distressed her. She did not recognize herself.

Danion must have seen the difference. Where was he, anyway? Here, he had said, in everyday life, as though he believed she was somewhere else. She should have been more specific; his sudden appearance had startled her, and on instinct she'd used the phrase she developed for Slava.

An image flickered before her eyes: a cave, and her husband sleeping on a scarlet mattress. She had no recollection of such a place, so rigidly free of decoration that it made her own room look ornate by comparison.

How she had horrified the Kazrati by stripping away their precious coverings and bibelots and insisting on plain white pillowcases and sheets. They had acted as though she meant to live in a tent. She had left the painted walls and ceiling alone. She hadn't demanded they remove the carpet, although it clashed with everything else in the room. Even so, they reacted as if she'd embraced some austere monastic regime. What would they make of this cave?

And where was the cave? On Tarkei, perhaps. The room resembled the priests' sanctuary, although darker than she recalled from her time there.

Odd, though. Danion seemed closer than that. The gold thread had strengthened in the hours since *Bayadère*. It did not measure distance exactly, but as a rule it became more distinct as they drew closer, thinner and less substantial as they moved apart. Nine months without a response from her would alarm him enough to send him in search of her, wouldn't it?

If Danion was here, or on his way here, Slava was right. They would need to stay alert.

Sasha sighed. If Danion came here, he would place himself in danger. If he did not, the three of them might spend the rest of their lives on Kazratan. In a pinch, they could escape the guards: Vestris and D'Toth had become pretty relaxed about their duties. Leaving the system without money or any idea of how to hire a ship or notion of where to get help had seemed daunting enough that no one had so far suggested it. Eventually, though, they would have to tackle the problem—unless Danion did make an appearance. Which, most likely, he would, with the bond reforming.

And what a relief that was. She had spent weeks drifting in and out of consciousness. In her befuddled state, she could not tell whether Danion was not there or hidden behind a barrier created by her injuries. Then clarity returned, but the bond remained so faint that at times she would have sworn it had disappeared altogether.

Kazratan bordered Allied territory but lay far from Tarkei. She had tried to convince herself that distance weakened the link, but in the last two weeks the possibility of a more horrible explanation had become harder and harder to ignore. If Danion had died while she was unconscious, would she know? Would it feel like this?

She had no one to ask, so naturally she worried. And although the others worried for her, they had no chance to talk about the problem, for the Kazrati overheard every conversation. So Camille was reduced to obsessive questioning about her health, and Slava to his comments on the characters they played. The conversation this evening had been an extension of dozens of similar discussions.

But tonight she could stop driving herself crazy with thoughts that Danion had met a hideous end while she lay unconscious in a Kazrati hospital bed. The thread glittered in her thoughts, faint but clear, lighting everything it touched. She wanted desperately to see him, but only if he could reach her in safety.

Be careful, beloved, she said along the link. I don't want you captured or hurt.

As though he'd care, if he knew she needed him. I can take care of myself, he would say, then plow into danger if necessary—not heedlessly but with a perfectly clear head, and it would make her frantic just the same.

Oh, Danion, she said, what a tangle.

Danion did not respond. The link remained weak, so he could not be nearby after all. Too bad.

Pushing back the too-short hair, Sasha stood, glanced once more at the garden, then turned her back on the moonlight and prepared for bed.

Danion awoke to a scrabbling sound. He rolled onto his stomach, putting a hand over each ear. He had been dreaming of Sasha, and it was not the sort of dream he wanted interrupted, especially by a thirteen-year-old.

The golden thread was clearer this morning. For a moment, the illusion of his wife's presence felt so real, he thought he need only lift his head to see her smiling at him.

Instead, he looked around. A basket, apparently self-propelled, crawled into the cave under the cloth hanging. Danion sat up. No doubt Choli had many questions.

He straightened the bed and his sleeping robe and settled himself cross-legged on the coverlet. "Come in, Choli."

The child pushed through the curtain. "How did you know it was me?"

Danion welcomed her with an outstretched hand. "A reasonable guess. Most of the adults would not think to bring me breakfast, and Tamir would not think to do it silently. I thank you. Will you join me?"

Choli picked up the basket and plopped it on the pallet before him. Settling on the mattress, she helped herself to a flat, rolled-up bread, fragrant and appealing. "Would you like one, Danion? Natari made them, just a few minutes ago. They taste wonderful."

Danion picked one out of the basket. It warmed his hand. He pulled off a piece and put it in his mouth. It did taste wonderful, and it had a fascinating texture, soft and chewy at the same time. It made him think of an Indian bread Sasha used to love, grilled on the sides of a charcoal-burning oven—*nan*, she called it. "Did you want to talk to me, Choli?"

The girl fixed her eyes on him and ceased rummaging in the basket. "I wanted to ask you about Sasha." She enunciated each word as though she were choosing it with care. "Only I'm afraid I'll say the wrong thing, and you'll get mad."

Danion hesitated. What exactly did she want to hear? "I will not get mad, Choli. When have I ever shouted at you?"

Choli turned her right hand palm up, the Kazrati gesture of negation.

"Then what worries you?"

"Is she alive, your Sasha?" Choli tore off a piece of bread and chewed it.

"I think she must be," Danion said. "Otherwise, what is happening makes no sense."

"But you don't know?" Choli stared at the bread in her hands. "I thought if people were joined, they would know."

Danion glanced at her, but she did not raise her head to see it. "It's not quite so simple. Nirrtu says there is a time vortex between here and Chandar. Had you heard of it?"

Choli again signaled "no."

"If he is correct," Danion said, "it explains what happened to me. When Sasha entered the vortex, she vanished from that point in time, as though she had died. Only when I reached here, where she still exists, could the bond reform."

Choli hugged her elbows. "Do you think he's right?"

"I hope so." Danion spread his hands, the galactic symbol for uncertainty.

Choli tore off another chunk of bread. "I worried about you. You looked so strange."

An understatement, that. If he had not sent the child into hysterics, it was a wonder. "I expect I did."

Choli focused on Sasha. "And you can sense her now? Where is she?"

Danion touched the golden thread. He saw an elaborate ceiling, painted in greens and blues, on which Tarkenoid beings with diamond-shaped ears peered out from among more flora than he could have found on his entire home planet.

"I can," he told Choli. "I think she is here. I see a ceiling with people, similar to Tarkei, who do not live in an environment ever seen on Tarkei. It does not much resemble Kazratan, either, but old pictures of Orbfire show plants and animals of that type." He gave a small, self-mocking smile. "Not helpful, I know. On Tarkei, I could follow the link and find her that way. Here it is more complicated."

"What will you do, then?" Choli finished her bread and held the basket out toward Danion, who did not take it. She covered the remaining food with a napkin and placed the basket on the floor next to the mattress.

"I have asked Nirrtu to find out what we saw, and if possible, where Sasha is," Danion said. "Then I can decide what to do."

Choli avoided his eyes. Danion, remembering with sudden clarity how he and his sister had felt when their mother died, decided that perhaps he understood her real concern. He held out a hand to her. "I will not leave you, Choli. Whether I find Sasha or not, you are still my daughter."

Choli's face creased with worry. "Suppose she doesn't like me?"

Danion flicked her ear, his wife warm and alive in his thoughts. "That, my child, is nothing you need fear. Sasha will love you."

"You can't promise." Choli's hands twisted in her skirt.

Danion reached out, taking the closer hand in his. "I can. Have you forgotten already? Sasha and I are one."

The vivid little face lit with laughter, and Danion squeezed her hand.

❉

Almost on cue, Nirrtu's voice sounded from the other side of the curtain. "Danion, may I come in? I need to talk to you."

"Of course." Danion handed Choli a piece of fruit. "I'm sorry, I must send you away. Take this with you, and whatever else you like, and thank you for breakfast. We will talk later."

Choli rose, slipping under the curtain as Nirrtu entered the room. The older man sat on the bed and, at Danion's urging, took some of the food. "Are you still convinced your wife is alive?"

"Indeed," Danion said. "I sense her presence more strongly than before."

Nirrtu nodded, as though to himself. "It works, then."

Danion raised an eyebrow at his visitor, and Nirrtu explained. "Jonthar has just returned. He went out on the streets an hour before dawn, looking for news. Your ballerina was all over the public airwaves. The military governors 'requested' the program you saw."

Then he was *not* imagining things. Sasha was alive? After sixty years, it seemed too good to be true. Impossible. Fantastic. Wonderful. Danion, tempted to leap from the straw pallet and shout his joy to the world, was restrained by the grim expression on Nirrtu's face.

Then the meaning of Nirrtu's last sentence penetrated, and Danion realized how high a hurdle he and Sasha had yet to climb. "The military governors? You are certain?"

"Quite certain. The commentators repeated the report four times before Jonthar decided to come back and tell us about it. No doubt they are still talking about it. Such dancing is new to them. They were stunned."

As he was, although for different reasons. Danion, reminded of his wife's danger and the many barriers that lay between them, strove to project a semblance of his usual self-control. "I doubt they will see her like again—although she would classify much of that performance as no more than adequate. But where is she?"

Nirrtu's face remained grim. "All three are 'guests' of the government, their safety guaranteed by the secret police."

Not good news. Expected, but not good. "And how, precisely, did they become 'guests'?"

Nirrtu ran a hand through his silvery hair. "That is less certain. The ship crashed as it came out of the vortex. The initial news reports said that everyone died. Then the rescue workers found the three passengers, critically injured, in the wreckage. They were taken to a government hospital, where they stayed until they recovered enough to walk, then moved to a house in the city—that's what we have learned so far."

"They looked injured or ill." Danion thought of Sasha, bravely performing despite her pain. Slava, too.

Typical of dancers, and ballet dancers were the worst because their careers were so short—only tying them down could make them take their injuries seriously. That had been one of his tasks. "You do not know what kind of injuries?"

Nirrtu did not. More than ever, Danion wanted his wife here, with him.

"We must free them," he said. "To do that, we need more information. Their daily schedules, the number of guards surrounding them, and whatever else we can discover."

"Yes," Nirrtu said. "I will send Jonthar out again, to discover where the government is holding them and whatever else he can. It will be some time before we know enough to plan their release."

"It is a beginning, though," Danion said. "Thank you, Nirrtu."

The older man stood. "My apologies, Danion. I didn't believe you, you know."

"I know," Danion said. "But you sent Jonthar regardless, so I thank you anyway."

Smiling, Nirrtu left the room.

In the room with the elaborately painted ceiling, Sasha struggled to stay asleep. In her dreams Danion's arms enclosed her. Her cheek pressed against the warmth of his chest; she could feel the scratchy dark hair against her face. She tipped her head back. His mouth covered hers, and his hands—

A voice from outside intruded. She pushed her head into the pillows, trying to shut it out. It persisted, without regard for her reverie. "Grrr!" she said, and rolled over in response to the annoying call.

Slava yelled again. "Get up, Sasha! You'll miss class."

Class. Was the man nuts? Class was the last thing she wanted. She had enjoyed the performance—in the end, when the characters became real again—but it had exacted a heavy price. Every muscle in her body ached; her feet felt as though she had dipped them in hot lava.

Slava went right on calling, drat him. With a groan, Sasha hauled herself out of bed and limped to the window seat. There he stood in the garden, indecently fresh and ready for work.

A quick glance at the mirror behind her right shoulder showed nothing but dark circles and lines of pain. Ugh! She'd looked less haggard when they first let her out of the hospital. At least the too-short hair stayed neat, its only virtue.

"Time for class already?" she said.

Slava grinned at her. Fortunately, she had nothing to throw at him except the pillow. He dodged it, laughing. "That class ended hours ago. It's eleven o'clock. Camille gave you extra sleep because of the performance."

Sasha groaned. "I'm so stiff from yesterday, I can hardly move."

"The more reason to work the muscles, *ma belle*." Another voice from the garden. Camille. The dance mistress looked even more hideously cheerful than Slava.

"Have you no charity, you two? Am I the only one who felt stressed the last two weeks?" This attempt to evoke sympathy fell on even deafer ears than its predecessors.

Camille waved a cup at her. "Of course not, but now, mercifully, it is over. Come and see for yourself. It is a lovely morning. What better way to relax than to dance in the sun?"

Sasha put one hand to her forehead. Still no sympathy.

She gave up. Arguing with Camille was a waste of time. "All right," she said. "I'll be down in ten minutes. I suppose coffee's out of the question, but can you at least find breakfast?"

"It is here, in the garden." Camille pointed at the table. "We will wait for you."

"Ten minutes," Sasha said. In a fair world, the sigh she heaved would have reached the garden and blown her tormentors away.

7. Ballonné

TWO HOURS LATER, SASHA felt considerably better. Breakfast and something that, if not coffee, approximated it, followed by a gradual warm-up routine, had banished the various aches and pains that had afflicted her on waking. Her muscles had stretched out, and her feet— well, if she stopped dancing every time her feet hurt, she'd spend the rest of her life in a chair. Camille had told her to set the pointe shoes aside for a day; dancing in soft slippers was always a joy.

Vestris and D'Toth seemed happy this morning; perhaps their captives' success with the military governors had won them some points with the powers in their world.

Slava, restored by their success to his effervescent self, joked relentlessly; even if she'd wanted to, Sasha would have had difficulty retaining her morning gloom.

Best of all, the bond strengthened by the minute. A flick of her head, and Danion was there, at the end of the link, where she had wanted him to be throughout the long months of illness.

At this moment, Slava was pestering her to dance something lighter. "Have pity on poor Vestris," he said.

"Stuck watching Giselle and Nikia and Odette. She must think ballet is for mourning."

Such exaggeration. "What about Odile?" Sasha asked. "Or the character dances?"

"She didn't get to see them. But if you don't care about her, have pity on me. Come on, do Swanhilda. Or La Fille. Anything." One hand on his chest, head bent, he chasséed across the floor at a dirgelike pace, illustrating the effect of Sasha's solos.

"Terrible person," she said. "Honestly, Camille, how can you let him get away with this? And blaming Vestris, when it's his own idea. What do you think, Vestris?"

"It makes me sad, always," the guard said, "when you dance. I would like to see something livelier."

She might have guessed that Vestris would agree with Slava. Slava tended to have that effect on women; even Kazrati, it seemed, were not immune.

"Sad? Really? But that's wonderful." Sasha clapped her hands. Through the link, Danion was watching her. Oh dear, she told him, look at her! She thinks I've lost my mind. But Nikia was awful in the beginning. Did you see it?

I did, he said. Not awful, but somewhat mechanical. It improved dramatically toward the end.

Because you came. Revitalized by her husband's presence, Sasha laughed. Vestris looked alarmed, which only made it harder to stop. The ballerina walked to Camille and whispered in her ear. Camille nodded and went to the terminal that provided their music.

"You win, Slava," Sasha said. "Stop clowning around and get ready. Or get ready to clown to the music, rather."

He brightened. Sasha wouldn't have thought it was possible. She would have to peel him off the ceiling soon. "Ah, this is more promising. What have you chosen?"

"You'll see. Vestris, I'm sure you'll be able to guess what's going on. Kazrati can't be that different." Sasha grabbed the fan she had used in the flamenco, walked to one corner of the studio, and pointed a foot.

The music began. Sasha kicked high, then soared across the floor. Her back arched until the foot she flicked behind her almost touched her head. For you, Danion, she said.

So this is where it comes from, he said. She could tell he was remembering the day she did this for his friend Geoffrey and wondered, briefly, why it seemed so long ago.

This is it, she said.

While they were talking, Slava took Vestris by one arm and positioned her halfway between the door and the corner where Sasha had started. "Kitri," he said. "Much better. Just stand there, Vestris."

Camille walked to the other side of the studio and stood opposite Vestris. The Kazrati watched, puzzled, as Sasha came first to Camille, then to her, asking a question without words. Sasha made a desultory circle with her foot, walked away, and launched into a new series of steps. Slava went to Camille's side of the studio in preparation for his entrance.

As he approached Sasha, she covered her face with her fan. Slava sidestepped, stopped in front of Vestris, and bent his head as though engaged in conversation with her.

With her fan, Sasha slapped him on the shoulder. He turned. She sauntered away. He pursued her; she avoided him. He tried to kiss her; she used the fan as a shield. Vestris lost her bewildered expression. Slava returned to his conversation with the Kazrati, only to be slapped again. He renewed his chase, serenading Sasha with a pretend guitar.

D'Toth, who rarely paid attention to the rehearsals, sat up and took notice. Sasha swished her skirt in his direction.

She heard Danion's laughter through the bond. *Are you trying to make sure I come after you, kaleita?*

Well, of course! Sasha said. *What did you think?* Her own laughter vanished. *Just don't get yourself killed doing it. I'm on Kazratan. Where are you?*

The bond glowed, a gentle flame. *I, too, am on Kazratan, kaleita.*

You are? Why? Sasha asked, but before Danion could answer, Slava caught her in his arms. He tossed the pretend guitar over his shoulder. Sasha, hoping the shock did not show on her face, pushed other thoughts away and joined him in a flirtatious, flamboyant, sparkling dance, quite unlike anything associated with Nikia or Giselle. She could not tell whether Danion had not answered her last question or whether she had not heard him. She decided to ask him again later.

As the dance ended, Vestris smiled. "Happy?" Sasha asked Slava.

"Quite." Slava kissed her hands in the grand Slavic style. "Are you going to do Swanhilda now?"

"No." Slava did his best to imitate a puppy. Vestris clapped her hands against her knees—Kazrati applause.

"He's hopeless," Sasha told her.

"Down!" she said to Slava. "Go away. Good dog."

Slava put up his "paws" and begged.

"No!" Sasha said. He begged harder. "Oh, very well! What a pain you are."

"You spoil him, Sasha," Camille said. Even she was smiling.

They danced *Coppélia*, Slava as a particularly doddering Dr. Coppélius ("Talk about chewing the scenery," Sasha said) and Sasha as Swanhilda pretending to be a doll come to life. The Kazrati loved it.

According to the bond, so did Danion.

Commander Thuja Po, leader of the Fifty-fourth Airborne Pannthu Division, gripped her purple antennae in frustration. "He can't be!" she told her subordinate, who cowered in his chair, hands over his face, lilac teeth chattering.

Not because of Thuja, who barked with the best but struck terror into only the most timid of ensigns, and that only for the first two or three weeks. One might have said, she would not hurt a fly, if flies were not one of her favorite snacks—on the wing, preferably; so much more satisfying that way.

No, the cause of the subordinate's distress and the source of Thuja's frustration were the same: the elderly, wiry, implacable prime minister of Tarkei, who, according to the cringing subordinate, insisted on speaking to Thuja immediately and on line two.

"He is," the subordinate said, or so Thuja assumed. Six rows of chattering lilac teeth made it difficult to tell. She glowered at the still-empty screen, her antennae waving furiously, but a moment's reflection revealed no way out. Certainly, this spineless child would not be able to send Jenat about his business, and if she had to talk to him, she might as well get it over with. Much as she loved Danion, she did not enjoy conversations with Danion's father. No one did, in her experience, except her friend's long-dead human wife, who had handled the prime minister with the finesse of a Pannthu *chat* tamer. Like the *chat* tamer, she had had Jenat purring by the time she was done.

Enough. Sasha was gone, and Thuja, paying for whatever sins she had committed in her previous four lives, was here, with Jenat growing more impatient by the second. "Put him on," she told the subordinate, patting down her navy-blue hair and making sure her antennae pointed upward.

The screen cleared. Jenat had aged since she saw him last, becoming wirier and more leathered, as though the flesh were burning up beneath his ancient skin. The black eyes, so like his son's, shone as bright as ever, though; Thuja had no desire to cross him.

"Greetings, prime minister," she said with her jauntiest air. "May my crew and I assist you in any way?"

Not one for pleasantries, Jenat. He nodded curtly at her. "Thuja. I trust you are well."

He did not wait for an answer but said, "I need you to fly to Kazratan to collect my son and daughter and bring them back to Tarkei."

And while you're at it, why not throw in the two moons? Thuja would have glared at the screen, had anyone else been on it. "Prime minister," she said as sweetly as she could manage, "I would move worlds for your son, as I am sure you know, but he is better qualified to get himself off Kazratan than I will ever be. And his sister as well, if she is there." She pointed an antenna at him. "But why are Danion and Iqara on Kazratan?"

"Not Iqara," Jenat said. "Sasha."

Reflected in the view screen, Thuja saw her own antennae shoot sideways, at an angle, forming a vee with her head as the tip. Her entire crew was staring at her. They knew nothing of Sasha, but anything that could produce such a reaction in their commander had, if nothing else, wonderful potential as gossip.

Well, Jenat had lived a long time. She supposed senility must set in at some point—even among the Tarkei, not known for their mental or physical weakness. It would be unkind (and unwise) to point out to the prime minister of a foreign government that his antennae were curlier than a DNA spiral.

"Sasha," she said, buying time.

"No need to look at me like that, girl," Jenat said. Thuja straightened her face and her antennae simultaneously. So much for subtlety.

The prime minister was talking, his voice gruff. Startled, Thuja realized that the dragon did have a heart, just as Sasha had insisted he did.

"I received the intelligence report nine months ago," Jenat said. "The shuttle carrying Sasha and her friends went through a time vortex and crashed on Kazratan. Rumors at first, then confirmation. I didn't want to tell Danion, because I wasn't positive, and it's no secret what he went through when he lost her."

Thuja dipped her antennae toward him. She remembered, even though she had been spending most of her time acquiring a ship and organizing her crew. Geoffrey and Iqara, occasionally even Danion himself, had told her.

"So I sent him there on a mission, thinking he would find her, if the report was correct." Jenat tapped the edges of the view screen.

"And?" Thuja leaned forward in the captain's chair, determined to catch every word.

"She's there," he said. "No, I don't know if she's with Danion. Probably not yet. Last night our satellites picked up a video broadcast of Sasha and Slava performing in the capital of Kazratan for the assembled military governors. The government leaked the news to encourage us to negotiate for their release. Sasha, Slava, and Camille, the dance mistress—that's what the report said."

Thuja, eyes narrowed, antennae brushing her nose, stared at the screen. "Negotiate. What's the price?"

"The region surrounding Chandar." Jenat ran a hand through his silver hair, and Thuja saw an old man with too many problems to solve. "And Danion's life."

Thuja's antennae shot into the vee again. The crew would be talking about this for weeks.

Jenat answered the question before she could ask it. "He seems to have fulfilled the mission I set him too well. He's become the leader of their resistance movement, and the government wants him dead. The movement has grown as never before, despite its pacifist bent." He leaned back, glowering as usual, but his stern expression no longer fooled her. "That's why you have to go and get them out." He tapped his fingers on his desk once more. "I don't trust this situation, Thuja. Someone planned this, and planned it well."

Thuja scowled at her chair, thoughts running rapidly as tomorrow's dinner through her head. "Planned it. You mean someone kidnapped Sasha and took her to Kazratan to lure Danion there? To establish grounds to kill him? But why the pretense? Why not just assassinate him?"

"I can only guess," Jenat said. "I doubt that luring Danion was part of the original plot. Who would plan that far ahead? Reilu wanted to get rid of Sasha, and she succeeded. Others then saw an opportunity to exploit the situation once Sasha reached Kazratan. Danion is well known on many planets, well connected—considered a threat only on Kazratan itself. An assassination would incur significant sanctions, up to and including potential military strikes, whereas this way they can hope to dispose of him quietly."

Thuja's antennae had resumed their vee shape. Jenat must have read her reaction correctly, for he added, "Danion didn't tell you that Reilu was behind Sasha's disappearance?"

She shook her head, Tarkei- and human-style, so he would not misunderstand her.

"Yes," Jenat said. "That's why he threw her out. Good thing, too. I never made a bigger mistake than when I married him to that vithra. But the point is that this is too convenient for my taste. Danion's there, and Sasha's there, and the place is full of enemies—one of whom may be carrying a knife with my son's name on it. So I ask you, as a favor, to go to Kazratan. Will you?"

When he put it like that, how could she refuse? Danion had been her friend for seventy-five years. "I will leave at once, prime minister."

"Rig this ship for silent running." Thuja, hands on her skinny hips, gibbered her teeth at her assembled bridge crew, in case any of them felt like wiggling an antenna at the wrong moment. "Navigator, plot a course for Kazratan. Maximum speed."

She dropped into the command chair, ignoring the babble that broke out around her. The view screen, target of her ongoing irritation, shifted to a new display of stars.

"Heading for Kazratan, Commander," the navigator said. Thuja curled her lipless mouth at him for the benefit of the others; the navigator himself had served with her for years and knew better than to give her trouble, especially under such circumstances as these.

Also for the others' benefit, she snapped out the command, "Estimated time of arrival?"

The navigator's antennae stood straight above his navy-blue hair, the Pannthu salute. "Six days, Commander." His voice was brisk and businesslike. Thuja signaled her approval.

The ship sped toward Kazratan. Thuja glowered at the view screen, considering what Jenat had told her and wondering how to make contact with Danion.

The reconnaissance team reported to Danion every evening, but almost a week passed before they collected the information they needed. During that week, his bond with Sasha continued to grow. Danion saw her arguing with a shoemaker, laughing with Slava, sitting in a pretty garden under the moonlight. He shared her mischievous delight in her ornate room and enjoyed the return of her casual comments. He explained what he was doing on Kazratan.

Sasha was horrified. Danion did his best to reassure her, but angry and afraid, she pushed him for answers. He understood her anxiety, although he thought it exaggerated.

By the end of the week, the questions stopped. That was in character: Sasha seldom struggled against events she could not control, and Danion's involvement in the resistance movement predated the renewal of the bond. He was here, and soon they would be leaving; arguing over the past made little sense.

And arguing was difficult with the bond in its current state. The moments of contact came in fits and starts, short interactions of extreme clarity alternating with periods when he sensed only the bond itself. He could not predict when it would open, and as the days passed, he fretted at its failure to regenerate itself completely. To restore it, he needed only to touch her, but first he had to find her.

She was on Kazratan, that much was clear, and in the capital, where he was, which made things easier. Between her thoughts and Jonthar's discoveries, he felt reasonably certain that he could locate the theater where she practiced and the house where she was staying. The main unsolved questions involved timing and potential opposition.

Two guards, Sasha said. Always the same two. Between them, Sasha and Slava had a good chance of immobilizing them, but they needed to know when and where to go when they had.

Most of all, they needed the link, the only wholly reliable and untraceable form of communication. With it, planning was simple, but in its present form, they could not count on its working when they wanted it to. Communication had become like lightning flashes in a storm. Danion would use it if he could, but he also needed a backup plan.

❋

At the end of the week, an information and strategy meeting took place in Danion's quarters. Nirrtu arrived first, followed by Jonthar, the young man in charge of discovering Sasha's whereabouts.

Jonthar, a stocky young man with reddish hair and brown eyes, accepted Danion's invitation to speak. "The best time to strike is during the evening, when they leave the rehearsal area and return to the house where they are being detained. Both in the theater and at the house, we have to worry about building security of various types. Standard precautions, automatically activated, not directed at your friends per se."

"Why do you say that?" Danion asked.

"Because security in the streets is so lax," Jonthar said. "If they feared an escape, they would go by car, even though the distance is short. Or post more guards. As it is, they send only two, a woman and a man."

As Sasha had told him. "They are becoming careless. That should work to our advantage," Danion said. "And of course, they need not fear. The dancers will not try to escape unless they have somewhere to go."

"You will bring them here?" Nirrtu asked.

Danion glanced at the older man. "You think it would be unwise?"

Nirrtu spread his hands. "I am not certain. If they are traced, it endangers us all."

"Good point." Danion nodded at Jonthar. "We need someone to remove the transmitters. Undoubtedly, the secret police have implanted some."

He turned his attention to Nirrtu. "If not here, where would you take them?"

The white head tipped to one side. "Why, Danion, would you trust me with this wife of yours?"

Danion returned the stare. "Did I say I was giving her to you?"

Nirrtu's mouth quirked in acknowledgment, and Danion continued. "I would like to know where you think we should take them."

"Why not out of the city?" Nirrtu said. "I have a country estate, well guarded, where they could stay. If the transmitters were removed, no one would find them. You could go with them, if you wished."

"An interesting idea," Danion said. "I will consider it. Are there other issues we need to discuss?"

"Yes, one," Nirrtu said. "Were you planning to lead the rescue attempt? Because if so, perhaps you should reconsider."

Danion frowned. "Why?"

"You're older than Jonthar and his friends," Nirrtu said bluntly. "And you're the leader of the movement. If you're lost, what happens to the rest of us?"

Reasonable points, both, and worth addressing. "We could lead the attack ourselves." Jonthar straightened, breathing so deeply that his puffed chest made him resemble a large pigeon. A nice illustration of what was wrong with Nirrtu's suggestion.

"Except that Sasha and the others would not accompany you," Danion said. They should have seen that for themselves. "And it is hardly fair to ask you to take risks when I do not. In the worst case, I expect you will find another leader."

A round of protest greeted this suggestion.

"Let us compromise," Danion said. "This is what I propose."

8. Grand Jeté

THE TWILIGHT GLOWED A soft, deep purple. The two moons had not yet risen, and only Kazratan's sister planet lit the sky with its clear, pale light. Pleasantly tired after a full day's exercise, and exhilarated by the effects, Sasha and Slava strolled arm in arm along the city streets, Camille at their elbow. Vestris strode in front of them, more for show than anything else, Sasha thought. Her partner, stolid as ever, marched behind.

Onrushing night chilled the air, but it remained warm enough to make the short walk enjoyable, even relaxing. Alien blooms caught Sasha's eye, and exotic scents filled her nostrils, evoking hints of roses, hyacinths, and other Earth flowers. Sasha thought of gardens she had known and loved, including her own, and wondered if she would see them again.

The gold thread twanged. Danion. For the first time since she had awoken on Kazratan, it felt as though he were almost close enough to touch. She tightened her hold on Slava's arm. He glanced down at her, and she put a finger to her lips. He nodded and touched his other hand to Camille's waist.

Now, Danion's voice said in her mind. She pinched Slava, who whirled and knocked out the guard behind them with one well-placed kick. Sasha grabbed the largest rock she saw in the street and brought it down on Vestris's head. It made a sickening clunk.

Sasha winced. To her right, a window opened, and a long-fingered hand beckoned from it. She did not wait to see what she had done to Vestris. Instead, she grabbed Camille's elbow and ran, Slava behind her. A bolt of blue seared her left shoulder. She gasped and ran faster. As they approached the window, Camille pulled away.

Three steps and one grand jeté later, Sasha was in her husband's arms. Danion plucked her out of the air and kissed her, harder than he had ever kissed her before. The bond changed instantly from trickle to river.

Two thumps, and a window crashed shut. Camille and Slava, she guessed.

In the street, a laser gun was firing. Danion released her mouth, listening. The house was dark, too dark to see his face, but she didn't care. He felt warm and blessedly solid; she rested her cheek against his chest and wished she could stay there for the rest of her life. His arms encircled her; she wrapped hers around his waist and held tight. The gun fired again.

"Trouble," he said. "We have to leave." He pointed at a cloaked figure that stood nearby, an outline in the dim light. "Go with Jonthar. Stay with him until I come for you, and leave with no one but me. Understood?"

"But where will you be?" Sasha asked.

"I must let you go," he said. "The secret police will have tagged you, so allow Jonthar to remove the transmitters, or they will trace you. I must check on my students, but I will see you soon."

She stood on tiptoe to kiss him. I can't go until you release me, she said, making that difficult. He held her close.

I don't want to, he said.

His cheek, his mouth felt warm to her touch. Take care, Danion. Don't let them capture you.

He let go, pushing her toward Jonthar. Or you, *kaleita*. Quickly, now.

A cloak, like the one the mysterious Jonthar wore, enveloped her. By the time she had settled it around her shoulders and could see through the hood, Danion was gone. A hand closed around her wrist, and she hurried after her guide.

From behind a large flowering bush, Danion surveyed the damage. One member of the resistance was down, and two comrades had stayed to help her while the others fled back to the caves. Sasha's guards lay on the ground; a uniformed police agent kicked the woman as he walked by.

The crowd that lined the street had vanished, except for those who, dressed as civilians, were wielding guns. More than two guards, then. Had they always been there, and Jonthar and the others had missed them? Or had something warned the government of an escape attempt?

While he watched, the fake civilians split into two groups. One chased the fleeing members of the resistance, while the other remained to guard the three youngsters in the street. Danion hoped his followers would reach the caves before the secret police discovered where the entrance point lay.

His main concern was to free his comrades. Sasha was moving away from him again, as she should be, if Jonthar was following his instructions. Danion forced his wish to go with her into the back of his mind and focused on the present. He needed a diversion. Like most young people, the students reacted fast, and if he could provide the opportunity, he could count on them to seize it and run.

As if on cue, a puff of smoke rose from behind the building opposite Danion's bush. Minutes later, a boom of historic proportions sounded from one of the abandoned houses nearby (not Sasha's, Danion hoped), followed by a childish squeak, hastily controlled. The heads of the police officers snapped round as though pulled by a single string.

The two standing members of the resistance grabbed the one lying in the street and bolted round the corner. The remaining officers gave chase, only to be interrupted by a second boom, louder than the first. One, obviously the leader, cursed in Kazrati.

"You," he said, pointing to one of his subordinates, "after them. See where they go. The rest of you, with me." Without waiting for their acknowledgment, he turned and ran toward the burning houses, his five associates on his heels. The sixth hesitated, then raced after the students. Danion followed the man as quickly as he could without drawing undue attention to himself.

The crowd that had left the first street to congregate in the surrounding area was scattering. Danion could hear shouts and footsteps from the area where the explosions had occurred, although his own alley was deserted.

He ducked behind a house and peered around the corner. The secret police officer stood not six feet from him, looking from side to side in a puzzled manner. Danion drew back, intending to retreat, satisfied that his students had made their escape.

A hand tugged his sleeve. Danion whirled. He could hear his teeth grind as he tried not to yell.

Choli stood in front of him, Tamir at her side. One look at their soot-covered faces told Danion everything he needed to know about the source of the explosions.

His heart hammered. He held a finger to his lips. Choli nodded. Her wide eyes revealed that the escapade had frightened her. Tamir's broad grin told a different story, but they could deal with that when they reached the caves.

If they reached the caves.

Silently he drew the two children down the steps of the house behind them. As added insurance, he covered Tamir's mouth. The police officer passed within a hand's breadth of them, his head lowered except for an occasional glance over his shoulder. Danion, thinking of the kick administered to the man's fallen comrade, did not envy him; his commander would not be pleased that he had failed in his task.

A tile clattered to the ground. The police officer spun on his heel and came toward them. Danion pushed both children behind him, their backs against the wall. The officer stopped at the top of the steps.

He turned away, and Danion let out a silent breath of relief. Then the man apparently had second thoughts, for after another look over his left shoulder, he headed in their direction again. Danion grabbed his throat as he approached, throttling him into unconsciousness.

"Is he dead?" Choli whispered. He could see the horror in her eyes.

Danion gave the hand signal for "no" and pushed her toward the stairs. "Home," he said, "at once." She ran.

With Tamir's unsolicited help, Danion pushed the unconscious policeman into a convenient drainage ditch, presently devoid of liquid, away from the view of passersby. He grabbed Tamir's arm and jerked his head toward the caves.

Several twists and turns later, they caught up with Choli and the three members of the resistance. The one the secret police had shot lay, head lolling, between her companions. It did not take a doctor to realize that she was dead. Danion, identifying her as one of the many who had come in from the streets, sent a prayer to the suns of Tarkei, so much kinder than Kazratan's demon ghosts, to care for this young spirit dispatched too soon.

Tamir stared, shock on his face, the enormity of his danger striking home. "You saved them, Tamir," Danion said. It no longer seemed necessary to point out the risk the boy had run. "Without your diversion, all three would have been lost." He touched Tamir's short dark hair. "Myself as well."

Tamir looked up, his eyes troubled. "I didn't think," he said. "It was like a game. It could have been Choli lying there, or me."

"Thinking is usually preferable," Danion said. "We can discuss it later. For now, we must get home." He took Choli's hand in his and turned to his two remaining students. "Are there other injuries?"

One young man raised his arm. "I was wounded, but not seriously. Otherwise, I think everyone is unhurt."

"Take it to the healer as soon as we return," Danion said. The young man nodded. He and his companion turned, their fallen comrade slung between them. Danion touched Tamir's shoulder, indicating that the boy should go with them.

"And to think I expected to have trouble finding you," a familiar voice said. "So considerate of you to be out on the street when I arrived! I followed your scent the whole way here."

An overactive imagination—it had to be—but Danion was already reacting. Behind him, silence fell. Tamir, about to accompany the others as ordered, was staring at the entry to the last tunnel, where a skinny lavender being with navy-blue hair and fully perked antennae lounged against the rock wall. She turned her palms up to face the ceiling.

"It is well the police don't have your gift," Danion said. Then, to what he was sure would become the undying amazement of those present, he held out his arms.

Thuja leaped toward him, dangling from his neck as she always did. He could see the six rows of lilac teeth as she laughed at him.

"I am so glad to see you," he said as he returned her to her feet. "You could not have arrived at a more opportune time. Please, come with me. We must talk."

❋

Sasha followed the cloaked figure through what seemed like an endless procession of abandoned houses. From the street, she heard explosions, screams, running feet, and general commotion. Her guide quickened his pace in response to the noise, and Sasha did likewise, ignoring the ache in her shoulder where the laser beam had struck.

The bond had thinned again, although the memory of those moments with Danion remained strong, and the thread itself ran clear between them. She had only to reach out to touch him, but at the moment, she did not want to distract him. He could, as he would no doubt tell her, take care of himself. She worried anyway.

The cloaked figure Danion had identified as Jonthar beckoned impatiently, and Sasha ran to catch up with him. Her recapture would endanger Danion as well, and they would have the rescue to do over again. Her guide plunged down more dark hallways and doorways. How long would this last?

Finally, the Kazrati stopped and opened a trapdoor. Silent, cloaked, faceless, he stood like the cloistered ghost beloved of Victorian novelists, pointing at the hole in the floor. Sasha repressed a shudder, tried to forget every horror film she had seen, and dropped through the opening. While she had traversed this maze, Danion had found safety. She saw him standing in what looked like a tunnel with several young Kazrati, at least one of whom seemed to be no more than a child.

He had not been captured—a huge relief. As the trapdoor gave way to a dark, wood-lined passage and her guide, having pulled the door over their heads, pushed in front to lead the way again, Sasha needed as much reassurance as she could muster. The silence and the dark oppressed her, and her companion's sinister appearance did nothing to allay her fears.

From under his cloak, Jonthar produced a torch. Its feeble light made little headway against the encompassing gloom, but the sight of even that small beam cutting the darkness raised Sasha's spirits. But every step took her farther from Danion, which counteracted the benefit provided by the torch.

And where were Slava and Camille? Intent on her husband, she had not seen them leave, but not a whisper, not a breath, suggested they were nearby.

The tunnels twisted and turned. Sasha had long since lost her sense of direction. She reached out her hand to stop Jonthar and demand more information.

The Kazrati turned and grasped her shoulder at the exact point where the laser had struck. Pain lanced through her. She pulled back, trying to escape her attacker's hold, and for an instant, she slipped free. Not for the first time, a would-be assailant had underestimated her strength.

A door opened right beside her. Sasha whirled, intending to run, but strong arms encircled her. Jonthar again clamped a hand on her sore shoulder, and everything went black.

Her head rested on something soft. Everything else was moving, bumping and crashing around her. A hand stroked her hair. Her head hurt, and her shoulder as well. Concerned voices murmured above her. Was she in the Kazrati hospital?

At the back of her aching head, a bubble of concern floated. I'm well, she said to it. I think.

Sasha opened her eyes. Slava's warm brown ones looked down at her.

"Better, my dove?" He helped her sit up. What she'd thought was a pillow had been his lap.

She let her head rest on his shoulder. He put a brotherly arm around her waist. It was mean to wish that it could be Danion's shoulder and Danion's arm, but she did. The bubble of concern developed a multicolored sheen of amusement. Sasha sent her husband a kiss and did not share her thoughts with Slava.

"You're both here," she said. "How did you get here? I didn't see you in the passageways."

Over her head, Slava said, "We left with another of Danion's students while the two of you were saying hello." He prodded her in the ribs. "If you hadn't been so preoccupied, you'd have noticed."

Sasha elbowed him back. He grinned at her.

She looked at Camille, who knelt in front of her. Wherever they were was small, uncomfortable, and entirely surrounded by metal. And moving, as Sasha had noticed right away. Were it not for Slava's steadying hand, she would be rolling all over the place by now.

"Where are we?" she asked Camille. "Have you any idea what's happening?"

The ballet mistress raised a shoulder with the quintessential elegance so characteristic of her. "I do not.

We are in some form of ground transport. A truck, let us say." Like Sasha, she spoke French. A language the three of them shared but unlikely to be comprehensible to Kazrati, friendly or otherwise. They could have used it in front of their guards, except that Vestris and her partner would have become suspicious.

What had happened to Vestris—and worse, what would happen to her now that she had failed in her assignment? Guilt touched Sasha; she had rather liked Vestris. Not enough to want to remain a prisoner, but enough to feel sorry that Vestris might pay as a result of something Sasha had done.

"Does it hurt?" Slava brushed the spot where Jonthar had grabbed her.

"Yes," Sasha said.

"He was trying to get your transmitter out," Slava told her. "That's what he said, anyway. Apparently the secret police tagged us so that if Danion tried to rescue us, they could track us. It's him they're after; we're the bait."

"Oh." Sasha relaxed against her partner's shoulder. "Danion said that. Only someone shot me as I was running for the window. Right there. I couldn't figure out what he was doing, because it hurt like crazy."

"Does Danion vouch for him, *petite*?" Even in the dim light, Camille looked worried. "Because I must tell you, I am not so happy driving through the night with strangers."

Sasha queried the link in her head. Danion seemed happy—because of the renewal of the bond or something else? Improbably, purple antennae drifted in his thoughts. "He doesn't vouch for anybody," she said after a moment, "although he says Jonthar has been loyal until now. And to be patient; he will join us soon."

Behind her head, Slava's shoulder shifted. "Very well," the Russian said in his honeyed tenor, "but just in case, I think we should be prepared."

The truck drove on through the night as they made their plans.

Vestris came to herself to find one cheek pressed against the curbstone. Her ribs ached, as did her head. A tentative hand pressed against her temple came away streaked with dark brown blood. She shivered, although the night air was not cold.

Quiet enveloped her. She pushed herself upright and surveyed the scene. Not far away, D'Toth lay, unconscious or dead—she couldn't tell which. She ought to find out, but she felt weak and sick, not inclined to move.

What had happened? She had been walking down the street, with the three humans behind her, and her partner behind them. The same trip they had made a hundred times without incident.

She felt her own eyes widen in alarm. The humans! Where were they? The street was empty, herself and D'Toth incapacitated, the humans gone.

Vestris dropped her head in her hands and groaned. An escape attempt—and successful, it seemed. She and her partner had failed in their only task, to keep the government's hostages away from those who would try to free them. Her life would not be long, and the little of it that remained she could do without. She pulled out her laser gun, wondering if she should end it before her colleagues returned and did it for her.

The gun flickered in the reflected planet light, sleek and silver and deadly. Vestris held it to her aching head and put her finger on the trigger. I will press it, she told herself, but she could not make her hand move. She was not, it seemed, quite ready to die.

In the distance, she heard the sound of booted feet striking the pavement. Across from her stood a row of abandoned houses. As fast as her pain-wracked body would allow, she crawled to the nearest house before the police returned. Somehow, she managed to fall through the doorway. Once inside, she pulled herself up and, hanging on to whatever support she could find, slid from house to house, looking for a place distant enough, secure enough, that they would not find her. Indeed, where they would not even think to look.

At last, she saw a trapdoor. Perfect. With the last of her strength, she pulled it open and slipped through. She was not strong enough to hold it. It fell on her damaged head, knocking her out. Vestris tumbled down the ladder and lay at its foot, unconscious.

9. Échappé

THE TRUCK SLOWED, THEN stopped. The three inside heard voices raised in anger. Several male voices, their words unclear. Then blasts of laser fire. Tires screeched and an engine gunned as the vehicle took off, careening down the road, knocking them to one side, then the other.

More laser fire. The truck swerved, crashed, and skidded to a halt.

"We are prepared?" Slava said. Sasha nodded and saw Camille do the same.

The door to their compartment opened to reveal a cloaked figure holding a silver gun. Slava, about to pounce, stopped.

"Very wise," the figure said. A man's voice. "Jonthar is dead. You come with me."

The voice sounded familiar. Sasha listened, head on one side. Where had she heard it? Across from her, Slava was doing the same. Camille stared intently at the man.

He reached into the compartment and hauled Camille, who was closest to the door, out by one arm. He held the gun to the ballet mistress's head and said, "Out, both of you. Now."

Sasha raised her eyebrows at Slava, scowling like a lion whose selected antelope has put on a burst of speed and made a getaway.

So much for their plans, but she saw no real alternative. The hand that held the gun to Camille's head looked extremely steady. "Later," she said to Slava in Russian.

"Move!" The figure jerked Camille's arm. Sasha climbed out of the truck, followed by Slava. The gun was pressed against Camille's temple; it would be difficult to tackle this person before he pulled the trigger.

Difficult, but not impossible. He could not monitor three people at once.

"That way," the figure said, using his elbow to point to the right. Arm in arm, Sasha and Slava walked into the woods.

The thread between Sasha and Danion shimmered in the night. He could track her wherever this maniac took her. Sasha wondered if their captor knew about the bond and, if so, how much. Not enough, she hoped, to realize that he could not take Danion's wife to a place where he could not find her, or even cover up what was happening. The thread had thickened; Danion was traveling toward her. Good.

"He has left," she whispered to Slava in Russian.

"Quiet," the cloaked figure said.

That voice again. Sasha turned her head to glare at him. He still held the gun pressed to Camille's elegant dark head.

Sasha looked at her partner, who returned her gaze with the cool understanding so typical of him. They had known each other for a very long time. "Tombé, piqué, renversé," she said.

"Quiet," their captor repeated. In his irritation, just for an instant, he turned the gun away from Camille's head and pointed it at the two dancers. Slava dived for the man's legs, Sasha stabbed her foot into the ground and spun into him, knocking him over as Slava tackled his ankles. Camille hauled her arm free, stomped on the hand so recently pressed against her temple, and picked up the gun. The man yelled as her heel ground against his fingers. She gave the gun to Slava, who pointed it in a businesslike manner at their erstwhile captor's head.

The hood fell back, revealing white hair, a lined face, and brown eyes. "I was taking you to Danion," the man said mildly. "Jonthar was about to hand you over to the enemy."

That voice, so familiar. He looked familiar, too, although not enough that Sasha could pinpoint where she had seen him. Definitely, she did not trust him.

She glanced at Slava. Her partner was watching the stranger through narrowed eyes.

"I think," Slava said, "we will dispense with your guidance." Before anyone could protest, his right hand chopped across the cloaked neck. The old man fell.

"You didn't kill him, did you, *mon fils*?" Camille was staring at the old man's body.

"I'm not an assassin," Slava said. "I knocked him out. Let's go. I want to be far away when he comes round." He grinned at Sasha. "That was inspired, my dove."

"Thank you." Sasha returned his smile. "You understood me perfectly, or it wouldn't have worked. Do we tie him up?"

Slava shook his head. "If we move fast, he won't follow us. Danion can locate you, is that not so?"

"Of course."

"Then let us go, and quickly, before anyone else decides to offer assistance." Slava, gun in hand, turned and walked into the woods, keeping his distance from the highway.

"He's right," Sasha said to Camille. Together, they set off behind Slava.

❀

They walked for a long time. The evening air cooled, and the moons rose. No one pursued them. The woods, as silent and as deep as Robert Frost's, closed around them; the scent of something that smelled like pine needles rose from the greenery under their feet. Sasha kept expecting an owl to hoot, but no owls lived on Kazratan.

Danion was close now. Sasha forced her feet to move steadily, quietly, through the woods, not to rush into a refuge that might prove to be a trap. She whispered in Slava's ear, and he passed the news to Camille that their journey would soon end.

Sasha felt sure that anyone within a hundred yards must be able to hear her heart pounding. Her palms were moist with apprehension and anticipation; more than anything, she wanted to fling herself into her husband's arms. Her stomach was performing Odile's thirty-two fouettés.

Ahead lay a clearing, in its midst a stucco cottage. The moons struck sparks from the quartz that edged its gray tile roof. The windows gleamed. It looked like a dollhouse, exquisite and fragile, quite out of character with the surrounding woodlands.

Inside, Danion was waiting. Sasha touched Slava's arm, then Camille's.

Slava raised the gun, ready in case of trouble. Sasha walked down the narrow path lined with wood chips and opened the door. On the opposite side of the room, silhouetted against the moonlight, a still figure sat. In the moonlight, sparks flashed from a garnet earring.

Sasha stopped, just inside the door. Slava pushed her gently from behind. Camille stood at her right shoulder.

The figure on the other side of the room spoke, its voice calm—even, perhaps, tinged with amusement. "Really, Slava," Danion said. "Is the gun necessary?"

Everything seemed to happen at once. The gun clattered to the floor. Slava said, "You are alone, then?" and held out his hand. Camille shut the door, her breath rushing out in a huge sigh of relief. She pushed past Sasha and dropped onto the nearest chair. Sasha closed her eyes, overwhelmed with joy, and opened them again to find Danion walking toward her. While he was several feet away, she jumped, laughing, and threw both arms around his neck.

He caught her, of course—his reflexes were as good as Slava's. The bond glowed with delight and desire. Sasha gave her attention to greeting her husband.

When Danion put her down and she had leisure to look around, she found the others clustered in the corner, backs ostentatiously turned. Sasha leaned against that strong, beloved body, reveling in the sensation of her husband's arms around her waist. His chin rested on her short hair. The light was too dim for her to see his face clearly, but being able to touch him was enough.

"We must go," he said. "The farther we can get while it is dark, the better." In his thoughts, she saw he would have preferred to stay here. There was another room beyond this one, where they could be together.

That would be wonderful, she said. For hours, we've done nothing but run. How I want to be alone with you!

Soon, *kaleita*, he said, but he sounded wistful, as though he could not wait. Even now, he told her, we are not far from the highway. We have a long way to travel before morning.

Sasha wondered where they were going, but she had no opportunity to ask. Over her head, Danion was talking to Slava. "What happened to Jonthar?"

Slava raised his hands, expressing confusion. "Don't ask me. We were driving along, and it sounded as though someone stopped the truck. Then it sped off and crashed. Another would-be monk showed up in a cloak. He said Jonthar was dead and we should accompany him, and since he was holding a gun to Camille's head, we obeyed him until we had a chance to overpower him. Then we took the gun and came here."

In the moonlight, she saw white teeth flash against Slava's tanned skin. "We figured if we stayed with Sasha, you would find us." His grin vanished. "Luckily, no one else found us first."

"We must leave at once," Danion said. "This way."

"I recognized him," Sasha said. Her husband stopped, staring at her. "I don't know from where, but he sounded familiar. Looked familiar, too, although I don't know if that's because I had met him somewhere or because he reminded me of someone else."

"I agree. He did sound familiar," Slava said.

"And I," Camille added.

"Come." Danion caressed Sasha's ear. "You can tell me the rest on the way." One hand on her waist, he led her toward the back of the house.

Slava and Camille followed in silence. The sense of being hunted oppressed them, Sasha decided, as it oppressed her.

Behind the house, she saw a small shuttle painted in the particular shade of matte black that signaled the craft's ability to evade detection. A Tarkei ship, from its shape. Was this how her husband had traveled to Kazratan?

Danion opened the door, and the steps descended automatically. He lifted her up to the doorway, a habit of his that she had never succeeded in breaking, perhaps because she didn't make much of an effort.

She turned to fuss at him, playing her part, but he was handing Camille up to the door. Sasha went into the cabin and buckled herself into the seat next to the pilot's chair.

Slava and Camille settled themselves. Danion closed the door behind him, took his seat, and set the small craft in motion.

Surely now it was safe to talk. "Where are we going?" Sasha asked.

"Off planet." Danion aimed the shuttle's nose at the sky. "To a place of safety, if we can make it."

Not too informative. In the muted cabin lights, her husband's face looked strained, more lined than usual. Given the circumstances, that was not surprising. She reached out, touching his thigh, and saw his half-smile.

"An old friend stopped by," he said. The mischievous tone made it clear he would tell her no more. "I am delivering you there, before returning to the caves."

"You're not coming with us?" Sasha looked at her hands, curled into fists. Behind her, Slava and Camille echoed her protest, although not her unspoken wail.

Danion heard the wail. She saw him flinch, but she also sensed his determination. Damn. Convinced that a particular course of action was the right one, Danion could be immovable. After nine months without him, she had no desire to be carried off by whatever old friend he had managed to dragoon into transporting them while he went back into danger.

"I cannot, *kaleita*." He took her hand. "The attempt to recapture you demands my attention. Someone I trusted has betrayed us. Once your transmitters were removed— they were removed?"

Sasha nodded. "I think so."

She turned her head. "You said so, Slava. How did you know?"

"Jonthar told us," Slava said. "But I was not unconscious. I saw him take it out. Camille's, too. And yours. You fainted because your shoulder was injured."

"Then the secret police had no way to trace you," Danion said. "Unless someone told them where and how you would be traveling." He took her hand, his thumb making circles in her palm. "If I left, my students would be defenseless. They don't even know the danger they face."

Sasha clenched her teeth, refusing to yell at him in front of Slava and Camille. That caressing thumb was arousing feelings she both wanted and did not want, under the circumstances. She thought of pulling her hand away but could not make herself do it.

"We will discuss it later," Danion said. "I am not leaving tonight."

One blessing, at least. Sasha stared out the window on her side of the shuttle, fighting a wave of desolation. At the back of her thoughts, she sensed sadness, guilt, and Danion's overwhelming desire to leave the resistance movement to its fate.

He wouldn't do it, no matter what he felt: he was too much the Tarkei for that. And what could she say? If he were willing to abandon his commitments that easily, he would not be the Danion she loved. It would cost him, but he would do what he believed to be right.

The link flashed a vision of how much it would cost him. Sasha stared at Danion, who was not looking at her. Ahead of them, a tiny blip had appeared on the view screen.

Their destination, she hoped, not a Kazrati patrol.

His hand enclosed hers. Sasha squeezed it, signaling her forgiveness. Danion turned his head, bestowing on her the half-smile she loved.

Yesterday I was a prisoner, she said through the link. Thank you, my darling. You will not mind if I say I wish you would stay with me?

His hand tightened in response. And I, *kaleita*. I would give everything I have not to say goodbye again so soon.

That was the truth, she saw. His sense of their separation seemed infinitely greater than hers. Why?

She did not ask. Danion had returned his attention to his piloting. Ahead of them, the blip was growing. Soon they would know whether it represented friend or foe.

The potential for conflict had ended their conversation. This was not the moment to reinitiate it. Not even to talk about that strange sense she had had of recognizing the old man. Distracting Danion seemed like a bad idea.

It was odd, though. As the blip grew larger, she stared at it, her mind elsewhere. Where had she seen that old man before?

Danion released her hand, the better to concentrate on his task. Sasha clasped her palms together and watched, hoping the hunt was over.

Danion dipped the shuttle beneath the second moon and brought it into line with Thuja's ship. A hurried conversation, and a bay door opened. He docked the craft and watched the doors roll into place behind him. Until the hull was sealed and the air restored, they could not leave their vessel.

He had known Sasha would not approve of his plan to return to Kazratan. Her initial anger seemed to have given way to resignation. Danion doubted her silence would last and hoped her reaction would not spoil the reunion for which he had waited so long.

The whoosh of air returning was a welcome sound. The telltales on his console flashed, and he tripped the door. Slava, closest to the exit, went first, and Camille followed. He half-expected Sasha to scramble out behind them, evading his hand, but she did not. Instead, she followed him out, letting him swing her down.

Perhaps he had been mistaken, and she was not upset with him. More likely, she was biding her time, hoping to ambush him with a logical argument that he would find difficult to resist.

The lights in the starship's bay were bright, almost too bright to bear after the dimmed lighting of the shuttle. As his eyes adjusted, Danion realized that for the first time in that interminable day, he could see Sasha properly. He looked down at her. His hand caressed her too-short hair, the line of scar that ran down beside her ear. Her gray eyes looked huge in her thin, strained face.

She was staring at him as though he were the one who had come back from the dead.

What happened? Her shock reached him clearly through the link. *Did Kazratan do this? The resistance movement? You look years older!*

Her hand stroked his hair, where the glossy black mingled with gray. Only then did he realize that no one had told her how much time had passed since she left for Chandar. He looked at Slava, at Camille—they, too, stared at him as though he were a ghost.

Danion took both his wife's hands in his and held them against his chest. "*Kaleita,*" he said. He tried to keep his voice steady, but it refused to cooperate. The pain of those lost decades could be heard. "You were gone for sixty years." Her face went blank, emotion vanishing even from the bond. "The Kazrati did not tell you?"

Sasha shook her head. The hands he held trembled. Behind her, Slava and Camille looked equally bewildered, as though the whole concept was too outrageous for them to take in.

Danion tried again. "Your ship went through a time vortex and landed on Kazratan, sixty years after you left."

Between his hands, Sasha stood absolutely still, her eyes focused on his chest. Through the link he sensed her reaching out to him, questioning some part of himself that even he was not willing to acknowledge. Her head tipped back until she was looking straight into his eyes. The movement reminded him of Odile.

Her immobility vanished in a trice. Sasha threw her arms around his neck and burst into tears. You thought I was dead, she said through the link.

A floodgate opened, and despite his best intentions, the desolation of his years alone poured into her thoughts. Danion, his whole body shaking, buried his face in the too-short hair and held Sasha so tightly he was afraid he might hurt her.

She didn't protest, though. Oh, Danion, she said. I'm so sorry.

"That's why I couldn't sense you when I first woke up." Her voice was as shaky as his. He heard her take a deep breath and let it go. "I was so worried about you, but I had no idea. It never occurred to me that I might be the one who was dead."

"Fortunately, neither of us is dead." Danion could hear the tremor in his own voice. He stopped trying to control it and brushed the tears off his wife's cheeks instead. Behind her, Camille was sitting on the steps of the shuttle, her head in her hands. Slava sat next to her, looking stunned.

"Well met, everyone," Thuja said behind him. "Please don't think me heartless, Danion, but if you don't let go of Sasha and start piloting, the Kazrati are going to blast us out of the sky before we complete this rescue."

❀

Before Sasha had finished saying, "Thuja!" Danion stepped back.

"Take the command chair," the Pannthu called after him. "I'll settle the others and join you." Danion raised a hand as he went through the door.

Thuja held out her arms. "Well, Sasha-*chan*, you have outdone yourself this time." Her lilac teeth gleamed in the overhead lights.

Sasha hugged her, wishing the world would slow down for a moment so she could catch her breath. "Danion's taking the ship out?"

"He insisted on it," Thuja said. "Thank the seven goddesses. If he hadn't, I'd have had to hold him down until he did, because getting here was a nightmare. My crew is untrained, and I don't have his reflexes—let alone his calm. I can't imagine how he does it. The odds were split as to whether the helm officer would lose an antenna first or me."

Sasha hugged her again. "Thank you, Thuja. You don't know how much this means to us."

"And to me, Sasha-*chan*." Thuja dipped her head, bright purple with embarrassment, and changed the subject. "Then he's going back to Kazratan, he tells me. Unless you'd like me to knock him out or sabotage his shuttle." Her antennae drifted from side to side; the Pannthu was joking.

"I wish you would," Sasha said. "But he thinks he owes it to them, so you know it wouldn't do any good. He'd go back later, when we weren't expecting it, and then we'd have to come get him again."

Thuja produced her lipless smile. "So he would. A more stubborn man I have yet to meet. Except for his father, who will not be pleased when I explain why I have brought you but not Danion." Her face brightened. "You can explain. That is good."

A lavender hand on Sasha's arm turned her toward the door. "Come, let me show you to your quarters. Are your friends all right?"

Sasha glanced over her shoulder. "Are you? Personally, I'm too muddled to think." They nodded, although she did not believe them. How could they be? To Thuja she said, "Is it true? Were we really gone for sixty years?"

"It's true," Thuja said. "We thought you were dead."

Sasha shook her head, struggling with the idea. Camille, Slava's supporting hand under her elbow, walked over to join them—slowly, as though she was having trouble assimilating what she'd been told. Thuja embraced her.

Letting go of Sasha's arm, the Pannthu stood on tiptoe to hug Slava. "A pleasure to see you again," she told him. He kissed one lavender cheek, then the other, sending Thuja into an ecstasy of exclamation points.

"We thank you," he said. "You ran a great risk coming here."

Thuja grinned, her antennae waving happily. "Not compared to explaining to Jenat why I would not do what he asked." She led the way out of the shuttle bay.

"He still terrifies you, Thuja?" Sasha asked. "But he's such a sweetheart under that armor."

Thuja linked an arm through hers. "So you say, Sasha-*chan*. I expect you're right, too. He got quite choked up telling me about the report that you were alive. Nonetheless, I'd rather watch you explain to him why his precious son refuses to leave Kazratan. And first you can explain it to me."

They were halfway down the corridor already, Slava and Camille close behind them. "I'm not happy about it," Sasha said. "If I can talk him out of it, I will. But you know Danion. He thinks someone leaked information to the secret police about his plans to free us, and a man did try to recapture us, which is highly suspicious. And whether he's right or not, he won't leave until he finds out who the traitor is, and why they did it, and how badly the movement has been damaged—whether it's one person or a group. That kind of thing."

Thuja pressed the hand plate to summon the elevator. "But you three will come with me? You will not subject me to more heroics?" Her antennae dipped toward her nose. It made her look pathetic. "Please, Sasha-*chan.*"

She could not promise, although she had no more desire to return to Kazratan than to go into space without a suit. Still, she didn't want to leave Danion either.

"Let's hope it doesn't come to that," she said. Thuja groaned.

A neat little ship, Danion decided as the bridge doors opened. Five Pannthu heads swiveled in his direction. The navigator, whom he recognized and who straightened his antennae in salute, sat off to the right. The helm officer, whom he did not know, occupied a console in front of Thuja's command chair, flanked on either side by gunners;

the three of them looked like juveniles. On the right, behind the navigator, sat the communications officer. He, too, seemed very young.

"Mind your console," Danion said to him. "If you so much as see a star blink, I want to hear about it." The youngster's antennae shot up, but he stopped staring and turned back to his duties.

"I am Danion of Tarkei," he told the rest of them. "Your commander has asked me to pilot the ship out of Kazrati space. Thuja will arrive shortly, and she will expect to find you performing your assigned tasks." He dropped into the command chair and beckoned to the navigator. The other three heads faced front, as they should.

The navigator left his station to stand by the command chair. "Can I access the helm controls from here?" Danion asked.

The Pannthu pressed several indentations on the touch pad. "Now they are locked in." The buttons were marked in Pannthu, so he showed Danion which was which.

"I have it," Danion said. "Return to your station. We will leave at once and take the most direct route. Maximum speed." He gave the navigator the course heading and watched the man punch it into his console. Beneath him, the engines roared into life. The star field in the view screen changed.

"Your job, Communications Officer, is to notify me immediately of anything you observe." One pair of antennae dipped in acknowledgment. "And yours, Navigator, is to compensate for any course corrections I must make—the more rapid the corrections, the better." Another acknowledgment. "The rest of you, stand by."

The bridge doors whooshed behind him. Thuja tapped his shoulder. "We're underway, then?"

"Underway," Danion told her. "Sasha and the others are settled?"

"For the moment." Thuja pushed the young communications officer away from his console and took his place. "Sit there." She pointed to an empty chair between her seat and the navigator's. "And learn something. You, too, Helm."

Danion, watching antennae straighten around the bridge, suppressed his amusement and focused on the star field.

Sasha surveyed the quarters Thuja had assigned them. After the last twenty-four hours, she would gladly fall down, as soon as she found a place to fall. The quarters were pleasant: a central room with doors opening off it, one in each of the five walls, in the Pannthu pod style.

Three of the five walls were lined with bright red cushions, creating a sofa-on-the-floor appearance both colorful and welcoming. A large, low, triangular table stood in the middle, a food console visible on its gleaming marble surface. On the far side of the table, the young girl Sasha had seen in Danion's thoughts sat with her back pressed against the cushions. Straight black hair framed her face, and her dark eyes were wide. With her raised chin, she looked rather like an angry kitten.

Sasha, fighting exhaustion, exchanged glances with Slava and Camille, walked to the sofa, and dropped onto the red cushions. "I'm Sasha." She held out a hand toward the girl. "And you?"

The child lifted her chin even higher. "I am Choli. Danion's daughter."

She could be, too. Sasha had thought the girl was Kazrati, but she could just as easily be Tarkei. This wouldn't be the first time Danion had neglected to mention what she would consider crucial information.

But whose child was she? Not Reilu's, surely? Danion had made no bones about his refusal to sleep with the woman his father had forced on him, and Sasha had observed that he and Reilu sparked a peculiar antipathy in each other, as though all their synapses were out of alignment.

Still, much could change in sixty years.

"And who is your mother?" Sasha's voice sounded muffled in her own ears, perhaps because, almost of its own volition, her head had dropped onto her raised knees. She hugged them to her.

"My mother is dead," Choli said.

How old was she, anyway? Twelve or thirteen, at least. Danion had thought Sasha long gone by then. Would he have remarried? Or had a child, married or not? Neither sounded like him, but either was possible.

Sasha had expected Danion to be focused on his task, but her distress must have reached him, for he said through the link, My adopted daughter, *kaleita*. Please don't take offense at her manner. She spent many years alone, and she fears you will reject her.

Relief washed through Sasha like rain through the desert.

Kaleita, he said. How could you think such a thing?

Even though you believed I was dead?

I love you, he said with a finality that disposed of that argument. She heard Thuja's voice. I must go, Danion told her.

Sasha raised her head. Slava and Camille, concern in their faces, sat next to her.

"Let's start again," she said to the girl. "I am Sasha Sinclair." She pointed to Slava, then to Camille. "This is my partner, Slava Zoshchenko, and our ballet mistress, Camille Delagardie. It will be fine if you call us by our first names."

The child nodded, dark eyes wide in her small blunt face.

"Danion says he has adopted you," Sasha said. "That makes us your family."

Beside her, she felt Slava relax. Camille, too, released her breath in a long exhalation. The child before them did not react, except to draw farther into herself, the fear more visible beneath the hostile stance.

Sasha wondered what Choli needed to hear, and whether she could produce it after so long and stressful a day. Complex calculations were beyond her at the moment, so she settled for the simplest statement she could make. "I'm tired, Choli, but I'll try to be clear. I love Danion, and Danion loves you. You will always have a place among us. Only please, let's be kind to one another."

Choli's lip trembled. "I upset you. I'm sorry. Will Danion really go back?"

So she was scared, too. Sasha held out her hand again, and after a moment's hesitation, Choli took it. Sasha pulled the girl against the shoulder that had once held the transmitter and tried not to wince; it still ached. Hard to believe that had happened a few hours ago.

"It upset me to think Danion would have had a child with someone else," she said to Choli. "Even though that's not what you said. I'm having a hard time realizing that sixty years have vanished from my life—and on top of everything else that's happened today, it was more than I could cope with. As for Danion, I expect he will go back, although I'm going to try to persuade him otherwise."

Choli pressed her cheek against Sasha's shirt. Over the girl's head, Sasha's eyes met Slava's; she saw the sympathy there, for both of them. Sasha bit her lip against the pain and supplied what comfort she could.

"Suppose they kill him?" Choli asked. "I'm so afraid."

Me, too, Sasha thought. Aloud she said, "I expect he'll do just fine. He's good at looking after himself. And you won't be alone, because we will take care of you. I'm sure it worries you, though."

She flicked the child's ear. "I worry like crazy myself, but he always comes back."

The child wriggled farther into her arms. "Why does he want to get rid of us?"

Sasha laughed, brushing a hand through Choli's hair. "He doesn't want to get rid of us." Through the link, she touched Danion's thoughts. "On the contrary. He's taking the people he cares about out of harm's way, so no one can use us against him. Then he has only himself to worry about."

So Thuja had no need to fear, for Danion was no more likely to agree to take Sasha with him than to change his mind about staying.

Strap yourselves in, *kaleita,* Danion said. I anticipate a rough ride.

Sasha surveyed the room. How?

There is protective webbing on the beds, he told her, and harnesses behind the cushions.

Sasha passed the information along to her companions. On cue, the ship dipped and swerved, and she sighed. Someone was chasing them, or monitoring them, or something. Remembering what those course changes looked like from the bridge, she was glad to be spared the roller-coaster effect. She trusted Danion, but still, it meant trouble. Trouble she could neither control nor evade, that she had to depend on others to handle. If things went wrong, she might not even know. "I hate this part," she told Slava.

Camille, focused as usual on the present, interrupted before Slava could answer. "Well, *mes enfants,* here we are. Let us rest while we can, so that tomorrow we can practice, no?"

Practice. Sasha tried to guess what time it must be. They had ridden or walked or flown most of the night. She was so tired she wasn't sure she could get off the sofa to find a bed. And Camille could think about practicing.

She was searching for words when Camille pointed at Choli, whose head had not left Sasha's shoulder. "*La petite,* she may stay with me." She pushed herself off the cushions and stood up, then walked to the far right door, opened it, and peered in. "Excellent. Come, *ma belle.* Let us find this miraculous webbing that will keep us from being tossed about the ship."

"She means you," Sasha said, reasonably sure that Choli's upbringing hadn't included a short course in French endearments. "*La petite* is 'little one,' and *ma belle* means 'my beauty.' As you'll discover, Camille uses both liberally and applies them to all her surrogate daughters, including me." Sasha flicked the child's ear again. "It means you're family now." Choli raised her head.

"Feeling better?" Sasha asked.

The child stood, her face sad. "Thank you," she said in a voice as even as Danion's. "You are very kind."

Sasha watched her go, wondering whether she was seeing the effects of her husband's attempts at Tarkei training or something more troubling.

"She's trying." Slava grinned at her. "Poor kid."

He'd read her expression correctly, as he so often did. "Yes," Sasha said. "Dragged out of her home, dumped with a bunch of strangers, and threatened with losing the one person she can count on. It's not surprising she's touchy." She stretched. "It would be easier if I weren't so touchy myself."

Slava stood and held out a hand; she grasped it and pulled herself up. "I'm going to lie down," Sasha said. "See you in the morning."

Slava kissed her cheek. "Sleep well, my dove. You can be sure Camille will wake you in good time."

"She'd better not," Sasha said. "Not only am I completely exhausted, but if it's true that I haven't seen Danion in sixty years, I'm not getting up for ballet class!"

She heard Slava laughing as she picked, for no particular reason, the far left door.

❊

Danion, still in the command chair two hours later, experienced a sense of déjà-vu. To his right, Thuja called each obstacle, surveillance device, and scout ship they encountered. There were many: the Kazrati monitored their borders as a miser watches his gold; and they were as concerned about people leaving without authorization as they were about unwanted visitors. Thuja's ship did not look like a typical Allied vessel, and like the shuttle it was equipped to escape detection. Even so, evading the patrols demanded constant vigilance and short reaction times. Danion sent the ship up and down, left and right and into spirals, while the crew held onto their consoles and muttered prayers to the seven goddesses.

He was tempted to mutter a prayer himself, although of a different sort. As a rule, he loved the challenge of piloting, especially under such circumstances as these, but today he would gladly have sent the Kazrati to their demon ghosts' maw while he forgot the whole thing and went down to his wife. That he had been awake for forty-eight hours did not help.

Waiting for the next alert, he glanced around the bridge. The navigator, while not as quick as Geoffrey, did a good job of compensating for the numerous course changes. With Thuja, intent and focused, the three of them could bring the ship through. They would have to, for the rest of the crew were, to put it kindly, underprepared. The communications officer, deprived of his post, huddled in near-immobility, although intermittent prodding from his commander kept him from drifting into sleep. The gunners, barred from shooting anything, stared disconsolately at the screen. The helm officer seemed to swing between resentment and catatonia, although on occasion a daring move sent her antennae shooting upward. Danion wondered how they had made it to Kazratan. They must be an untried crew: Thuja was not known for her tolerance. It made her willingness to come after him that much more remarkable.

His friend gazed at her console, antennae touching her forehead. Between glimpses of the star field, Danion watched her, thinking about their long and, in some ways, improbable friendship. In personality, they were not alike. Of course, he and Geoff were not alike either, and they were just as close.

For a moment, he wondered why Thuja was still captaining a ship after so many years. Perhaps it satisfied a part of her nothing else could touch, or maybe she could imagine no alternative. She had several pods of children back on Panntha in the care of their fathers but no established household. No steady friends, except himself and Geoffrey. Danion clasped his elbows, reminded again of that long-ago trip to Xantera. Here he was in the pilot's chair, Thuja monitoring for enemy traffic, but no Geoffrey to navigate. Danion missed his human friend. Another reason not to tarry on Kazratan.

The link glittered in his thoughts. Geoff was not here, but Sasha, whom he had thought lost forever, was waiting for him three decks down. How strange life was.

"Astern," Thuja said.

They must be close to the perimeter. "How far?" Danion asked, fingers hovering over the controls. Against the star field, he saw one last scout ship, putting on a burst of speed. He didn't think it could catch them.

"On my mark," Thuja said. "No need to compensate. Navigator, alert. Wake up, Communications. Helm, pay attention. Gunners, stand by. Five, four, three, two, one. Boundary." The ship, free of pursuit, flashed across the imaginary line separating Kazrati and Allied space. The scout ship screeched to a stop on the other side of the line and trailed them along the border. They continued to travel away from it, and after a few minutes, the scout ship fell back.

The purple antennae dipped in his direction. "Thank you, Danion," Thuja said. "I will tell anyone who asks that you're still the best pilot in the fleet." She glared at her helm officer, who cringed, antennae drooping. "I hope you took notes."

Danion gave her his half-smile and stood. "Be careful, my friend. You may yet see a scout ship or two, although this is not a disputed region. Meanwhile, I will be with Sasha." At the door, he turned. "If my father calls, don't wake me."

Thuja, six rows of lilac teeth showing, grinned at him. "If you insist. Shall I tell him you'll call him back?"

Danion raised a hand. "Do that." The bridge doors closed behind him.

At last, he could be alone with his wife.

10. Sissone

DANION FOLLOWED THE LINK to Sasha. He thought she must be asleep, but when he cleared the protective webbing and lay down beside her, she rolled over and put her arms around his neck.

What a day, she said, sounding drowsy. Her fingers tangled in his hair. I'm so glad to see you. We made it through?

We are in Allied territory. Danion rolled onto his back, pulling Sasha on top of him. Unless we encounter another vortex, nothing should trouble us. His hands, exploring her, found fabric. What is this?

It came from the bureau drawer. Sasha giggled. In case Choli came in or I had to get up for some reason. I have no clothes of my own except the ones I had with me.

None are necessary. Danion tugged at the robe, and Sasha pulled it over her head. Her skin, soft against his own, almost convinced him she had never been away. Almost. He stroked her back, feeling ribs sharper than they should be, with odd bumps here and there marking recently healed breaks. Her short hair curled around his fingers, silken as a baby's, but beneath it he could feel the rough edges of scars that had not been there before, delicate new skin with crinkly, burned edges. How close he had come to losing her.

As, indeed, he had believed for so long. The contrast intensified the pleasure of holding her, alive against the odds.

On her shoulder, he touched the blister left by a more recent wound. Sasha flinched, and Danion apologized.

It's nothing, she said. One of the police agents fired at me as I was running for the window. I treated it before I came to bed.

I will be careful. He brushed the scars again. You have had a good deal of pain, I think.

Through the link, he could see how much, but Sasha shrugged.

It was not pleasant, but it is over. She flicked his chin. And you're here. Not being able to reach you was worse than the injuries, and I didn't even know about the sixty years.

My Altanai, he said, referring to the rare desert plant that was their metaphor for the joining. It is true, we are together.

It seemed unreal. For not much more than a week, he had known she was alive, but until certain of her rescue, he had not dared to revel in the understanding that his years of solitude were over.

Sasha's fingers traced the line of his collarbone; her lips touched his ear. He sensed her listening to his thoughts, trying to understand what had happened during those years alone, to see the impact of her own absence, her own return. Her hand brushed back black hair frosted with gray, caressed lines she had not expected to find. He heard her wondering how he had changed, whether she held the same place in his life.

So much experience, she said. It's like getting to know you for a second time. I missed you, and I thought we were apart for only nine months. I try to imagine what it was like for you, and I don't know where to start. I have so many questions.

I love you, Danion said. The short hair rubbed between his fingers, soft and fine. I have always loved you. That will never change. An image of Reilu's marble face shimmered at the back of his thoughts. He shivered, in the way that humans claim marks a goose walking over one's grave, and banished it to the ice palace where it belonged.

Sasha was watching him. Her fingers stilled against his cheek. Where did that come from?

Her eyes were warm—sympathetic, even. He might as well tell her; she would find out soon enough. She lived with me, he said, for several years after you disappeared. I had no contact with her, and eventually I threw her out.

He hesitated, biting his lip. You will think it an excuse, perhaps, but in those days it took everything I had to maintain the façade of self-control. I had no energy to fight Reilu.

Sasha's thumbs pressed against his temples, her fingers returned to bury themselves in his hair. How far did it go? Her voice had the same tone it had had when she asked about Choli's mother—idle curiosity masking the potential for deep hurt.

Danion pulled her against his shoulder, showing her what had—more accurately, had not—happened between him and Reilu. As the truth communicated itself to her, he felt her relax in his arms. Watch out for her, though, he said. She intended for you to die, or at least to send you to a place where I could not follow you.

Sasha's head snapped up, and the gray eyes that seemed too big for her face met his. *She* arranged it?

My father had proof, Danion said. That was when I threw her out. Even now, fifty-seven years later, his anger bubbled at the thought.

Sasha freed a hand and caressed his cheek. Then her eyes narrowed. Not alone, though. Who was her contact?

Danion thought. Had Jenat told him? I don't know, he said. Father may not have found out. But you're right, she must have had one.

He could hear Sasha thinking; the bond, clear as a river of gold, flowed and curved and washed between them. So many levels, each with its own joys. Touching her mind was as precious as sharing her body. After so many years, both had become pleasures as rare as the altanai he called her.

Danion stroked his wife's back. There's a thought there, she said, but it will wait.

Sasha kissed him, her mouth warm and soft. Her tongue flicked his, and Danion closed his eyes. When he tightened his arms, her nipples pressed into his chest.

Sixty years is a long time to wait to make love with one's wife. Yet he had not forgotten the broken bones and papery skin. You were injured, he said. You will not let me hurt you?

You won't hurt me like this, Sasha said.

❈

Danion heard voices outside their door. Sasha lay on top of him, her head heavy against his shoulder. He straightened an arm that had fallen asleep and tightened his hold.

Sasha raised her head. She was awake. With one hand, he made sure that the blanket covered them.

The voices did not come in or even pound on the door. Danion, rolling sideways with his wife in his arms, thought gratitude.

Sasha's laughing face looked up at him, just as it had in his dream—was it only a week ago? Choli wants to see you, I'm sure, she said, and Camille's undoubtedly itching to start class. Slava probably told her I threatened not to get up as long as you were here.

Thus ensuring that one person will be glad to see my back, if only so she can get you into the studio? Assuming that Thuja has such a place. Danion tapped her nose.

If there's a floor, Camille will make a studio, you can be sure. That woman frightens me. She stroked his face. As for the other part, she has to reach you first. What makes you think I'm planning to let go of you any time soon?

He ran his fingers through her hair. Alas, my Sasha, you must. The farther we travel into Allied space, the longer it will take me to finish my task.

You're determined to do this, then?

He caught the hand she stretched out toward him. Through the link, he sensed sorrow and apprehension, perhaps a sense of rejection—as rigidly controlled as though she were the one who had been raised on Tarkei but present nonetheless.

He hated to disappoint her, especially under the circumstances. Suppose he failed and was captured, realizing her worst fears? No one knew better than he what she would endure if that happened.

And even if it did not, he had already spent too many years without her. If he had not believed her dead, he would not have gone to Kazratan in the first place. He would have let the resistance movement take care of itself.

Sasha lay in his arms, soft and warm and loving. Danion caressed her ear with his thumb, letting his desire flow across the bond, so she would know he did not want to leave her.

But you will, Sasha said. He would have liked to protest, but there was no point. What he might have done when the resistance movement was a group of faceless fighters, he could not do now. People depended on him, young people unaware of the betrayal that threatened them. Sasha was not the only one who needed him, although she was the most important.

It hurt, to face such a choice. He felt pulled in both directions, after just starting to feel whole.

And you won't take me back with you, his wife said. She sounded as though she knew the answer.

I can't, Danion said. You have already been used as bait once. I can operate freely only if you and your friends and Choli are safe, and the more freely I can operate, the sooner I can finish what I need to do. You were right about Xantera, he said, seeing that objection in her thoughts; let me be right about this.

Sasha traced his cheekbone with her fingers. I don't want you to be right. I want you to stay with me and be safe.

He had no answer to that, so he made none. Instead, he caught the exploring hand and held it against his chest.

Sasha kissed him. We will take good care of Choli.

Thank you. She was trying to be helpful. It should have made him feel better, but his sadness remained.

Sasha pulled her hand away and snapped a finger against his face. Just make sure it isn't permanent, or you're going to be one sorry ghost!

He caught her hand in his again, the sadness fleeing as laughter bubbled along the link. I promise, *kaleita*. I can—

Take care of yourself. She reclaimed her hand and circled his neck with both arms. I love you, Danion.

And I love you, Sasha. He kissed her. No one said we had to get up this minute.

By the time they did get up, the others had finished their morning meal. They sat, in various stages of relaxation, on the red sofa cushions: Camille ramrod straight, her back nowhere near the wall; Choli curled in a corner, her feet tucked under her, neat and self-contained; Slava sprawled, propped on one elbow, across an entire bank of pillows. Sasha requested coffee and yogurt from the food panel and settled at the far end of Choli's section. Danion, a plate of vegetables and what she always thought of as Tarkei tortillas in his hand, joined her.

He flicked Choli's ear. "Did you rest well, little bird?"

Choli blushed and nodded. Sasha watched with interest; this was the first time she had seen them together. The first time she had seen Danion with a child, for that matter. It made her realize how short their marriage had been.

"Good morning," she said to Choli, and received a shy smile in return. "You two look much better," she told Slava and Camille.

Slava stretched. With his blond hair and tanned skin, he resembled a tawny lion. "Yes, another century or so, and I will be quite recovered." One long arm ruffled Sasha's too-short hair. "Not that I had your source of rejuvenation, my dove."

Sasha aimed a kick at his shins, but he rolled aside. Danion seemed more amused than embarrassed.

"That's for you to fix, not me," she said. "And you, Camille? I heard you up indecently early, given how late we went to sleep. Or did it just seem early?"

"It is past noon, *ma belle*," the ballet mistress said. "I slept as long as necessary. Indeed, I have already found a place to practice. The crew is converting its exercise area for our needs. We will start when you have finished your breakfast."

Told you so, Sasha said to her husband.

"Later, please." Sasha saw Camille's hands move in instinctive protest. She did not owe Camille an explanation, but she offered one. Camille cooperative was preferable to Camille obsessed with rehearsal. "Danion has to leave, and before he goes, he needs to hear whatever we can tell him—about the accident, our treatment by the Kazrati, the people we met, the attempt to recapture us, everything."

As she talked, Sasha glanced around the room. Each of her companions reacted to her words in his or her own way. Slava nodded and sat up, his languor replaced by intensity. Camille raised her hands, bowing to a logic she could not deny. Choli withdrew into herself, wrapping her arms around her thin body as though she could rely on no comfort but her own. Danion responded, reaching a hand toward the child. Choli pulled away from him. Her chin quivered; she looked small and scared.

Should I not have mentioned it? Sasha asked her husband. I wanted Camille not to fight me over the practicing.

Choli knew, he said. She wants me to leave no more than you do, but she understands.

I think, he added. Sasha sensed him watching that rigidly contained small form.

It frightens her, because she has been abandoned before, Sasha said. So much he had told her last night.

Yes, Danion said. He looked sad, but she could not help him. It was for him and Choli to work out. Instead, she talked about the accident, the hospital, their recovery, the performance—whatever she could remember that might give him the information he would need to come safely home.

Slava and Camille broke in with details she had forgotten, but none of those details revealed why the old man whom Slava knocked out had seemed so familiar.

"Tell me again," Danion said. "He told you he had killed Jonthar."

"He implied that he had killed Jonthar. He said Jonthar was dead, after trying to turn us over to the secret police." Sasha looked at Slava. "Isn't that right?"

"He said, hand us over to the enemy." Slava frowned, as though trying to remember. "I assume that's what he meant. And that he was taking us to you. Had rescued us, in other words."

"But you did not trust him?" Danion looked curious, the "I am Tarkei, I have no feelings" pose that bore little resemblance to his real self, the cross-legged pose left over from his days as a priest. He neither lounged like Slava nor kept his back ramrod straight like Camille; rather he sat as though being centered and still were the most natural things in the world. He seemed focused on the conversation at hand to the point that, had Sasha not known him as well as she did, she might have thought he had forgotten Choli.

Glancing at the girl pressed into her corner, her crossed arms a barrier between her and the rest of them, she wondered if Choli understood that he had not forgotten, could not forget. His determination to fulfill his commitment to the resistance movement was, in itself, proof of that.

Slava was answering Danion's question, his voice dry as the Tarkei desert. "By then, I trusted no one but you, and at times I wondered if you were not acting under duress."

Danion quirked an eyebrow in response. "An old man, you said, with brown eyes."

"Do you know him, Danion?" Sasha asked. "Whoever he was, I don't think I saw him here. Unless he was in the hospital, I suppose, when I first woke up."

Her husband shook his head. "I would doubt that." He glanced at Choli, who avoided his gaze. "It sounds like Nirrtu, don't you think, little bird?"

Choli hugged her arms closer to her chest. "Yes."

"A friend of yours?" Slava asked, drawing everyone's attention except Danion's.

Hands in his lap, Danion watched Choli. "In a sense. Nirrtu joined the resistance movement long before I arrived. He was the one who asked Father for help."

He touched Sasha's temple; she heard him querying her thoughts through the bond. "Definitely Nirrtu," he said.

Sasha sat with her back against the wall, supported by the cushion. "If that's so, there's no way I would have seen him before, is there?"

"It seems unlikely," Danion said. "Perhaps he reminds you of someone. Sendar, for example. I have often noticed a resemblance."

"Perhaps," Sasha said. She did not believe it but, being unable to suggest an alternative, let it go.

Danion flicked a finger against Choli's ear. "You will do fine, little bird."

The child sat cross-legged on the red cushions, pleating the fringe of a pillow in her fingers. The dancers had left the two of them alone, ostensibly to check on the practice facilities Camille had found.

"You said you would never leave." Choli would not look at him. "Now you want to go back to the most dangerous place I know."

While I stay with these strangers. Danion filled in the missing part of the sentence without difficulty, but how to reassure her? Sasha would accept her—had already accepted her—and not only because he requested it; she and Camille collected waifs and strays as readily as they breathed. Slava, too, exhibited a brotherly concern. Choli had that effect on people. She didn't realize it, however, and he doubted it would comfort her if he told her. Instead, he tried to explain his reasons for going.

"I cannot take you with me, Choli." He wished she would look up, but her eyes remained focused on the pillow as though it could solve her problems. "I need to ensure that you will not be captured or hurt. If the secret police has infiltrated the movement, you are not safe anywhere on Kazratan. They will use you to get to me. They know how much you mean to me."

Complex thinking for a thirteen-year-old, even one raised on the streets. Danion hoped she would focus on the last part and feel comforted.

Instead, he saw her thin shoulders shake. Danion placed a finger under her chin and tipped her head back. "Oh, little bird," he said, seeing the tears, "I will come back."

She felt warm and light in his arms. "Do you love me, Danion?" Her voice came in bursts as she found control and lost it.

He patted her shoulder. "Of course. Did I not say so? You are my daughter."

The sobs eased. "I wish you wouldn't go."

"I would rather stay, my child, but I can't leave the movement without a leader, and in such disarray. I swore to help them, too." She sat back on her heels, and Danion brushed the hair back from her forehead. "You will like Sasha, I promise."

"It isn't that," Choli said. "I like her already. I was mean to her yesterday, and she didn't yell at me or anything. And the others spent the whole morning with me. Camille even said she would teach me to dance." She sniffed.

Danion made no comment. Since the day she heard the story of Sasha's shoes, Choli had talked about how much she wanted to dance on her toes, but at this moment, she sounded as forlorn as though Camille had threatened to feed her bread and water for the rest of her life.

"You will like that, I think," he said after a while.

Choli looked at him. Through the tears, one dimple showed. "Not if it means you will leave me." She no longer sounded as though she had lost her only friend. Danion gave her his half-smile, and she threw her arms around him. "Hurry back, Danion."

"As soon as I can," he said, hugging her. "I assure you, I am not eager to extend my stay on Kazratan."

He repeated the same assurances to Thuja, who dangled from his neck with her usual abandon and threatened to return to collect him if he had not appeared within three months.

"There is no need for you to enter Kazrati space," he said. "If you would like to meet me beyond the perimeter, however, I will not object. I will tell Sasha when I leave." He deposited her on the floor of the shuttle bay and flicked one antenna. "It will be pleasant to see you again so soon."

"Very well," she said. "I would protest more strongly if my crew were better trained, but I don't think two hours of watching you pilot will teach that wretched child of mine how to fly. I will wait for you in the area where you broke through this time."

"Yours," Danion said. "Literally?"

Thuja produced a sigh that could be heard on Tarkei. "Literally, alas. She fancies herself a helm officer, and I have hesitated to disillusion her, but soon, I think, I must. The communications officer is mine, too, from the same pod. Fortunately, some of the others show greater aptitude. Two have their own ships."

"Congratulations," Danion said, letting his affection show in his voice. "I am certain these two must have aptitude as well, if not for helm and communications."

"Oh, I think they would profit from a stint on someone else's ship," Thuja said. "They don't listen to me. But perhaps you're right, and they belong in science. I will suggest it." She tapped his ear. "And I will wait for you, Danion, when Sasha says you are leaving, so do not tarry long."

"I won't." Danion felt like a stuck computer program. "Thank you, Thuja. I look forward to seeing you soon."

Saying goodbye to Sasha was most difficult of all. Having accepted that she could persuade him neither to stay nor to take her with him, his wife, as was typical of her, wasted no time on recriminations. Not that she hid her feelings; Danion could have identified them even without the bond. Grief at the shortness of their reunion, fear for his safety, hope for his rapid return, love—everything he might expect to find in such circumstances was there. She hugged him and cried. Danion kissed her and wished that he himself could cry. "I'll be home soon," he told her.

"You'd better be," Sasha said. "Otherwise, I'll talk Thuja into bringing me to look for you."

Alarm rushed through him. Then he saw the rueful smile, the tilt of her head. "I didn't mean it," she said. "I remember why you brought us here." She hugged him again. "But I do want you back in one piece, and soon. Agreed?"

"Agreed," Danion said. "A few months at most. Once I find out what happened and train a successor, I can return."

Sasha stepped back. "I'll be waiting, Dani-*chan*, so don't disappoint me."

She had never used his nickname before. He flicked her ear in farewell.

"May you bask in Danar's rays, my love," she said. "May the stars always smile."

Danion kissed her once more and boarded the shuttle.

"He's gone?" Thuja greeted Sasha as she came through the bridge doors. Sasha nodded, trying to hide her grief. The Pannthu probably guessed; an antenna dipped in her direction.

"We must call Jenat, then." Thuja looked like someone faced with the news that a serious illness has been declared terminal.

Sasha waved an airy hand at her. "Call him. I'll talk to him. I'm sure he'll understand."

The lilac teeth gleamed in the bridge lights. "I'm sure he will, if you explain it to him, Sasha-*chan*. I just don't want to do it myself."

Sasha raised her eyes to the ceiling. An expression wasted on Thuja, who had no equivalent. Off to one side, she heard the communications officer place the call.

In a remarkably short time, given the distance between their present location and Tarkei, the screen cleared. Sasha subdued a lump in her throat and smiled at her father-in-law. The contrast between the Jenat she remembered and the old man before her made clear—even more than the change in her husband—how many years had passed since she had last seen any of them.

What must her brother Tonio look like these days? Was he even alive?

Alive and lively, Danion said along the bond. The last time I saw him, in any case, which is not that long ago. Danion's mind revealed a Tonio she barely recognized: the bright brown curls a shock of white; the face lined; the body wiry and thin, not unlike Jenat's; but the eyes a brilliant, sparkling brown.

A thought tapped her brain and withdrew, a flash of recognition that disappeared as fast as it had shown itself. She straightened her face so that Jenat would not misread her reaction and set the thought aside to puzzle over later.

"Father," she said to the man on the screen, "I am delighted to see you. Thank you so much for sending Thuja to help us."

"My daughter." Jenat extended a hand toward the screen, his voice unsteady. "This is a joyful day indeed. Are you and yours well?"

"We are," Sasha told him. "Slava and Camille are with me, and we bring you a granddaughter—Danion's adopted Kazrati child. Her name is Choli, and she is thirteen years old. But I must tell you, Danion himself has returned to Kazratan. He brought us past the perimeter, but he is concerned that the resistance movement has no credible leader and may have been infiltrated by the secret police. He promises to return in a few months."

The elderly face crumpled. Jenat, prime minister of Tarkei, fought for control and found it, but to Sasha, who had never considered him unfeeling, his pain was clear. Another thought drifted by—this one she hid from Danion, committed to another course of action: could it be that Jenat did not have a few months?

She hoped not. Sasha loved her father-in-law, despite his grumpy façade.

"I know," she said, wondering if she did. "I, too, wish he were here."

"He seemed to be in excellent condition, however," she added, hoping he would detect the mischief and be comforted.

His dark eyes lit with the humor he rarely expressed. "I am pleased to hear it, my daughter. And you are well? You look somewhat..." He stopped, apparently searching for words.

"I was injured," she said. "The shuttle crashed coming out of the time vortex. I am much better now, though. And you?"

"I am old, dear child," he said. "Otherwise, I have no complaints. Do you come to Tarkei?"

Sasha glanced at Thuja. "I go to Earth, father. I must see my brother. Can you meet me there? Or should I come to Tarkei as soon as I can? I have much news."

Jenat talked to someone Sasha could not see. "I will meet you on Earth. In San Francisco?"

"Please." She turned back to Thuja. "How long will it take us?"

"Four, five days," Thuja said. "We are closer to Earth than to Tarkei."

"I will meet you at the Tarkei Consulate, in a week, or whenever suits you," she told Jenat. "If you are delayed, the ballet school will know where to reach me."

Thuja whispered in her ear. Sasha said, "Commander Po asks me to tell you that she is planning to return to meet Danion whenever he is ready to leave, and that he's still the best pilot in the fleet."

Two Tarkei eyebrows lifted, but Sasha knew he was pleased.

"Naturally. Why else would I have sent him to Kazratan?" Jenat raised a hand. "But I thank the commander for her assistance, past and future, and I will see you, my child, one week from today."

Sasha blew him a kiss. "I look forward to it, father. Take care of yourself."

"And you, my daughter," he said.

Jenat vanished as the connection was cut. "Incredible," Thuja said.

Sasha grinned at the circling antennae and left the bridge.

11. Promenade

CHOLI, SPELLBOUND, WATCHED THE two dancers. They began with simple knee bends and progressed through what was obviously a planned routine to more complicated steps. Even the knee bends interested her, though; they turned their legs right out to the sides, and they went down so straight. Without moving from her chair, she imitated the sideways stance. When Sasha pointed her feet, Choli pointed hers too, trying to imagine how the movement would feel if she were standing.

Once when they were between steps, she saw Camille watching her and quickly turned her head. A few minutes later she glanced back. Camille was still watching her.

What had she done? Here in the studio, the dance mistress made her nervous, for she jumped on Sasha and Slava for every error, even though most of them were too small for Choli to see. Not that the dancers seemed to care; they took the corrections in stride, except for the occasional muttered comment.

After a while, Choli saw why: Camille cared a great deal that her students do well. In some ways, she reminded Choli of Danion, although she had a vivid, expressive warmth that Danion permitted himself only in rare instances—primarily, Choli thought, when Sasha was around. She felt a rush of jealousy, which she suppressed as unworthy of Danion's daughter.

"Now stretch," Camille said after a whole series of exercises. "But, Sasha, one moment please."

Sasha came to stand beside Camille.

"Look." Camille pointed at Choli, who panicked.

Oh dear, she had done something after all. But what? She hadn't moved!

Sasha looked, and her eyebrows rose. "My, my." She walked over and lay down in front of Choli, her feet drawn up, knees and heels both on the floor. "Can you do this, Choli?"

The girl lay down on the floor beside her and copied her pose. "Of course."

"Of course." Sasha sounded as though she might break into laughter at any minute. "Did you hear that, Slava? Of course."

She turned back to Choli. "There's no 'of course' about it, my lamb. We call those 'frogs,' after a Terran amphibian, and 99 percent of the population can't do them to save their lives. The gods have blessed you with natural turnout. Stand up."

Choli stood, puzzled. It seemed she had done nothing wrong. But what was natural turnout?

Sasha led her to the makeshift barre they had placed beside the shuttle wall. "Here. Hold onto this with one hand. Pull your stomach in as tight as you can and kick to the front, like this." She watched as Choli did as she asked. "What do you think, Camille?"

"Definitely," the Frenchwoman said. "Definitely. She is not too old to begin?"

"With that physique?" Sasha tapped Choli's stretched knee. "I doubt it. Kazrati age more slowly than we do, remember. In physical terms that puts her closer to nine than thirteen."

Camille, a hand on her chin, nodded. "That is so. Then ask her whether she is interested. If she is, who makes the decision? Danion?"

"We do. He left her in our care. I'm not going to bother him with something like this when he has so much else to handle." Sasha had begun stretching while she talked. It made the conversation oddly choppy, but it looked beautiful.

"Choli," Sasha asked, "would you like to learn to dance like me and Slava? It takes a long time and it's tons of hard work, but it's almost the most fun you can have and remain legal."

Choli was dying to say yes. Ever since she had found Sasha's shoes, she had longed to know how it felt to dance like that. The flash of jealousy that had plagued her vanished in the light of this new and fascinating opportunity. "You mean dance on my toes, like you?"

"One day, if you want to." Sasha, one foot on the barre, bent forward from the hips and laid her cheek against her shin. She spoke to Choli from under her raised arm. "You need years of training first. Would you like to learn, though?"

Choli thought. "Yes," she said, "I would. Could I?"

"I will teach you," Camille said. "We have a school for dance and many other things, like those you learned from

Danion. The students come from throughout the allied planets, and they belong to many species. Even Tarkei, although that is rare. I don't know how many students the school has now, but Danion said it exists. You would be welcome to join it."

"They would let me in?" Choli asked. She meant, "They would admit a Kazrati?" but it didn't seem to occur to the dancers that that might be a problem. Slava burst out laughing. Choli stared, unaccountably hurt. She had thought of him as a friend, or at least not a stranger.

"Don't laugh, Slava," Sasha said. "Choli doesn't know you yet; she'll think you're mocking her."

Slava laughed harder, until he was holding his sides. "Choli, I'm sorry," he said in gasps. "That's not it. I am laughing because I cannot imagine Sasha's brother, even at—how old is he now?—having the nerve to tell Camille he would not take a student she recommended."

He stopped long enough to grin at Camille. "No one would." Camille smacked his hand—lightly, making a point.

Sasha stared at him. "How old is Tonio? I hadn't thought." The white-haired man in Danion's thoughts flashed before her eyes, filling her with dismay. "Sixty years, gone like that. I'm thirty-one, so what would that make me—ninety-one? Tonio must be ninety."

"Ninety." Slava repeated the number, his eyes on the studio wall. He was no longer laughing. For once, Sasha could not tell what he was thinking.

"How can he be so much older than I am? He's my little brother." Sasha's stomach tightened, until she had to fight not to throw up. "Half the people we know will be dead." The thought that had hovered around her while she spoke to Danion's father returned, drifting just out of reach. She chased it, but it eluded her.

Meanwhile, even Camille had fallen silent.

"It will be very strange," she said at last. "Very strange indeed." Sadness showed in her dark eyes, before her relentless practicality reasserted itself. "But for you the world will always have a place, so for now let us continue. Later we can consider what else we must face. Choli, please return to your seat. You will like to watch this, I think. When they are done, I will give you your first lesson. Agreed?"

❀

Danion parked the shuttle as close as he could to the city without attracting attention either to it or to himself. The ride in had been easier than the passage out, not least because this craft was much smaller than Thuja's ship and thus much better at evading detection. A short woodland path, a rapid run across open space, and he had reached the tunnels that traveled under the abandoned houses.

He was in no hurry. The thought of what awaited him in the resistance movement, however strong his conviction that he had to deal with it, was infinitely less attractive than the family he had sent away on Thuja's vessel.

Had he, after all, made the right decision? He had been gone more than two days. A determined informer had had plenty of time to destroy the resistance. Suppose the movement was already dead?

Jonthar and Nirrtu. One had lied, but he did not know which. One had betrayed him—possibly both. Jonthar was dead, if Nirrtu told the truth, but Danion had no independent confirmation of that. Nirrtu, most likely, lived.

And how many others wore the faces of friends but served the enemy? Tamir? The young man whose friend had fallen during the first rescue attempt?

Not Choli. He was sure of her loyalties. And she was gone from the caves. In that he had succeeded.

Ahead he saw the ladder that rose to the trapdoor. At its foot, the dim light of the lantern he carried revealed a body that thrashed and moaned.

Danion crept closer. The body belonged to a woman in a police uniform. She was unconscious, although her erratic movements suggested she might recover consciousness at any time. He heard a muttering, like delirium. Gently he turned her over, feeling for injury. Near the crown of her head, he discovered old blood.

He shone the lantern on her face. Even drawn in pain, it triggered a moment of recall. Danion had last seen her in the street, lying in front of the house where Sasha had jumped through the window and into his arms. The woman assigned to guard the prisoners, whose life was now worth less than nothing to those who had employed her.

Danion stood, looking at the body on the floor. He was not so far from the caves that he could not carry her; although stockier than Sasha, she was a good four inches shorter. But she was a police agent. Even in its disordered state, the movement deserved better than for its leader to bring a police agent into its camp.

Yet without care, she would die. Danion could not find it in himself to leave anyone, including a police agent, to die when he had the means to help.

Perhaps he could make use of this and assist her at the same time. Danion picked up the woman and, with some difficulty, maneuvered her up the ladder and onto the floor of the silent house above. He slung her over one shoulder and went on, taking a roundabout route into a section of the caves known only to the inner circle. There he laid her on a straw pallet and settled down to consider his next move.

"San Francisco." Sasha stretched as she disembarked from Thuja's ship. After a warm farewell, Thuja herself had remained on board, chivvying her crew through its preparations for departure. "As lovely as ever. Look, Choli, the Golden Gate Bridge."

The child twisted this way and that. At any moment, Sasha expected to see her swivel her head full circle like an owl. Choli bounced with excitement, but her hunched shoulders suggested fear as well. Sasha hugged her. "It'll be fine, you'll see."

Slava hailed a skimmer and piled bags into its trunk. "Come, ladies, San Francisco awaits. Choli, this is the hilliest city in North America. That capital of yours is so flat, I shouldn't think you've ever seen anything like it."

Out of pure devilry, Sasha decided, he plotted a route that traversed most of the city, including a trip down Lombard Street that had Choli covering her eyes.

"Beast," Sasha said. "Couldn't you break her in gently?"
Slava just laughed.

❀

Years ago, when she danced with her brother's company in San Francisco, Sasha had owned an apartment. Despite the many ways in which her husband had parted company with his planet's traditionalism, the instinct to hold on to property remained, for he had told her that it was still there, available for her use. With Slava, Choli, and Camille in tow, Sasha walked into a home that she had not seen for sixty years (although it seemed like less than one) and found it almost exactly as she remembered it.

It was eerie, in a way, to know that so much time had passed but to see so little evidence. The appliances were more modern, like the ones on Thuja's ship. Otherwise, although the apartment must have been repeatedly painted and polished, it looked the same. Not a stick of furniture had been moved nor an ornament displaced. It was also meticulously neat, although not for long. Slava piled the few supplies they had brought in a corner, kicked off his shoes, and threw himself onto the couch. Bought for Danion, it accommodated his six-foot-plus frame without difficulty.

Camille requested tea from the food panel before sinking onto a chair. Choli stood in a corner, looking scared and lost. Sasha hugged her, and Camille, noticing, said, "Come, *ma belle*, do not despair. We will take good care of you."

She held out a hand to Choli, who took it and came to sit beside her. Seeing the child settled, Sasha walked to the window.

San Francisco spread out before her. Along the link, she sensed her husband. He was back in the caves, alone, except for what seemed to be a person sleeping nearby.

Vestris, he said. That is what you called her, is it not? Your guard. She is injured, but she will recover.

I'm glad, Sasha said. That I didn't kill her, that is. Have you made any progress in finding the spy?

I have not, Danion said. I have brought Vestris here, so that she cannot harm the members of the resistance nor they her and so that I can reveal my presence at the most opportune moment. The movement still exists. The police either did not discover the entrance to the caves or have as yet refrained from using it. More than that I do not know.

It is a beginning, I suppose, Sasha said.

I suppose. Danion sounded wistful. I would prefer to see the end. And you? Are you well?

I am not in danger, Sasha said. The apartment looks wonderful. It feels as though I never went away. And I will see your father soon—today or tomorrow.

Make my excuses, will you? He went to considerable effort on our behalf, and I'm sure he is not pleased that I did not take advantage of it.

Sasha's laughter, audible only along the link, was rueful. None of us are pleased, beloved.

Ouch, Danion said. I see I must accelerate my pace.

Only if it brings you home safely, Sasha told him.

❋

A search of the apartment produced a trunk of clothes left over from Sasha's previous time here. Wondering how they had survived sixty years unattended (had Danion not lived there after she disappeared?), Sasha gave some to Choli and Camille and set the rest aside for herself. The most conservative she put on right away: after considerable debate, she had decided to visit the consulate first. If Jenat had not arrived—and, being the soul of punctuality, most likely he would not for two days—she could call on her brother with a clear conscience.

It seemed like a good plan, until her request to see her father-in-law was referred to the Tarkei secretary for protocol. On entering a pristine office arranged with rigid symmetry, Sasha found herself staring at the one face she least wanted to see.

Reilu's marble countenance did not change, although her clear green eyes narrowed for an instant when Sasha was announced.

Obviously, Danion had not known. Jenat probably did not either; even the prime minister cannot keep track of every diplomatic functionary. In any case, Reilu was here.

The human spread her hands. "Well, isn't this awkward? I take your husband, or so you believe, and you try to have me killed. And now here we are, face to face."

Reilu leaned back in her chair. One hand indicated the seat opposite. Sasha took it, although she had no intention of staying long.

The green eyes regarded her steadily. "Danion told you that, I suppose."

"It's not true?" Sasha hadn't expected denial.

"You are here," Reilu said, as though that were an answer.

"No thanks to you."

The nonexpression in the green eyes did not change. "Are you sure?"

"My benefactress," Sasha said dryly. There seemed little point in continuing. She stood. "I came to see Jenat. Please tell him, when he arrives, that I am in San Francisco and will return in a few days."

"Where shall I say he should reach you?" Reilu, relaxed in her chair, gave such an appearance of calm friendliness that Sasha wondered if they had misjudged her.

She could not think of anyone she less wanted to have her address, however. "He knows."

The green eyes flashed with an emotion Sasha could not distinguish. It could have been anger or scorn or respect for a worthy opponent, but whatever it was, Reilu controlled it immediately. "A pleasure seeing you again."

"And you," Sasha said, matching the other woman in indifference. "An experience I cannot begin to describe." She gave Reilu her sweetest smile and had the satisfaction of seeing those marble lips tighten. Still smiling, she closed the door behind her.

Safe in the corridor, she leaned against the wall to catch her breath and settle her pounding heart. In the room behind her, she heard Reilu prowling.

Sasha left as fast as she could. The last thing she wanted was to run into Danion's first wife again.

❃

Less than an hour later, Sasha faced another difficult task. Fortified by the presence of Slava and Camille, she stood outside the building that housed the Xantera Ballet School and tried to control the butterflies in her stomach. No matter how often she'd thought it through during their journey, she hadn't found a way to tell Tonio of their return without giving him the emotional equivalent of an electric shock. Now that the moment had arrived, nightmare visions of her saying, "Hello," just to have him drop dead in front of her pranced before her eyes.

"Courage, *ma belle*," Camille said.

"I'm trying." Sasha touched her hand to Camille's elbow. "Let's get it over with, shall we?"

The inside of the school had not changed in any appreciable way. Sasha could see the same big airy studios, filled with eager students and company members in rehearsal; the same dingy offices; the same profusion of dancers' belongings in the hallways—toe shoes spilling out of bags, leg warmers tossed to one side, towels hanging from chairs placed here and there. Except for new paint on the walls (not that new, either), the building matched her memories of it with uncanny perfection. Like her apartment, it obscured the fact that six decades had vanished.

The visitors checked each studio in turn until, about three-quarters of the way down the hall, they found Tonio. Even if Sasha had not seen him in her husband's thoughts, she would have recognized him: a wiry man with Tonio's shock of curls, now white, and vivid gestures undimmed by the intervening years. The half-dozen young dancers inside stood awestruck, as though regarding a prophet, while he demonstrated a step with surprising vitality for someone of such an advanced age.

"*Bozhe moi*," Slava said. "He looks like Balanchine. Balanchine with a perm."

"Doesn't he, though? At least he seems healthy enough. I'd been imagining a frail old man."

Slava grinned. "Old man, definitely. But frail, I doubt it. Look how he's got those youngsters gaping at him. I bet he's loving it, too. Let's go in and startle him, shall we?"

Sasha took a deep breath. "We may as well. Ready, Camille?"

The Frenchwoman was scowling through the window. The young women inside were imitating the step Tonio had shown them, adding speed and height. Camille tapped her foot at the result, then flung open the door and said, "Anthony Sinclair, why do you not correct that child's *attitude*? Can you not see she is dropping her knee on the turn?"

Tonio whirled so fast the stool behind him crashed to the floor. "Dear God in Heaven! Camille? Am I losing my mind?" He looked around him. "Does anyone else see people standing there, or did I go right past my second childhood and end up in Ghostland?"

The dancers shot confused looks at one another, but a pretty girl with light brown hair stepped forward. "You're fine, gramps. Three people just walked in."

Tonio shook his head, quickly, as though to clear it. "Well, that's a start. Bella, tell me what they look like."

Bella rolled her eyes and looked over her shoulder at her classmates, but she obliged. "There's a woman who has dark hair with a streak of white down the right side and black eyes, another woman with short dark hair and gray eyes, and a blond man who looks like Viacheslav Zoshchenko."

"Excellent," Slava said. "I am Slava Zoshchenko." He bowed to the astonished Bella, who stared at him, and held out a hand to Tonio. "We wondered if you could use a pair of unemployed but fit dancers—and an extra ballet mistress."

Tonio, looking dazed, shook the hand. To Sasha, who had moved to stand in front of him, he said, "Didn't you do this to me once before? Next time I'm not even going to stage a funeral. I'll just wait for you." He held out his arms.

Sasha, tears streaming down her face, hugged him. "I am so glad to see you, Tonio. It was terrible, and I'll explain later, but oh, it's good to be back."

He let go of her and hugged Camille. His face grew serious. "Come into my office, and let's talk. I can use the three of you. It's been a long time since I had a genuine prima to work with."

Bella's face took on an expression of outrage. Tonio turned to the dancers. "Take a break, kids. Rehearsal's over for now."

Sasha, following her brother out of the studio, turned at the doorway. Bella looked furious. I see Tonio hasn't learned tact in the last sixty years, she told Danion. If I had to guess, I'd say he's knocked somebody's nose right out of joint.

D'Toth stood, straight as a sword, at attention in his supervisor's office. His commander paced, window to door and back, his steel-gray head sweeping from side to side. D'Toth silently thanked the demon ghosts for the many hours during his training when he had been made to stand motionless. Today he needed it.

"You say Vestris is responsible?" The commander had mastered the knack of spitting out his words until they echoed the growl of a hunting patika. "She betrayed us?"

D'Toth took a deep breath. This, the weakest part of his story, would determine his fate. On Kazratan, power did not tolerate failure, but anyone could fall prey to treachery. If Vestris remained missing long enough, he was safe; otherwise, he could expect to die—horribly.

"She failed us, Commander," he said, sounding as reluctant and as vague as he could manage. "Had she done her job, the humans would not have escaped. Now she is dead." And so she would be, if D'Toth caught sight of her.

He hesitated, acutely aware of his supervisor's gaze, then made himself look more reluctant than ever. "She did treat them with excessive familiarity, I thought. As though she had developed a liking for them."

"But you did not see fit to report it?" The supervisor's bark cast shivers down D'Toth's spine. His cultivated expression of embarrassment became real apprehension.

"I could not imagine that she would forget herself in that way. Sympathizing with humans!" He let his gaze drop to his boots. "I realize the extent of my error, Commander."

"Hmmm." The commander sounded thoughtful now, and D'Toth dared a glance, if only through his eyelashes.

"And now?" his supervisor said.

D'Toth produced a calibrated and elaborate shrug. "Could we not turn it to our advantage? Our informant in the resistance movement says that Danion of Tarkei has left Kazratan. Without its leader, the movement is vulnerable. There is no indication, even, that the fighters know they have been betrayed. They are ripe for further infiltration."

"Do it." The commander still scowled, but it was a reprieve, at least temporarily. D'Toth controlled his sigh of relief and listened.

"Your responsibility," his supervisor said. "Bring me the traitors. Vestris, if she lives. Danion, if that information turns out to be false. Otherwise, the current leader. I am determined to break this movement. Fail, and you can expect no third opportunity to disgrace us. Is that clear?"

"Yes, Commander." D'Toth saluted and marched out.

"It's not the dancers," Tonio said when the explanations were done and it was his turn. "The chain of instruction was broken when Elasi died."

"I'm so sorry." The interruption came in three separate voices.

"Was it long ago?" Sasha added.

"Long enough, Sasha. More than fifty years. She was forty-one—old for an Argosian. Anyway, with Camille gone and Elasi dead, I had no one in the company who could take over. For a while, I survived by bringing in people from the outside, but, good as some of them were, they didn't have the immersion in our traditions, our special way of dancing. It's a rarity these days: most companies mix the various styles to the point where the ability to perform true classical ballet has almost disappeared."

"Is that so bad?" Slava said. "It expands the horizons."

"Of course," Tonio said. "As a choreographer I love the freedom, but as artistic director I can see the price we're paying. I couldn't name a single company, including ours, that could credibly stage a nineteenth-century ballet, let alone something like *Romeo and Juliet* or *Cinderella*. They do Balanchine, sometimes, and in a way that's worse, because Balanchine without the spirit isn't real Balanchine, if you know what I mean. I need you three—Camille to teach these kids how to dance, and the two of you to show them. As it is, the company's hanging on by its teeth. Ticket sales have dropped steadily the last ten years, and who'll invest in a company without a box office?"

Camille nodded. "I saw it, there in the studio. I will begin at once. Also, I have brought you a student. A thirteen-year-old Kazrati girl named Choli. Danion and Sasha have adopted her."

"Thirteen? Seriously?"

"She has natural turnout," Camille said. "The first day, she lay down on the floor and did 'frogs' with Sasha, and she learns—well, you will not believe it until you see it. Not since *la belle*"—she pointed at Sasha—"have I seen such dedication. I tell you, she is a born ballerina, or do you not trust me?"

Tonio laughed. It took sixty years off his age and made him look strikingly like the younger brother Sasha remembered. "I'm not in my dotage yet, whatever I look like. If you vouch for her, she's in, and welcome to her." He tipped his head toward his sister. "So you saw Danion? Everything fine there?"

"Except that he's gone back to Kazratan." Sasha raised her hands in pretended helplessness. "He swears he'll be home in three months."

Tonio looked sympathetic. "Tough, when you'd just gotten back together again. Although it must be worse for him. I don't suppose he told you, but he pretty much fell apart when you disappeared. Went off to that sanctuary of his and didn't show his face for ages. I worried about him, and we weren't that close. His pal Geoff and his sister were frantic."

"I sensed that." Sasha shivered. "Although you're right: I don't think he told me the half of it."

Uncomfortable with the discussion of Danion's grief, she changed the subject. "Speaking of pain, was that your current prima glaring at me in the studio? Isn't it going to be difficult for her (and her male counterpart, whoever he is) if you reinstate us?"

"Isabella? She's my granddaughter. Your grandniece. I lived with another dancer for a few years after Elasi died." Tonio's mischievous brown eyes were wide and open, igniting instant suspicion in Sasha. "It won't hurt Bella to endure a few slings and arrows. Besides, she isn't prima yet, although she is my chief soloist. Needs must. Child's all flash and pyrotechnics; she has the emotional range of a carrot. Running into you and Camille will do her a world of good."

"Aren't you being dense, Tonio?" Sasha said. "Just because she shouldn't care doesn't mean she won't."

Tonio's eyes sparkled. "You going to turn down my contract, sis? What about helping your family in its hour of need?"

Tonio's appearance might have changed, but his personality had not altered one bit. "What a shameless blackmailer you are. No, of course not. I'm sure I can handle an irate grandniece or two. I just wanted you to think before you acted."

He grinned, unrepentant. "I'm ninety, you know. Don't you think I've learned a few survival skills by now?"

"They aren't obvious," Sasha told him.

"Maybe not." Tonio's impish expression gave way to a contemplative stare. "Now, let's see, what will I do for your premiere? Something with a real stretch to it. Something that's going to remind people what Xantera Ballet used to be."

"*Swan Lake*?" Slava suggested.

Tonio shook his head. "I want something no one has seen live since the three of you disappeared. Something unique."

"*Giselle*?" Camille asked. "Always, the public thinks of Sasha and Slava in connection with *Giselle*."

"Hmmm, perhaps." After a few more minutes of staring, another grin, this one positively wicked, spread across Tonio's face.

"Now you really look like my younger brother," Sasha said. "What are you plotting?"

His eyes gleamed. "You're worried about Bella, right? That she'll feel displaced?"

"I am rather."

"Suppose I let her kill you?"

Sasha felt her eyes widen. For a moment, she took him seriously. Then she realized what he meant. "Oh, Tonio, you wouldn't."

"Why not?" Tonio spread his hands, palms up. "She's perfect for Gamzatti: all that whiz-bang and no feelings worth the name. Except anger, which being displaced should give her plenty of. Nikia, on the other hand, she couldn't manage if Camille trained her for the next quarter-century. What do you say? *Bayadère* for openers, and we go from there."

"Can the corps handle it?" Camille asked. "It is difficult, that third act."

Tonio waved a hand. "I think so. You'll have to whip them into shape technically, but it doesn't demand much otherwise; they can get by with looking ethereal. Most of them can do that. And if you can't give me a decent Water Carrier by the time that curtain rises, Camille, I'll declare on the spot that you're an imposter."

Camille drew herself up and glared down her aristocratic nose at him. "I do not care how old you look, Anthony Sinclair; I diapered you. You will not insult me. I go to get Choli, and then I return. Give me the cast, and I will have them ready."

Tonio nodded, his eyes bright with laughter. "Glad to have you back, Camille."

12. Petits Battements

THE CAVE, DANK AND chill, offered few amenities. It was not the cave he had originally chosen; Danion had already decided that he would be foolish to trust his fellow leaders more than his students. So he had moved Vestris farther into the tunnels, into an area that no one in the movement used. As he had for the last three hours, he sat and watched her, lying unconscious on the opposite side of the room, while he considered his next move.

At the back of his thoughts, he heard his wife talking to her brother. Danion closed his eyes, reaching out to her. The choice to leave was his, and he could envision no other; even so, their separation hurt. Living without her had become a state of being, so familiar he had almost forgotten the alternative. Now he could no longer pretend that love belonged to the past or that his emotions had vanished with his youth. The imprint of her body remained in his arms, the taste of her on his tongue. He might not see her again for months. It seemed beyond bearing, although the link remained, a current of gold running clear in the darkness.

He should focus on the present, the sooner to finish his task and return. Vestris was wounded and required care;

for that, he needed supplies: food, water, and medicine—and someone he could trust to carry them. Someone clever enough, quick enough, to avoid being caught, someone likely to be loyal to Danion himself.

He turned names over in his head. It would help if he knew what had gone on during his absence, but to find out he needed a reliable informant, and that brought him full circle. Once he would have trusted Nirrtu—not to tell the whole truth but to tell his own truth, at least. After the events of the last few days, he could no longer count on that. Nirrtu had killed Jonthar or seen him killed—or worse, lied about his death to cover up some scheme of Nirrtu's own. Sasha and the others had not seen Jonthar's corpse; they had reported what Nirrtu told them. Either way, he distrusted Nirrtu—and Jonthar, who, if not dead, also had questionable loyalties. Most of the others were untested; Danion would not give this task to any of them.

That left Tamir. Not even Tamir was 100 percent reliable, but Danion knew him well enough to risk contact—providing he could convince the boy to hold his tongue. Tamir took to gossip as readily as the Pannthu.

Danion, watching Vestris, made his plans.

Sasha lay on the bed she had once shared with Danion, admiring San Francisco at twilight. Through the open windows she saw the city lights and the familiar outline of buildings against the darkening sky. In her exhaustion, she thought it looked like a postcard of a friend's vacation, pretty but remote. The encounter with Reilu, the shock of seeing Tonio, the separation from Danion, the stress of instant mothering (although Choli was a charming child)— these various sources of emotional upheaval pressed in on her, clamoring for her attention.

At least Camille had relaxed her obsession with practicing for today, although the routine of eight o'clock class would soon be reinstated. Tonio's dancers would never know what hit them.

It would have helped to share her inner turmoil with Danion, but it must be night on Kazratan, for he was dreaming of her. Sasha assumed he was sleeping and sent him pleasant thoughts. Reilu would have to wait for another day. Nothing pleasant there: he would be writhing in nightmares if he learned that he had worked so hard to get them to safety, only to deliver them into the hands of the one person who most wished them harm.

Better to think of *Bayadère*. Was Tonio right about his company's ability to handle that complicated choreography? In Sasha's experience, he usually had a good feel for the dancers he worked with—and of course, he could re-choreograph the whole ballet on the fly if necessary—but Camille was right, too. His current crop of dancers needed significant improvement before they would be ready for the Entrance of the Shades. Could Tonio himself have forgotten how difficult *Bayadère* was to dance?

Which brought her back to the issue of Tonio's age, so much greater than her own. On the surface, she saw little change, but it must be there. In Danion, too, although Tarkei aged so much more slowly than humans that the differences seemed less obvious; on the surface, he looked no more than fifty to her thirty. Yet the signs of emotional development were clear. In their short time together, she had sensed it: no fundamental personality shift, but a steadiness, a self-confidence, that had not been there during their marriage—wisdom, perhaps.

Tonio's emotional development was more questionable, but he must also have life events, interests, that he took for granted and she knew nothing about. The relationship with Bella's grandmother, for example.

So many years gone in a flash, like the smoke from a genie's lamp.

The thought that had been teasing her since her stay on Thuja's vessel emerged with crystalline clarity. Tonio was older, Jenat was older, even Danion looked older, but when she had tried to identify the man in the cloak, it had not occurred to her to search her memories for someone younger. She had not learned of the time difference until she reached Thuja's ship; and even when they discussed it with Danion, the idea seemed so strange that she had failed to realize its implications.

Sasha conjured up an image of the old man with the laser gun and tried to imagine what he would have looked like sixty years ago. Her husband had called him Nirrtu, a name unfamiliar to her. Danion had also noted the man's resemblance to Sendar, and that was true. Their faces were similar.

For that matter, the old man had looked quite like Danion—Danion in thirty years, perhaps. Although not related, Sendar and Danion bore a strong resemblance to each other. A Tarkei "type," she supposed.

Their voices, however, were quite distinct. Neither sounded anything like Nirrtu's. Sasha closed her eyes, listening. Voices do not change much in sixty years. What images did it call up?

A garden planet, pristine and beautiful, its people destroyed by invaders. A voice pounding into her ears, demanding information she did not want to give him. Layers of overlapping memories, poured into her mind by the voice—confusing her, stripping her of identity, turning every interrogation session into an encounter so muddled she could no longer separate what she had told the voice from what the voice told her. Overwhelming guilt, desperation, and an escape that led, eventually, to Danion.

Sasha fought down a wave of sickness and curled into a ball. She understood why the old man looked like her husband, why she and Slava and Camille had instinctively mistrusted him, why they seemed to remember him despite the odds against them having met him before.

When she could, she pushed herself off the bed and walked through to the living room, where Slava lay asleep on the couch. She shook his shoulder, ignoring his groans of protest, until he glared at her.

"The old man in the woods," she said. Slava stopped glaring and sat up. "I know who it was." She whispered a name in his ear.

Slava frowned, not in anger but in puzzlement. "It couldn't be. The eyes."

Sasha shrugged. "He changed his name. Why not his eyes?"

Slava held his blond head in his hands. "Of course. You wouldn't think I'd spent half my life on the stage. Are you sure?"

"You tell me." Sasha held out her hands. "It didn't occur to me at first, because I can't grasp how long ago that was. But the voice." She shivered. She couldn't help it. That voice still held the power to terrify her.

As Sasha herself had done, Slava closed his eyes. "Yes," he said after a while, "you're right. It's the same." The warm brown eyes met hers. Slava held out a hand. "Let's go and tell Camille."

"It can wait till morning. If we go in now, we'll wake Choli as well." Sasha squeezed his hand. "Thank you, Slava. I don't know how you put up with me. I shouldn't have woken you, either, but I needed reassurance that I wasn't going crazy."

Slava tapped her cheek with one finger. "Go to sleep, Sashenka, and don't worry. That's what friends are for, no?"

"Thank you," she said again. "You're a sweetheart, Slava."

Danion left the unconscious Vestris to wend his way through tunnels of rock. As he approached the main caves, he became more cautious, slipping into side crevices whenever he heard footsteps. Sasha was dreaming about Xantera, the home the Kazrati had invaded a few months before he met her—he wondered why. It made a disturbing backdrop to a difficult journey.

He heard light footsteps, moving with Tamir's characteristic rapidity. Tamir ran more often than he walked; although sixteen, he exhibited the perpetual motion of a much younger child. Danion peered around the edge of his crevice of the moment, established that the runner was Tamir and alone, and grabbed the boy as he came past, wrestling him into the crevice while placing one hand over his mouth. "It is I, Danion," he said—quietly, to keep Tamir from crying out.

The boy wriggled free. Danion did not stop him. Tamir had one hand over his own mouth, and his eyes were wide with amazement. He touched Danion's face. Danion watched, not speaking.

Tamir beckoned. Danion followed, back the way he had come, away from the main caves. Curious. A situation that could make Tamir wary was a situation worth watching.

"We thought you were dead," the boy whispered as soon as they were far away from the main tunnels. His hand gripped Danion's arm, as though he did not quite believe in his mentor's existence. "You've been gone for days. What happened to you?"

Danion released the death grip on his arm and led Tamir to a corner of the cave where passersby would not notice them. "I'll explain in a moment. Tell me first what's been going on in the caves."

Tamir shuddered. "Nothing good. Nirrtu took over after you left. He told us you were dead and that you'd appointed him leader. Then he ordered us to stay within the caves and not to leave the main area without permission."

"You were outside the main area when I caught you," Danion noted. The boy hung his head but made no attempt to defend himself, a sight Danion did not recall seeing during his nine months in the caves.

"It will serve me well if you can get beyond the bounds without being seen," he said. Tamir raised his head; from his expression of gratitude, he had expected a reprimand. "If the others believe me dead, do not correct them. That will be difficult for you, Tamir. Can you do it?"

The boy bit his lip. "I think so."

"It's vital that you do," Danion said. "We have a spy in the movement. It may be Nirrtu." The boy's eyes widened. "Has he done more than take over the leadership and order you to stay in the caves?"

Tamir scuffed his toes against the pebbles that littered the cave floor. "He appointed a deputy, a man from the streets. I don't like him. And he has meetings, many meetings, with a small group of followers. They discuss plans—for an armed uprising, I think. I haven't managed to get close enough to overhear everything they say."

"An armed uprising." Danion struggled to restrain his consternation. "It would be suicide." But that was the point, obviously.

"And Nirrtu himself does not stay in the caves," Tamir said. "He leaves, once every two or three days, at least."

To report, probably. Danion thought it unwise to share that possibility with Tamir. Instead he said, "Be careful of him. He had no reason to spread the story that I was dead. No reason to think I would not return to the caves, for that matter. That is why you must tell no one that you have seen me. *No one,* Tamir—no friends, no instantly regretted confidences, no statements shouted in anger. The merest hint that I am here, and the spy, whoever it is, will be warned."

Tamir's air of maturity vanished, leaving a frightened child. "How do you know there is a spy?"

Danion patted his shoulder. "Someone tried to recapture my wife after we removed the police transmitters. It may have been Jonthar, and Nirrtu saved them. Or it may have been Nirrtu, who killed Jonthar to provide a cover for his own actions. Or a third party, who killed Jonthar and whom Nirrtu eluded. I don't know which." He frowned. "Although Nirrtu's actions since then suggest the second."

Tamir said nothing. Danion tapped the shoulder he had just patted. "I need food and water and medicine, suitable for someone with flesh wounds and concussion. Can you obtain these things?"

"I will bring them," Tamir said. "You needn't worry. I won't tell anyone." His gamin face lit with enthusiasm as he slipped through the entry. "I've always disliked Nirrtu."

❋

Danion sat, hands loosely clasped in his lap, sending reassurance to his sleeping wife through the link and waiting to see if Tamir deserved his trust.

Sasha's dreams mutated from Xantera to the woodland house. He had been waiting then, too. They shifted again, pictures of ballets—Nikia and Solor, he thought. Then the dream period passed and she slipped into delta sleep.

Running feet alerted him long before Tamir appeared. The cave echoes made it difficult to distinguish numbers, but it seemed unlikely that the secret police would move so fast.

Just in case, Danion wedged himself into a smaller tunnel with a ready exit.

Footsteps entered the cave and stopped. Silence fell. Danion stepped out of his tunnel to find Tamir, a covered basket over one arm, staring about him as though he had been seeing visions.

"No one followed you?" Danion asked.

Tamir shook his head and held out the basket. Danion checked it quickly. "Excellent." Tamir seemed nervous but not guilty, and thus probably had nothing to conceal.

"I need an assistant," Danion said. "When Nirrtu leaves the caves, or whenever is convenient, but at two- to three-day intervals, I would like you to leave a similar basket here, in this cave. Not in a way that endangers you: I want you to protect yourself first. But if you can. If you find out more about Nirrtu's plans, or if anything makes you suspicious, please write a note and leave it for me. If you are in danger, search for me." He pointed back in the general direction of the cave where Vestris lay. "You will find me over there. I cannot tell you exactly where, but I expect you will discover it. Can you do this? Will you?"

"I will," Tamir said. His uncharacteristic maturity had returned.

Danion hoped it would survive Tamir's youthful idealism. "Very well," he said. "I am counting on you." He took the basket.

"But what will you do?" Tamir asked.

Danion flicked his ear in the farewell to family. "I will return."

Tonio surveyed the roomful of dancers. "This," he said, indicating Sasha, on his left, with a sweep of his hand, "for those of you who don't recognize her, is my sister, Alessandra Sinclair, better known as Sasha. And this," he pointed to Slava, on his right, "is her partner, Viacheslav Zoshchenko. I assume everyone recognizes him. He didn't chop his hair off." He grinned at Sasha, who obliged him with a dramatic sigh.

"I gather you met Camille Delagardie this morning," he went on. A few stifled moans rose from the audience, and Tonio grinned again. "Camille is resuming her position as dance mistress, effective immediately. Sasha was our prima ballerina before she disappeared, and I'm reinstating her in that position, with Slava as premier danseur. Those of you who haven't seen them dance will soon find out why. Those of you who have, I suspect, don't require an explanation."

Bella muttered something to her companion, but Sasha sat too far away to hear what it was.

Tonio ignored his granddaughter and continued his speech. "In honor of their return, we are adding a new ballet to the fall season. More accurately, an old ballet, one not in the current repertoire of any company, major or minor. We used to have great success with it, and if we do a good job of advertising it, it should go a long way toward restoring both our finances and our reputation as the galaxy's top ballet company. It will, however, demand very hard work from every one of you. Rehearsals begin today and take precedence over your other assignments. The corps, in particular, must show up every day; Camille will set the principals' schedules after she has had time to evaluate your dancing. Camille?" Having yielded the floor, he returned to his stool and watched.

"*La Bayadère*," Camille said. "The Temple Dancer. Are you familiar with it?"

Heads shook around the room. "It is a classic," Camille told them. "Music by Minkus, choreography by Petipa. Known primarily in the Russian tradition, but adapted by Makarova for the Royal Ballet and American Ballet Theatre. Since then, many companies have danced it, including this one. We will use our own adaptation, which draws on the Russian version but eliminates certain offensive characterizations.

"The story comes from an Indian legend. Nikia, a young temple dancer, loves Solor, a famous warrior, and he loves her. The Brahmin who rules the temple first sees Nikia on the day when Solor has come to the temple to visit her, and the Brahmin too falls in love with her. He declares himself. Nikia is shocked. She rejects him, and later he sees her and Solor together. Jealous, he vows to destroy Solor. This marks the end of Scene I. In Scene II, the Rajah summons Solor and orders him to marry the princess Gamzatti. Solor tries to decline, but the Rajah will not listen, and in the end Solor capitulates. Meanwhile, the Brahmin, hoping to eliminate his rival, tells the Rajah that Solor loves Nikia. Gamzatti overhears him. The Rajah does not care whom Solor loves; indeed, he wants to kill Nikia. Nikia then arrives, bringing congratulations from the temple. A scene ensues between the women. Gamzatti orders Nikia's death."

A gasp ran around the room. Camille waved a regal hand for silence and continued her plot summary. "Act II celebrates Solor and Gamzatti's approaching wedding, with much character dancing. At the end, Nikia, sent by the temple, must dance in honor of her lover and his bride. Gamzatti and the Rajah send her a basket of flowers containing a poisonous snake, which kills her. Solor is heartbroken and remorseful. In Act III, unable to sleep, he takes opium and dreams that he sees Nikia among the ghosts that inhabit the Kingdom of the Shades. You, *mes filles du corps*, have a most famous and dramatic entrance in arabesque penché, which we will practice until you hate me, but you will be perfect. In his dream, Solor and Nikia are reconciled. We begin tomorrow. Company class, eight o'clock. All will attend."

Renewed groans came from the audience, and Camille regarded them sternly. "Miss it, and I will cut you from the cast. To dance with greatness, one must have discipline. Do you think the Royal and the Mariinsky allowed their dancers to skip class? Eight o'clock, here in the studio, boys and girls together. Girls in slippers. Pointe class begins at nine o'clock sharp, when you are warmed up. Tonio, you will take the boys at nine?"

Tonio nodded. Camille stepped back, and Tonio took over again. "Sasha dances Nikia, with Slava as Solor. They've done this before and, with Camille and myself, can help the newcomers figure out how to play it."

Bella muttered again. Tonio continued to ignore her. "Slava partners both Sasha and Bella. Bella, you are Gamzatti; you act in the second scene and you have a grand pas de deux in Act II, as well as assorted walk-ons. The ballet depends on you as much as Sasha; you must create a credible character, not a caricature. Camille will help. I will cast the Rajah and the Brahmin tomorrow, as well as assorted other parts such as the Golden Idol and the Head Fakir."

He swept a hand in the direction of a group clustered near the mirrors. "The women's corps has a great deal of dancing throughout. The men's corps gets short-changed, except in Act II. Otherwise, it's primarily fakirs and soldiers—and priests who stand around doing nothing. We'll make it up to you later. Schedules will be posted by tomorrow morning. Costume fittings start in a few weeks, once I adjust the choreography for this cast; we may need to change parts here and there. We open with this in three months, so show up regularly and on time, people. Xantera Ballet may not survive another season if we don't make this a success."

Amid a circle of shocked faces, Tonio sat. When they did not move, he waved his hands at them. "The corps stays. Everyone else can go. Except Bella, Sasha, and Slava."

With backward looks over their shoulders, the dancers straggled out.

Vestris lay where Danion had left her, motionless on the straw pallet that he had fetched from the storage area attached to the cave to which he had initially brought her. He doubted anyone would miss it; the inner circle used that area only for the occasional meeting and as a fallback location in case of invasion from without. From what Tamir had told him, the main danger at present came from within—and must resolve itself long before those in charge worried about missing mattresses.

Wishing he had his sister's medical knowledge, he knelt next to his patient and washed the blood from her head. She stirred under his hands; he had to hold her chin to keep her steady.

The basket contained an antiseptic, which he applied, and a healing compound. Danion sprayed the air-activated bandage onto the wound and sat back to assess the results of his rough-and-ready doctoring. He did not expect her to recover so fast, but if this did not work, his options were limited.

Bread and some vegetables, also from the basket, satisfied his hunger. Danion moved to his own mattress and rested his head against the wall, reaching for his wife. As usual, Sasha sat in the middle of a ballet studio, but she was not dancing; instead she was watching others. Touching her thoughts, Danion saw Slava, also observing; Tonio and Camille; and a young woman with light brown hair and a sulky expression whose appearance struck a chord of memory, although he could not recall her name.

Bella, Sasha said on cue. My grandniece, Tonio says, although she can't be more than five years younger than I am. She's unhappy that I've shown up and taken over. And how are you, my love?

As well as can be expected, Danion said. I have reached the caves, but for the moment I am staying away from the others while I try to find out what happened during my absence. I am caring for Vestris, who is on the road to recovery, I hope.

Must you care for her yourself? The bond developed sharp blue angles of anxiety. She is a police agent. Suppose she turns you in?

She will not turn me in at the moment, he said. She is unconscious.

You know what I mean. Sasha's sigh reached him across the vast distance that separated them. I'd like her to recover, though. I thought her superiors would blame her for our escape, and although I didn't trust her, she was pleasant to me.

It is better this way, Danion assured her. I will not allow her to hurt me. Tell me what you have been doing.

She told him about meeting Reilu and about recognizing the old man. Appalled at the first and skeptical of the second, Danion urged her to take care.

Sasha's astonishment rang clear across the link. You're telling *me* to take care? When you're the one in the middle of a vipers' nest?

The wave of remembered grief struck Danion without warning. He dropped his head to his knees.

I'm sorry, beloved, Sasha said. I will not walk into the lion's den, I promise. Or in this case, the lioness's. Anyway, soon your father will arrive.

On the opposite mattress, Vestris twisted her head back and forth. I may need to leave soon, Danion told his wife. Please show me the image of the old man again. You are certain that you identified him correctly? The eyes are different.

The bond shimmered with indecision. I can't be certain, Danion. It was sixty-three years ago, and many Kazrati may sound like that. But Slava agreed they could be the same person, and so did Camille when I had a chance to ask her. Eye color can be changed with contact lenses; blue to brown is easiest. Why? Does it seem to you that it couldn't be?

Danion shook his head, before realizing that she might not see it. The bond varied in intensity from moment to moment; only Sasha's response confirmed what she had heard, although thoughts and emotions traveled more reliably than expression and surroundings. It does not, he said. It is quite possible. I wanted only to know how convinced you were of the identification. A hidden identity is suspicious in itself.

Eighty percent? Close to that, I'd say.

Across the room, Vestris was watching him. Her eyes had the peculiar stillness of the very ill. He raised an eyebrow at her to gauge her reaction. She tried to lift a hand in response, but only the tip of one finger left the mattress.

Vestris is awake, Danion told Sasha. Thank you for what you have shared with me. You will watch out for Reilu?

Yes, Sasha said. If you will watch out for Nirrtu, and for Vestris.

I will, Danion promised. Take care of yourself, *kaleita*.

And you. Sasha returned to her dancers.

A flask of water in his hand, Danion walked over to Vestris.

❋

Sasha removed a plate from the food panel and handed it to Choli. "Curried spinach with chick peas," she said to the machine, "and *nan*." The food panel made a jingling sound and produced another plate. Sasha collected it and moved to the table. "And I thought that would challenge it. It's wonderful. Much better than the one we used to have."

Choli sat beside her. "It's so different from the caves."

Sasha thought she heard wistfulness in the quiet voice. "Are you homesick, Choli?"

The girl hesitated.

"It's natural, you know," Sasha said. "We won't take it personally. Even when home's dreadful, it's familiar, and people miss it."

"Life in the caves wasn't dreadful." Choli pushed the food around her plate. You would have thought it was the most interesting object in the world.

Sasha waved a piece of *nan* at her. "I meant, even if we'd brought you here straight from the streets, you'd miss the old life from time to time. Didn't you ever miss it when you were with Danion? The freedom, for example—not having anyone give you orders or make you learn lessons."

Choli flushed. "I did, sometimes, when it seemed I couldn't do anything right. I felt terrible about it, because I didn't want to go back there. I thought if I told anyone, they'd throw me out, and there I'd be, hungry and cold again. And Danion did so much for me, I felt ungrateful even to have such thoughts."

"There, you see." Sasha patted the girl's hand. "And if you felt that way about the streets, how much more likely it is that you'd miss Danion and your friends and Kazratan itself."

"I suppose." Choli relaxed, her shoulders visibly dropping. She stopped pushing the food about and tasted the panel's effort at making what she'd said was her favorite dish.

"How is it?" Sasha asked. "I told it to start with chicken burritos, use whole-wheat tortillas, double the jalapeños, and subtract the cheese. Did it come close?"

"It's not bad," Choli said after a moment. "A bit mild, perhaps."

Sasha held bread coated with spinach inches from her mouth. "Kazrati must have asbestos taste buds. We'll ask it to use habañeros next time, and if that fails, Scotch bonnets."

"Scotch bonnets?" Choli touched her head, as though imagining a tam-o'-shanter. Pretty impressive; Sasha hadn't expected her to know what a bonnet was, never mind a Scotch one.

"Distilled fire." Slava joined them at the table. "How was your first day, little bird?"

"Good, I think. I liked the dance classes, although it felt strange. Most of the other girls aren't more than ten, and they're better than me."

"They don't learn as fast, though," Sasha said. "Because they're younger. You'll soon catch up. What about the other classes?"

Choli shrugged. "Danion taught me lots of things, so it wasn't as bad as I expected. Some of the girls were nice, and some said rude things about my clothes and because I didn't know much about Earth. But I showed them in math, and for the rest, I tried to look at them the way Danion would."

"Good for you." Sasha licked spinach off her fingers. "Thirteen-year-old girls can be vicious. On Kazratan, too, probably, although I can't see Danion tolerating that sort of thing. Let us know if you need help, but the more you tackle it yourself, the less trouble you'll have with them in the long run."

Choli dropped the spoon she had been using to consume the redesigned burrito. "I spent seven years on the streets, Sasha, and two months in the girls' dormitory. I bet I can out-nasty those spoiled brats any day."

The two dancers smiled at her.

"I bet you can, little bird," Slava said.

Vestris accepted the water, and some broth Danion found in another flask, although she was too weak to do more than swallow a few sips. Danion tested her temperature and made sure her pulse was steady, then gave her medicine to help her sleep. The sprayed bandage would protect her wound while it healed, unless his delay in treating her had caused infection to set in. If that happened, he would have few options but to take her to the healer; his own skills and supplies were limited to providing first aid.

After the liquid and before the medicine took hold, Vestris managed to croak out the traditional question as to where she was. "In the caves," Danion said, not wanting to burden her with specifics. Her eyes closed, and she turned her head toward the wall without saying anything else. Soon, no doubt, she would want to know who he was. What should he tell her?

If she did not ask, of course, it meant that she already knew the answer. Not a comforting thought, that.

13. Pas de Chat

CLASS BEGAN PROMPTLY AT eight o'clock. By 8:30 half the corps was in tears, and as for the other half—a little telekinesis and Camille would have had more spikes sticking out of her than a hedgehog. By 9:30, when they reached pirouettes in fifth, Sasha wanted to hide behind the piano so that the ballet mistress could not ask her to demonstrate any more correct positions of the knee. Bella looked ready for spontaneous combustion, despite having received a grudging nod for her technique in the turns, while the corps, as far as Sasha could tell, had subsided into depression.

At 9:50, Camille gave them ten minutes to rest. The women streamed from the studio, some collapsing in boneless heaps on the floor, pointe shoes pressed against the wall; some flowing into the dressing room; some inhaling water from the fountain; some burying their heads in the nearest towel. The men, who for the last hour had endured nothing worse than a sense of inferiority as Slava did grands jetés around the studio, his legs in a straight line, regarded the hysterical ballerinas with sympathy.

Tonio arrived. The grin he bestowed on the gasping dancers did nothing to raise his sister's estimation of his tact. Sasha watched her partner shake his head at Tonio's back.

Camille came to the door.

"Very well, boys and girls, break is over," she said. Yelps of anguish sounded from the crowd on the floor, but they dragged themselves up and straggled back into the studio. Bella, among the few who had remained standing, waited until the last minute before sauntering with elaborate languor into the room.

"And now," Camille said, "we discuss characterization. This is a classical ballet company. When you come to class with me, you will perform the steps as I showed you this morning. Often a choreographer will ask for something different; then you will provide it. If the choreographer says, 'Turn in,' you turn in. But if no one tells you, you do the step in its classical form. And why is that?"

No one answered. Sasha assumed they did not dare. Personally, she thought she had attracted enough attention, so she kept quiet; Slava's hunted expression suggested that he felt the same. Tonio, perched on his stool, watched them with bright, beady eyes. He gave the impression of enjoying himself hugely.

"That technique is your foundation," Camille said. "When you need no longer think how to produce the step, you have the choice to alter it in subtle ways. Sasha, Slava."

Bella scowled ferociously as the two older dancers exchanged small shrugs, then got up and went to the front of the room. "Can't wait for this," she muttered to Alyssa, who sat on her left.

Alyssa treated her to a glance filled with pity. Bella's anger grew. That she had worshiped her grandaunt since the day she did her first plié didn't help; on the contrary, it made her feel worse. If only they'd stayed dead. Then she could have appreciated them as they deserved.

Camille waved an imperious hand. "Sasha, demonstrate. Slava, support. Arabesque, pose variable. *Giselle*, Act I. Observe."

Sasha sprang onto pointe with the effervescence of a young girl in love, right arm swept above her head, left leg stretched behind her.

"Act II."

The leg came down. She returned to fifth, then, Slava's hands around her waist, drifted up onto pointe as though too light to remain on the ground. This time her right arm stretched forward and the left extended from the shoulder, a classic first arabesque. After a moment, she came back to fifth.

"*Bon*. Odette."

Sasha brought her right foot to her left ankle, stretched it forward with swanlike grace, and balanced on the toe, arms in the broken-wing position that had so affected Danion.

"Odile."

Without changing position, the arms stiffened. Sasha looked over one shoulder, testing her effect on Slava, who assumed a besotted expression. In response, she swept her head down until it almost touched her knee. As she came up, she brought her arms above her head, opening the left to the side as she gazed regally at her partner. In the spirit of the dance, Slava turned her on pointe.

"God, she's good," Alyssa said in a whisper. "Did you see that?"

Bella glowered at her. "Traitor. You think I couldn't do that?"

Alyssa did not answer. Bella felt a flash of satisfaction, but a treacherous thought slid under her defenses; in her heart, she knew she could not do that. Alyssa spoke the truth. Sasha was good. Better than Bella.

She shook her head quickly, pushing the thought aside. She felt small, which made her angrier still. She'd show them. She didn't have to stay and take this. Gramps wouldn't even care if she left, now he'd got his precious sister back.

Camille smiled warmly at Slava and Sasha, which did nothing to improve Bella's abysmal state of mind. "It is well," she said. "One more, and I will have made my point. Kitri."

The captive audience, presumably expressing its mixed feelings about the new regime, had watched so far in silence, but Kitri overwhelmed the dancers' resistance. The pose matched Giselle's first, but an indefinable shift in Sasha's placement—the fingers? the tilt of the head?—created a quite different persona. In that one pose Bella, fuming, saw Kitri: a flirtatious, self-confident young woman; a playful Giselle; an Odile who lacked the Black Swan's malice. The dancers, her friends until today, gave way and clapped.

Sasha, glad to be finished, came back to the floor to find heads nodding around the room.

"You see, my dove," Slava said with quiet satisfaction in her ear, "we are not yet beyond the hills."

"I suppose not. I doubt we'll ever face a tougher audience."

"Gamzatti, however, remains unconvinced." Slava jerked his head in Bella's direction.

That young lady was glaring at them. "There's always one heckler in the crowd," Sasha said lightly, then stopped to listen to Camille, who was explaining how the principle she had just demonstrated should carry through into one's final bow. The dance mistress selected "volunteers" to practice this concept, Bella among them. Slava and Sasha grabbed their chance to blend into the crowd on the floor.

The explosion followed the most trivial of corrections by Camille.

"Almost, you have it," she told Bella. "It needs only a little more sweep of the arms, so." She caught Bella's wrist and raised it half an inch.

Bella wrenched her arm from Camille's grasp. "That's it!" She stormed toward the door. "I'm not going to spend the rest of my life under this kind of petty harassment! I can dance with any company I want."

"Now, Bella—" Tonio said.

Camille stopped him with an outstretched hand. "Let her go, Tonio. She is right. She is a good technician, and from what you tell me about the state of *la danse*, if she wants no more than that, she can find other work."

"If she leaves," Tonio said, "she'll stay a soloist, whatever they call her."

Camille moved only her shoulders. "Better that than misery. I teach those who want to learn."

Bella stood—uncertainly, Sasha thought—near the door. "As opposed to what?" she said with bitterness. "Staying here to play second fiddle to Aunt Sasha?"

Camille looked at her, a small smile on her lips.

Sasha had seen that smile before. So much for the grand exit.

"You think that is what I want?" Camille said. "A copy of Sasha? But I have the original. What good is a copy to me? You have the talent; already I can see it. You need only to grow up a bit. Give me five years, and I promise you, the public will flock to you as they do to Sasha. Not to Sasha's niece but to you, Isabella Sinclair. You will carry on the great tradition of your family. You will be prima."

Bella wavered. She had stopped clutching the doorknob, but her feet seemed reluctant either to go or to stay.

"It's your choice," Camille said. "But what I offer, you cannot get elsewhere. I will push you as hard as I can, and sometimes you will not want to see my face. But if you leave, you will never know how good you could have been. So decide. I do not teach the halfhearted."

As though the confrontation had not occurred, Camille turned back to the openmouthed dancers. "Sinara, if you please. We will begin to imagine *La Bayadère*. You are an Indian temple dancer. How would you make your *révérence*?"

Sinara thought for a moment, then curtseyed, hands together, fingertips touching her forehead, in the Indian gesture of respect.

"Excellent," Camille said.

Unremarked, Bella walked back to her place.

❋

"Come on, Slava, don't be a pig. It's not that far." Sasha shook her partner's shoulder. "Danion will be horrified if I go by myself. He's convinced that his first wife got rid of me once and will do so again, and while he could be wrong, he has enough on his plate. I don't want to add to his troubles unless I have to."

Slava moaned. His feet hung over the arm of the couch, a result of his having collapsed onto the furniture without bothering to position his head on the cushion. "Heartless woman. After the day I had, you want me to go visiting? If Camille had said, 'Slava,' just once more, I would have left and returned to Kazratan. If an entire company must hate me, I prefer to bring it on myself."

Sasha put her hands on her hips and glared at him. "After the day *you* had? Where was I? With young Bella breathing smoke like a dragon at my head, I thought I'd need an asbestos suit to get out of that studio alive. Not to mention the fifty-nine arabesques and the eighty-four pirouettes I did showing those wretched children what alignment means. What were their teachers thinking? I don't know if I want Choli in their miserable school. It looks like she won't learn anything but bad habits!"

Slava's blond head lifted as he repositioned himself, then collapsed back onto the couch. "I don't think you need worry. When I left, I heard Camille telling Tonio to make the teachers attend company class from now on. By the time Choli can do serious damage to herself, they'll either have shaped up or moved on. Camille's a tyrant, but she does know her stuff."

To that there was no argument. "In any case," Sasha said, "it's not only because of Danion that I want you to come with me to see Jenat. You know what a sweetheart he is, and it'd do us both good to change scenes."

The blond head rose again, this time so that its owner could stare at her. "Sweetheart? Your father-in-law? You must be kidding!"

"He is. It's protective coloration. He's not nearly as grouchy as Dad could be, and you loved him." Sasha pulled at his arm. "Do come."

Slava sighed so deeply she could see his chest rise and fall. "All right, give me fifteen minutes to catch my breath, and I will. Satisfied?"

Sasha kissed his cheek. "I knew you'd see it my way. Fifteen minutes, then. I'm going to take a shower. If I show up in a leotard, Jenat will be shocked."

Fifteen minutes later, however, Slava was asleep. Shaking his shoulder and whispering in his ear had no effect at all. Sasha frowned at him, then left him alone. What kind of company would he make, as exhausted as that?

"Rats," she said to Camille. "I'll have to go by myself after all. Tell Slava he owes me one."

The Frenchwoman, involved in helping Choli decipher a history lesson, muttered an acknowledgment without looking up. "Franz Joseph II," she was saying as Sasha walked to the door. "Was he from Alpha Centauri?"

Whoops. She and Slava had better review Choli's homework from now on.

At the doorway she stopped, realizing that here lay a solution to her problem. "Choli," she said, "how would you like to meet your grandfather?"

Choli looked up from her book, alarmed. She obviously remembered Danion's description of his father too well.

Sasha smiled at her. "Don't worry, my lamb. You'll find out he's a lot like Danion underneath. And I'll be with you, so you have nothing to fear."

This time, Sasha did not recognize the protocol officer who greeted her. The young man regarded her with disdain when she asked to speak to the prime minister and demanded various pieces of documentation before proceeding. Then he left her and Choli in his office while he went off to check with his superiors. Sasha stood at the open window, looking out on the garden, wondering what her house in Tarkakhan looked like these days. Did the altanai still bloom after sixty years?

The garden was lovely. The brilliance of a normal California spring, when bulbs of different varieties bloom simultaneously and blend with succulents and other native flowers, was exaggerated by the addition of plants from Tarkei and a dozen other planets. Even some of the birds looked imported: magenta feathers tipped with white drooped from the tree opposite, and iridescent wings sparkled in the sun, misted by the fountain in which they were bathing. Big splashy desert blooms vied for space with heart's ease and daisies while old-fashioned pink roses, cousins of the red and white over which Lancaster and York once fought, sent their perfume into the air.

Choli came to stand beside her. "So pretty. I don't remember anything like it on Kazratan, although they say the rich have gardens."

Sasha hugged the thin shoulders, responding to the edge of anxiety in the young voice. "It will be fine, you'll see. They're wonderful people, the Tarkei, and they care for their own."

"But I'm not their own," Choli said.

"Yes, you are. Danion adopted you; that makes you family." Sasha gave the shoulders another squeeze. "I know. It's almost as intimidating to acquire a whole family overnight as it is to have no one. But believe me, family is better in the end."

Behind her, the door opened. "Sasha-*chan!*" It was a woman's voice, lightly accented, with a warmth and lilt that one would not expect in a lifelong resident of Tarkei.

Sasha whirled. "Iqa-*chan!*"

Iqara—tall and slender, if not quite the fashion model she had been sixty years ago, the short blond hair frosted with silver—held out her hands. Sasha took them, laughing, only to have her sister-in-law drop them both and flick her ear in the Tarkei greeting to family.

Sasha hugged her. They had become good friends during her two-year marriage to Danion. That she had not expected her sister (the Tarkei did not separate in-laws from birth ties) to travel to Earth heightened her pleasure. "I had no idea you were coming. How wonderful to see you!"

Iqara pulled away, looking her over. "What, did you think I would sit home and wait for my sister to drop by? But look at you! By Selassa's rays, were we ever so young?

Or so thin? You find the fountain of youth, and it takes you to Kazratan. How can life be so unfair?"

"You haven't changed a bit, Iqa." Sasha, laughing, hugged her again. "Is Father here?"

"I am." The voice, deep and cool, sounded so much like his son's that Sasha shivered in her sister's embrace. Iqara stepped back, and Sasha walked toward her father-in-law, hands held palms up in respect.

Jenat touched them with his own and flicked her ear as Iqara had done. He did not smile, but his eyes showed moist at the edges and his gaze was soft. "My daughter," he said, the deep voice not quite steady. "Too many seasons have passed since we met."

It sounded like a ritual greeting, but Sasha didn't know the correct response. Danion's mind brushed hers. *Thank you, beloved,* she told him. She stretched out her hands again. "Indeed, father, the suns have not blessed us."

Jenat nodded, apparently reassured by her response. But reassured of what? Her identity? He had not tested her when she talked to him from Thuja's ship. What had happened to change his mind?

"Do you doubt me, father?" she asked. "You cannot think Thuja so easily taken in."

Jenat snorted. "That one! Decades have passed, and she still cannot look me in the eye. Although I admit, she proved of great assistance in this instance." He pinched Sasha's arm, not hard but enough to establish her reality. "Forgive the fears of a foolish old man. That vithra who married my son was here when I arrived. She suggested you might have misled Danion—be a shape changer or something, I don't know what she thought. I did not want to believe her, but where the Kazrati are involved, one does well to make certain."

His hand again flicked her ear. "It was not impossible that Danion might see what he wanted to see. He took his loss hard. Blamed himself for your disappearance. For a time, I thought he would return to the mountain, and I would lose you both."

Sixty years later, and the cost of this remained audible. "I am sorry, father," Sasha said.

She placed a hand under his elbow and walked with him toward the seating area. "All of you suffered. I feel so bad about that. Everything collapsed around me, and I awoke in a hospital. I didn't find out about the time difference until I reached Thuja's ship. But Thuja told me you saw me dance. Did that not confirm my identity?"

Jenat eased himself onto a straight chair near the couch. Sasha beckoned to Choli, who walked toward her, then stopped, uncertain. Jenat and Iqara had not yet noticed her.

"As I said, my child, I wished to be sure." Jenat's eyes lit with a joy he would not express in words. "But you are here, and I am pleased. I should have guessed Reilu was trying to distress me. It is her way."

Iqara caught Sasha's wrist and indicated the cushion next to her. With her creamy café au lait skin and those big brown eyes, she looked much as she had six decades ago. Her hemlines were lower (they could hardly have risen), but the style and the grace were as remarkable as ever.

As Sasha settled herself on the couch, she imagined inviting Iqa to the studio to give Tonio's dancers an opportunity to appreciate the intrinsic sense of self that can transform the simplest action into something unique. Iqa was not a dancer, but she had the manner of one.

At the moment, Iqa was scolding Jenat. "I'm disappointed in you, father. Listening to Reilu! How could Sasha deceive Danion? They were joined."

"Are," Sasha said. "We are joined."

Jenat's eyes fixed on her, bright in his leathered face. It reminded Sasha of Sendar, Danion's mentor, who had manifested the same contrast between wrinkled skin and undimmed soul. "The bond survives, then? And how is my son? What is he doing?"

Sasha thought. "He rescued one of our guards. I hit her over the head with a rock during our escape, and I felt terrible about it, because she had been nice to me. Danion found her on his way back to the caves and took her to a safe place. He found someone to help him get food and medicine, and he is caring for her. She recovered consciousness a short while ago, but he has given her a sedative and she is sleeping again." She smiled at him. "He says to flick Iqa's ear and tell her not to worry, and if you didn't think I was real, why did you send him to Kazratan?"

"Tell him to mind his tongue." Jenat's eyes twinkled. Sasha did not bother to relay the request. Her father-in-law held out his hands again. "Welcome, my child, and let us say no more about it."

Sasha touched her palms to Jenat's. "Think nothing of it, father. I am glad to see you, too, and even more glad to see you well."

Iqara left her chair and returned with a flask of golden juice and three small cups. She poured the juice and handed each of them a cup. "To family," she said, lifting it.

"Indeed," Jenat said.

Sasha echoed him, then sipped her juice. It was from Tarkei; she remembered its sweet-sour tang. "Speaking of family, Choli has been standing there near the window since I came in. Come, daughter, and meet the rest of the clan."

Iqara jumped from her seat and extended both hands, as she had with Sasha earlier. The honey-brown eyes were alight, her face as vivid as Sasha's. Choli decided on the spot that her aunt was the most beautiful woman in existence.

"This is she?" Iqara said over her shoulder. She turned back. "Welcome, Choli-*chan*. I am your Aunt Iqara."

Choli blinked. Danion had told her that the Tarkei did not express their emotions openly as humans and Kazrati did. He had repeated it many times. Trying to imitate him, she made an effort to control her own, although her success so far was patchy.

Sasha must have read her expression. She said, "Honestly, Iqa, give the child a chance." To Choli she added, "This is Danion's sister. Pay no attention to her manner; she refuses to act like a proper Tarkei."

Iqara stepped forward to flick Choli's ear. Looking more closely, Choli could see her new aunt's resemblance to Danion: their ears were the same shape, and there was something in her expression that reminded Choli of Danion in the rare moments when he allowed his amusement to show. Although this looked more like mischief. It was difficult to imagine Danion mischievous.

"I'm pleased to meet you," Choli said to her new aunt. "Danion told me about you."

Iqara laughed. "That must have been something. Perhaps you'd better not pass it along. Instead, say hello to your grandfather."

The old man in the chair did not look much like Danion, or even as Danion might look in fifty years. The stern face and piercing black eyes, the contrast between shoulders that had been broad and powerful and today's gaunt frame, the way he looked her over, as though she were merchandise being presented for his inspection— Choli found him quite intimidating. Remembering Camille's teaching, she lifted her chin and stood straight, keeping her eyes fixed on his.

But after what seemed like hours of scrutiny, she saw his eyes lighten. Jenat's mouth curved in a half-smile that could indeed have been Danion's, and he extended his hands, palms down. She stepped forward and placed her own hands, palms up, under his, as Danion had taught her.

Jenat glanced at Sasha. "I can see you and Danion had the raising of this one." His tone was cool, but Choli, used to Danion's restraint, heard a note of pride in the level voice.

"Danion, primarily, and he only for the last couple of months," Sasha said. "I would love to take credit for her, but I think it must go to Choli herself."

"I am not sure of that, my child," Jenat said. "Already she has your style." He looked at Choli, his eyes bright with suppressed laughter. "And your courage. You wouldn't hesitate to tell the truth to an old man, would you, my bird?"

Choli swallowed. "No," she said. It seemed like the safest answer.

Jenat ruffled her hair. "I didn't think so. Come, granddaughter, and tell me of yourself." A lordly hand waved. "Iqara, a cup of juice for my granddaughter, if you please."

Behind her, Choli could hear Iqara laughing. "Right away, father," her aunt said.

Jenat beckoned Choli toward the couch. Sasha moved to the end to make room for her.

"You know, then, that Reilu is working here," Sasha said. "Danion has been worrying ever since he found out. He's convinced she was responsible for my disappearance and that she still intends to harm me. Is he right, do you think?"

"About the first, unquestionably." Jenat placed his cup on the table, his back not touching the chair frame. Camille would approve. "I had proof of her involvement. Regarding the latter, I don't know. It would not surprise me. But you can tell him to relax. Within half-an-hour of my arrival, she discovered an urgent need to return home. She left this morning. I had the young man who greeted you take her to the space port, just to be sure."

Iqara, restored to her seat, was laughing again. Sasha joined in. "I see. Well, Danion said you hadn't lost your touch."

Jenat shook his head. "Such disrespectful children. I don't know what I did to deserve the three of you. Tell me, daughter, what you can about Kazratan, and what we must do to get that son of mine home."

Iqara poured her another cup of juice. Sasha curled her feet under her and began to talk.

❀

Danion looked up from his deliberations over what Tamir had told him to find Vestris watching him. She looked better—her eyes clear, her skin more normal in color, her hands with a tighter grip on the cover. The strain in her face remained. No surprise there: he had not expected her to heal overnight.

"I owe you my life," she said. "That places me in your debt. Who are you?"

Danion regarded her steadily, refusing to let the question fluster him. He had predicted it. "I am Sasha's husband," he said in Kazrati.

"Sasha." Vestris frowned. "The human dancer? Sasha is not a Kazrati name."

"The human dancer." Danion offered her the flask of broth. "Just sips, until you're stronger." He checked her wound, turning her head to one side so that he could examine it. It was healing well under its protective skin. He held out two pills.

Vestris looked wary.

"An antibiotic and a sedative," Danion said. "I did not save your life so that I could kill you."

Vestris did not move. "One can do worse than kill."

She had a point. Danion placed the pills on the mattress beside her head and sat back on his heels. "I am not a torturer, nor can I profit from making you addicted to drugs. If you refuse them, nothing will happen, except that you will heal more slowly than necessary."

She looked as though she might put his words to the test, but after a moment's staring, she picked up the pills and swallowed them. Danion kept the satisfaction out of his face, thinking she might see triumph where he intended none. She was capable of rationality; that was a good sign. It would make their future dealings much easier.

In response to the sedative, Vestris soon fell asleep. Once he was sure she would not wake for a while, Danion went to collect Tamir's next basket from their chosen cave.

14. Temps de Flèche

VESTRIS AWOKE TO FIND herself alone. She surveyed the bare cave, wondering where she was. The man who had cared for her earlier must plan to return: she could see another mattress like the one she was lying on against the opposite wall. At the end of the pallet stood the basket from which he had pulled flask and medicine. Otherwise, except for two or three candles and a pile of clothes, she saw no possessions, no signs of habitation. Everything was meticulously arranged, although she supposed even the messiest person would look organized in a situation of such austerity.

The man who had identified himself as Sasha's husband looked familiar. Where had she seen him before?

Sasha, the human dancer. Sasha had not mentioned a husband. At first, Vestris had believed that Sasha and Slava were lovers. D'Toth had continued to think so, but Vestris had soon accepted that they were not, despite a closeness that at times seemed almost like mind reading. Reviewing her three charges' more obscure conversations, she realized that they had on occasion referred to a fourth person, so obliquely that she had missed their meaning—as they had, no doubt, intended.

And by some quirk of circumstances, not only had she met Sasha's missing and unanticipated husband, but he had saved her life. By the customs of Kazratan, he owned her, unless and until she could cancel the debt by doing the same for him.

Vestris scowled at the stone ceiling. Did he understand that? She had seen no evidence that he did, no proprietary air or hidden triumph. Even when he talked her into taking the pills, he had not touched her, and the pills had done exactly what he said they would do. The finger that had turned her head had been quite impersonal, the casual care any healer would give. Which meant that Sasha's husband, although he looked Kazrati, most likely was not.

That made sense, because the government had kept Sasha under constant observation since she recovered consciousness, so the idea that Sasha could have met and married a Kazrati was as absurd as its alternative, that she had married one before she arrived. Kazrati and humans did not mingle; even in diplomatic negotiations, the Tarkei represented the other side, expressing the two governments' conviction that their shared heritage gave them a communications advantage.

Privately, Vestris wondered. Her limited acquaintance with human history suggested that her people might have much more in common with certain Terran nationalities than they would ever have with the Tarkei. She kept those views to herself.

But if Sasha's husband did not come from Kazratan, there was really only one person he could be. No wonder he looked familiar: she had seen his picture a dozen times.

Vestris felt her own eyes widen, realizing that she must be in the caves occupied by the resistance movement.

Silence enfolded her like a blanket of fog. In the caves, but far from the resistance fighters, then.

Which also made sense. No fool, Sasha's husband, whether he was protecting her or his colleagues. Or both.

With any luck, only Sasha's husband knew she was here. Even her supervisors might believe her dead. Vestris let her breath go in a whoosh. Had she stumbled over the opportunity for which she had hoped for so long?

Tamir was waiting when Danion reached the cave where they had agreed that the boy would leave supplies. A loaded basket covered in a flecked towel sat in one corner. Tamir sat in another, dangling his feet from a large rock.

Danion raised an eyebrow. "Do you have news?"

Tamir's hands twisted in his lap. "I don't know. Nirrtu and his lieutenant keep making new rules. First, they sent most of the children and their mothers out of the caves. Then they demanded that the rest of us attend daily meetings and training sessions for the armed uprising. I'm to go tomorrow." He shivered. "I don't want to kill anyone, Danion. Helping you and the others escape was different— like playing. When I came here, I wanted to learn, not to fight."

"Would you like to come back with me?" Tamir looked so disconsolate that Danion felt he had to ask, although he half-hoped the answer would be negative. Gathering supplies would become much more difficult without

Tamir's help. It was a testament to his teaching, though, that the boy saw more to life than combat. Not many Kazrati could say the same.

"Later," Tamir said. "The uprising is not due for several weeks." His characteristic enthusiasm rebounded. "It'd be useful to know how to fight, so long as I don't have to hurt anyone."

"An essential skill, unfortunately," Danion said. "You have a sense of where to find me if necessary?"

Tamir pointed in the right direction. "You told me. Over there."

"Good." Danion nodded. "Don't hesitate, if you feel yourself in danger." He picked up the basket. "Thank you for this. Let me know as soon as you hear more."

Vestris was awake when he returned—propped against the wall in a pose that reminded him of his early encounters with Sasha. Her balance seemed shaky, like that of a baby learning to sit. Clearly, she possessed an excellent constitution.

And a not inconsiderable intellect. She examined him with the probing stare that his father had developed into an art form; give her a century, and Vestris, too, might scatter subordinates before her.

"Sasha's husband," she said by way of greeting.

Danion bowed.

"You arranged her escape." Vestris searched the cave with her eyes, winced, and touched the bandage.

"My wife is a woman of resource." Danion responded to her action rather than her words. "In this case, I fear, she hit you with a rock. You might say it was my fault for taking her by surprise. She was concerned that she might have killed you. She seems to have taken a liking to you."

Vestris touched her wound and winced again. "May the ghosts have mercy on those she does not like." She rubbed the opposite temple, as though her head ached. "Nonetheless, I liked her too, and I respect strength. She is not here?"

"I sent her home." What else should he say?

"Is that why you saved me?" she asked. "Because your wife liked me?"

"In part," Danion said. "I am not in the habit of leaving bodies in my wake."

"I knew you were not Kazrati." She assessed him from head to toe. "You are Danion of Tarkei."

He tipped his head in acknowledgment. "And you are Vestris, is that not so?"

"Sasha told you my name?" Vestris regarded him with a certain superstitious fear. It provided an odd contrast to her otherwise rational demeanor.

"Yes." Danion saw no need to explain the joining. "And what made you guess my identity? Was it only my lack of bloodthirstiness?"

Vestris, improbably, smiled. Her face crinkled, and her dark eyes lightened until she looked like an older version of Choli. "That, and the earring. And the fact that you cared for me, a stranger, instead of leaving me for my own to claim."

Danion touched his earlobe, somewhat self-conscious. He had worn the garnet for so many years, he often forgot it was there; a relic of his life in the priesthood, it had no counterpart in Kazrati custom.

"And how else would you have married a human?" Vestris went on. "You forget. I was with her from the day she recovered consciousness until her escape. My superior warned me to watch for you, that you had helped her on Xantera and might do so again. But he did not mention the marriage."

"Would it have made a difference?"

Vestris rubbed her temple once more. "I might have prepared better, I suppose."

"I saw no lack of preparation." Had he overreacted in suspecting the movement contained an informant? The secret police had, it seemed, anticipated that he would try to rescue Sasha. It did not need his comrades to supply information.

But that did not explain what had happened since—the attempt to recapture Sasha and the peculiar situation in the caves. Not to mention Nirrtu's double identity.

"I was unprepared," Vestris said bitterly. "So was D'Toth. I saw his body in the street when I woke up. I heard the firing in the distance, too. My superiors didn't bother to tell me they'd sent reinforcements. I feel like the designated sacrifice." Her coffee-colored skin flushed a deeper brown.

Her superiors had kept her in the dark—but to what extent? Could she tell him whether the secret police had contacts within the movement, and who those contacts might be? Aware of how little trust lay between them, he did not ask. "I apologize if we harmed a friend of yours. And for the damage to yourself, naturally."

"D'Toth was no friend of mine. I thought of him more as my jailer, although in theory I was in charge. He defied my authority whenever he could and reported on me to our supervisor. If he survived the attack and the interrogation, I'm sure he blamed me for losing your wife." She stopped, fingers restlessly pleating the cloth Danion had used to cover her. She looked like someone deep in an internal debate.

Danion, who had plenty of time and an equal amount of patience, watched her wrestle with herself.

"You suspect me of wanting to harm you." Vestris closed her eyes, one hand brushing her temple. Danion guessed that sitting up for so long was making her dizzy.

He placed a cushion behind her head. "If you overexert yourself, your recovery will take longer. Shall I help you lie down again?"

"In a minute." Vestris breathed deeply and opened her eyes again. "This is important."

Danion returned to his pallet. He sat cross-legged, as the priests had trained him to do, hands in his lap, waiting with the patience of the mountain—a pose so natural he did not notice it until Vestris remarked on it. "Do you always sit like that?"

Danion looked down at his own knees. "Often." He shrugged one shoulder. "I seem to have an affinity for living spaces without chairs."

The Choli-like smile again lit Vestris's stern face. The vivid expression revealed how young she was—in her mid-twenties, he guessed.

"Once I was a police agent," she said. "No longer. You saved my life, so I owe my loyalty to you. That is our custom."

"But not mine," Danion assured her. "Your person and your conscience are your own."

"By the ghosts, a man I could serve from conviction." Vestris's voice, surprisingly light, drew a half-smile from Danion. "Perhaps I will join your movement after all."

"If you wish," Danion said. He did not trust her, but he could withhold judgment; some time would pass before she would be capable either of joining him or betraying him; in the meantime, he expected he could discover where her true loyalties lay.

"I will prove my worth," she said. "Did you know that the man who invaded Xantera is here, in the caves?"

Danion stood and walked toward her. "As my trusted lieutenant."

She nodded. "I suspected it," he said. "Sasha identified him, but she last saw him long ago. You have given me confirmation. For that I thank you."

Vestris closed her eyes again. Danion eased her onto the mattress. "It is time to rest. Whatever your goal, you must rebuild your strength."

She did not answer. The closed eyes had dark circles beneath them; it seemed she had pushed herself to her limits. A characteristic of hers, perhaps.

Sasha spoke to him, telling him of her meeting with his father, her previously unexpressed concern that Jenat might have fewer months left to him than his family would wish, and her joy at being proven wrong.

He listened, pleased to hear that his family was safe. The news that Reilu had left brought relief; Camille's run-in with Bella yielded amusement. But beneath these surface exchanges, a current ran, too deep and turbulent to ignore: the yearning to leave Kazratan and go home, where Sasha waited.

I love thee, *kaleita*, he said in the ancient language of Tarkei. May Selassa hold thee close.

I would rather hold you close, Sasha said. I miss you. Do come home soon. Those stars can't smile forever!

Danion sent his laughter along the link. That would be too much to expect, although I hate to think what Thuja would tell them if they desisted. Be patient, my love. Matters are progressing. You were right about Tendak, it seems. A few weeks, and I will be done.

I'm counting the days, Sasha said.

As am I, Danion told her. As am I.

Through a window that could have used a wash, the late afternoon sun cast deep orange shadows on a face previously restricted to a communications console. A jowly face with cruel lines and an air of dissipation. Gray hair and steely eyes, a stocky frame like the desert predators of Tarkei. Reilu repressed a shudder of distaste. Despite the man's military bearing, she perceived a lack of self-restraint in his under-polished decorations that extended to the disorderly office. Its lack of symmetry struck her as a deliberate affront.

Her contact leaned back in his chair, balancing it on two feet, and stared at her as though she belonged under a microscope.

She stared back, chilling him with hauteur. Two could play that game. Even if one of them was a high-ranking officer in the Kazrati secret police.

The inconsiderate boor had not offered her a seat. She aligned the cleanest one with the bleary window, placed herself at the exact center of the chair, adjusted her skirt to hang evenly on both sides, and had the satisfaction of seeing his mouth tighten. Refusing to submit to the overwhelming air of casualness, she sat as her mother had taught her—upright, feet flat on the floor.

"I don't need you," the boor said. "Danion has left the caves, and I have the movement right where I want it."

"He has not left the caves," she said. "Or Kazratan. You are misinformed." How had she descended from the cultural heights of Tarkakhan to educating this halfwit amateur?

One more burden to heap on the shoulders of Danion and his detestable human wife, who did not even have the grace to vanish when required. "Perhaps your present informers do not deserve your trust."

The boor's glare intensified. He reminded her of a Terran animal she had seen during her stay on Earth: a wild pig with sharp tusks, red eyes, and an attitude that no doubt served him well in this hellhole. His voice, too, had a roaring quality. "What's it to you?"

"That is none of your concern." She dropped the temperature of her own voice as his rose. "Danion is here. I have it on the best authority. I will deliver him to you. What happens to him after that is your business." She raised her chin, letting the contempt she felt for him show. "Since your precious troops could not take advantage of the gift I sent them, one would think you would accept any assistance I choose to offer."

"We're not in the habit of relying on women." The boor looked her up and down in a manner so insulting that were it not for her mother's training and the honor of her lineage, she would have gouged out his eyes. "Until a few years ago, we had the sense to keep them out of the military, and we were much better off, if you ask me."

"I did not ask you," Reilu said in her most arctic tone. "Nor am I requesting favors from you. I propose a deal in which we both get what we want. Surely even a woman is capable of that."

The boor squirmed in his seat. Good. He needed to develop respect.

"Very well," he said after a long pause. "What do you want?"

Bella sat in the rehearsal room. What had she agreed to in consenting to stay? Dance she understood. The choreographer said, "Do this, do that," and she obliged. If the choreographer was Gramps, he might ask for many different steps or change his mind when he saw how they looked. He would grumble about putting her heart into it, but if she repeated the steps often enough, he stopped hassling her and rewarded her with praise.

This Camille woman, though. Three weeks into rehearsal for *La Bayadère*, she hadn't shown Bella so much as a step. Instead, she and Sasha (Bella had stopped even thinking of her as Aunt Sasha, because a grandaunt who could pass for your sister was too absurd to contemplate) went on and on about Gamzatti's past. Her relationship with her father, the Rajah; her thoughts about Solor and Nikia; what her childhood had been like; whether she had friends; what kind of education she would have had.

They might as well discuss what she ate for breakfast, as far as Bella was concerned. So it went, until Bella felt like imitating the girls in the corps who ran out of the studio and screamed into towels whenever Camille let them loose. What good did it do to imagine how Gamzatti felt about being the Rajah's daughter? It didn't show up in the ballet, did it?

But after her previous outburst, Bella didn't quite have the nerve to say that to Camille, so she humored them in the hope that eventually they'd tire of quizzing her and teach her the steps.

Sasha ceased talking and gazed at her niece. (Like Bella, she had decided the grandniece business had to go.) Camille tipped her head in silent inquiry.

"You have no idea why we're putting you through this, do you?" Sasha asked.

Bella's head snapped back. "Of course I do." She flushed. "No."

Camille opened her mouth, but Sasha waved a hand at her. "*Bayadère* isn't one of these abstract ballets so popular now. It's like a novel on stage, like a play. The audience has to know *why* Gamzatti is so angry, why she'd kill Nikia. That means you have to show them, and without words. To get that across, every gesture, every expression has to fit. When you make that entrance, you have to *be* Gamzatti. You can't do that unless you immerse yourself in her first. How does she think? How does she move? What makes her unique? You don't have to feel everything she feels. I hope you won't do everything she does. But you do have to feel something of what she feels; you must be able to imagine why she makes the choices she does. Without that, the steps have no meaning. They're just pretty pictures."

"I can't do that." Bella sounded sulky. "I never have."

"You never have," Sasha said. "But you can. How did you feel when Tonio said he didn't have a prima?"

"Furious." Bella was pouting at the memory.

Sasha raised her hands, palms up, to show her understanding. "Who wouldn't? He insulted you. Not deliberately, but so what? He took something you thought belonged to you and gave it to someone else."

Bella hesitated, and Sasha wondered if she had pushed too hard too fast. They didn't have much of a relationship yet, and the answer demanded real honesty.

"Yes," Bella said at last. "Worse, he told me I was inadequate. I hated that."

Progress. Bella could identify her own thought process and the emotions it generated.

"That's how Gamzatti feels," Sasha said.

Images of Reilu entered her mind: sitting in the office of the Tarkei Consulate, denying the truth; kneeling in the garden, dragging Danion's altanai out by the roots—that was his memory, not hers.

"We don't know what drives her," she went on, forcing herself to focus on Gamzatti and Bella, not her own self-proclaimed rival. "Maybe she'd always wanted to marry Solor. Think of it, a young girl in a society where she has no say in picking her husband, and there's that picture of the handsome young warrior on the wall. Who could blame her for daydreaming? Or maybe she's Daddy's darling and whatever she wants, she gets, so when he says she's to marry Solor, Solor becomes hers. Maybe she's been pleading with Daddy from the beginning. What a catch to show her girlfriends! Who knows? Pick whatever interpretation you like. That will make her yours—you see?—not anyone else's. But whatever her reason, when Gamzatti discovers that Solor loves Nikia, she feels robbed. She can't understand it. What's wrong with the man? Why fall for a silly little temple dancer when he could have a kingdom?"

For the first time in three weeks, Bella, a finger under her chin, looked truly present, as though she might be considering what her aunt was trying so hard to explain.

"So she tries to buy Nikia off," Bella said. "And Nikia throws it in her face. He loves *me,* she tells Gamzatti."

"Because she's hurt." Sasha spread her hands as Nikia might have done. "The priests send her to bless Gamzatti's marriage, and she comes and dances and does her job, then discovers Gamzatti's going to marry the man who has sworn an oath to Nikia. Gamzatti's furious and betrayed, but so is Nikia. She fights back, as you say, by throwing in her rival's face the one unanswerable truth: that Solor loves her. She attacks Gamzatti with a knife. Nikia is not Giselle. Solor wrongs her, but she doesn't give up and die. She fights. Now do you see why Gamzatti wants to get rid of her?"

Bella nodded. "She thinks that if Nikia dies, Solor will forget her. That she, Gamzatti, can win his love."

Good. Insight to match her technique. What a blessing they had come along before that bright talent went to waste. "Whereas if Nikia lives," Sasha said, "Gamzatti will have no peace. Whether Solor goes after Nikia or not, she will stand between him and Gamzatti. She will not submit and go away."

"But killing her does the same, doesn't it? In a sense, it immortalizes her."

Sasha again thought of Reilu—her extraordinary self-centeredness and her absolute refusal to accept that the husband assigned to her by tradition did not want her.

"You're right," she told Bella. "Worse, it freezes Nikia in time, so that she becomes eternally desirable. She can never irritate Solor as a living person would. What does it say about Gamzatti that she doesn't realize that?"

Bella chewed the side of her finger and considered the question. "That she's impulsive. She thinks ahead, but only so far. She sees the immediate gain but not the long-term cost. She's a child, in a way."

Sasha nodded. "Good. You got it."

"Think about that for a moment, then stand up," Camille said. "Make the gesture that says, 'I will kill her.' Let me see the rage."

Bella cast her mind back to that day three weeks ago when Sasha had returned from the dead and upended the world that Bella had taken for granted since she graduated from school. How she had hated Gramps for his callous remark. How she wished a hole would open in space and swallow Sasha up. How even the touch of Camille's hand on her arm had felt like a violation.

She stood, one pointed foot crossed behind the other, and let the righteous fury fill her. She felt strong, invincible.

I am the Rajah's daughter. With savage grace, she extended her left hand from the shoulder, palm down, pointing at the absent Nikia. *That woman has injured me.* Her right hand came over her head. Fist clenched, she slammed it down. *No one takes what is mine. Kill her!*

Camille jumped to her feet and clapped. "Brava! Bravissima!" For the first time, Bella saw the dance mistress's stern face break into delighted laughter.

Camille hugged her. "Now I will teach you the steps."

15. Piqué

VESTRIS'S HEALTH CONTINUED TO improve. As her wound healed, her strong constitution took over, and she made rapid strides. Within the week, she was exploring the caves. Danion felt like a bird with one chick. Most of the time, he managed to restrain his urge to tell her to slow down. On occasion he forgot, and she looked at him as though he were her grandfather, brushing off his concern.

Lacking other forms of entertainment, they engaged in long conversations about her past and his, Tarkei philosophy and life in the secret police. She revealed that she came from a family of intellectuals. Dissident intellectuals: her father, a scientist, had asked the wrong questions; her mother wrote poetry that did not glorify the state. When she was ten, the police killed her parents and forced her into a government school, then into service. Many of her peers had given in, accepting the government's values. Some destroyed themselves through rebellion or drugs; a few committed suicide. Vestris adapted, or so she claimed.

At first, Danion did not believe her, but as their discussions continued he watched her shed her façade of compliance, releasing her essential self. She was younger than he had thought—young enough to put the past behind her and create the life she had wanted for years. Although she had longed for an exit, leaving the secret police was almost impossible. But if they thought her dead, they would not search for her.

Faced with Vestris's openness and her clear-sighted assessments of everyone from her supervisors to the street people, Danion's skepticism yielded to reluctant admiration. Vestris gave no sign of recognizing that she had convinced him; she focused on the achievement of her long-desired freedom.

A thought fluttered by, then lodged in his head, strengthening with each passing day. Vestris, if she could be trusted, was intelligent and resourceful and courageous. Skilled in many areas that could prove useful to the movement. She would make a worthy successor, if she were willing.

Then Tamir arrived with a new problem. Arrived in the flesh, wending his way through the passages until he found the cave that housed Danion and Vestris.

Danion gestured him in. Tamir had been running; sweat beaded on his forehead, and his chest was heaving. He looked scared and unhappy.

"Come in and sit down, Tamir," Danion said. "Catch your breath. Were you followed?"

Tamir made the "no" gesture, gasping for air. He dropped onto the end of Vestris's pallet, narrowly missing her feet. She moved them out of the way, and he exhaled something that sounded like an apology.

"Meet Vestris," Danion said. "I have been helping her since she was injured. As have you. She has recovered, for the most part. Vestris, permit me to introduce my friend Tamir. He has kept us in food all this time."

Vestris bowed her head toward Tamir. "Thank you."

Danion noted the formality with amusement; he had become used to more freedom of expression from her.

Tamir was staring at Vestris, horror in his face. Danion, puzzled, looked from one to the other. He had become so accustomed to Vestris over the last ten weeks that several minutes passed before he realized that Tamir was reacting to the police uniform she wore. Extra clothing was not easily obtained in the caves.

"She was a police agent, Tamir," Danion said. "But not by choice. She is working with us now."

Tamir moved farther away from Vestris. He did not voice his protest, but he made it clear that he did not trust anyone from the organization that had killed his parents. Danion would have been more concerned if he had. As long as Tamir continued to trust Danion himself, things would work out in the end.

"The police killed her parents, too," Danion told him.

Tamir shivered, avoiding Vestris's eyes. "Nirrtu has set the date for the uprising. Five days from now. And he has brought someone new into the caves. She says she is Kazrati, but I don't believe her. No Kazrati acts like that, even in the police."

His mouth twisted, and he shot Vestris a passing glance, muttering, "Sorry."

"I am not offended," she said. "Danion spoke the truth. I want to escape from the police."

"Oh." Tamir focused on the hands twisted in his lap.

"Go on, Tamir," Danion said. "Tell me more about this woman. Why don't you think she is Kazrati?"

Tamir fidgeted. Danion waited while his young friend sorted out his mingled impressions. Although not as quick as Choli or Vestris, Tamir had a good sense of the incongruous; if he suspected this woman, others would do well to pay heed.

"She is too cold," Tamir said after a minute or two. "Other people show what they think in their faces. She does not." Danion, seeing the boy's eyes fixed on him, felt his stomach contract. A nasty thought slid by; he acknowledged it without stopping it and forcing it to produce its papers. "Even less than you," Tamir added.

There was one way to find out the truth. "Tell me," Danion asked, "does she have green eyes, this woman without expression? And perhaps an extreme need to arrange her possessions—indeed, whatever she touches— in a symmetrical design?"

Tamir stared as though Danion had started a second career as a fortune teller. "How did you guess?"

Vestris's formality vanished in a grin that made her look Tamir's age. "Don't be a dope. He recognizes her from your description. Who is she?"

Danion did not return the smile. The rock bit into the back of his head as he rested it against the wall. "My personal demon."

Tamir's superstitious awe turned to fear. Danion sent Vestris a rueful glance. "I don't know how she got here, and I shudder to think why, but my fears for Sasha's safety appear to have been exaggerated."

Vestris's smile faded. "Who is she?"

"My first wife," Danion said. That startled them both. "Sixty-one years ago, she set this whole series of events in motion by arranging to have Sasha sent through the time vortex. When I learned of it, I thought she took advantage of an opportunity to rid herself of a rival. But if she is here, that suggests she has something else in mind."

"Not to your benefit, I would guess," Vestris said.

Danion nodded. "An understatement. Of that, I think, we can feel confident."

Rehearsals became more intense and more frequent. Sasha maintained contact with the consulate, apprising her family of Danion's progress, but her hours were so unpredictable she kept in touch mostly by videophone, often leaving messages late at night. Another eight weeks passed in this way, making nine since her arrival on Earth and ten since her husband's return to Kazratan.

Most of the time, she tried not to think about his absence, losing herself in the minutiae of preparing to dance Nikia. It worked during the day, although the evenings were long and lonely. She sent Danion wistful thoughts and received many in return; although better than the months of silence, they did not compensate for his absence.

One day she received an urgent message from Iqara, unusual in that relaxed and cosmopolitan soul. Wondering what her sister had to say, Sasha agreed to meet her at a café a few blocks from the consulate. One rehearsal lasted longer than expected, and the next was postponed, so Sasha arrived first. The café, quiet in the early afternoon, had a typical California prettiness: an open patio with white metal furniture and vines drooping from the trellis that substituted for a ceiling.

Sasha ordered vegetable curry and iced tea and watched the crowd on the street. Her early arrival had assured her of this perfectly placed seat; back to the café wall, she knew no one could slip up behind her, while the closest table stood too far away for eavesdropping. Iqa had expressed concern that they might be overheard at the consulate, although whether the concern was general or limited to their father, Sasha could not guess. The cloak-and-dagger tone was peculiar enough, considering the source.

A swirl of butternut flowers splashed against a dark brown background dropped onto the seat opposite her. Iqara reached across the table to flick her ear. Sasha returned the greeting. "How are you, Iqa-*chan*?"

"Well, I thank you." Iqa beckoned the wait robot with an imperious finger. It rolled over to her and waited, its scarlet sensors extended, giving it an air of anticipation. "Tarento tea," she said. "And what's that, vegetable curry? It looks good. I'll have some." The robot blinked in acknowledgment and rolled away. "I didn't have lunch either," Iqa told Sasha.

"You were busy?" The curry came with a roll. Sasha broke off a piece and put it in her mouth. It was delicious— richly textured whole wheat mixed with currants, the aroma an invitation in itself.

"I was shopping."

Sasha giggled. Iqa loved to shop; the first time they met, she had taken Sasha around the Tarkei capital in search of much-needed clothes, some of which Sasha (thanks to the sixty years away) was wearing today. "I thought you said this was urgent."

The wait robot was back, a pot of tea and one tea glass in a brass holder on its retractable tray. Iqa took the objects off the tray and patted the robot on the head. It rolled away again. "You're not easy to reach, Sasha-*chan*. I had to get your attention. It's unpleasant but not earth-shattering."

"Not enough to keep you from shopping, I see."

Iqa pantomimed a wince.

"It's not Father, I hope. How is he?" Sasha helped herself to a bite of curry. The taste of coconut and chili peppers filled her mouth. Hot, but not hot enough to be inedible. Choli would no doubt describe it as bland.

Iqa turned as the wait robot arrived with her food. The robot stood, scarlet sensors flashing with confusion. Iqa lifted the plate and deposited it in front of her. "Fine," she told the robot. It departed, and she answered Sasha's question. "Father's the same as usual. Curmudgeon on the surface, soft as butter underneath. He's delighted you're back and glad to have met Choli—you should bring her again, by the way—perhaps dinner tonight? He worries about Danion, although he won't admit it. Just grumps about how his son should stop fooling around on Kazratan and come home."

Sasha took another bite of the roll. "And his health? I can't get over how old he looks, compared to the way I remember him."

"Oh, he's fine." Iqa was his doctor. "He's only 136. He'll still be here giving us trouble fifty years from now." Her eyes sparkled in the California sun. "You were the one we were likely to lose early. You and Geoffrey." The sparkle dimmed.

"Danion says he's healthy." Sasha touched her sister's hand. "You can hope for another three decades with him. Maybe more. Although I understand he's traveling a lot. That must be tough."

"It makes it worse, yes. I worry more, and naturally I miss him. But I don't want to discourage him. He might die of boredom. As for the rest, it's the price of marrying a human." Iqara ate curry. "Danion went through it early, but if this thing with the vortex hadn't happened, he would be in the same situation as I am."

"True." Sasha and Danion now had comparable life spans—she hadn't realized that until Iqa mentioned it. The average Tarkei lived to 180, whereas humans were ancient at 130. Not much consolation to Danion, except in the sense that grief is always better in the past than in the future, but since they could not escape growing older, it would be pleasant to go through it together.

"Will Geoffrey come for the performance?" Sasha asked. "I know Danion wants to see him. Me too, of course."

Iqa brightened. "He says he will. His students have exams, so he's asking someone else to administer them. I'm expecting him next month."

Sasha squeezed Iqa's hand and let it go. "That's good. Tell me why you asked me to meet you here."

"Word came this morning." Iqa, her face intent, tapped her fingers against the tablecloth. "Reilu did not return to Tarkei. We don't know where she went."

Sasha was glad she had put the cup down; she might have dropped it at this news. "She didn't go to Tarkei?" She tapped a finger against the table as she considered the implications. "She's up to something."

"Yes," Iqa said. "The question is what. Did she sneak back here?"

"She must have, don't you think?" Sasha stopped tapping her finger and rested her head against the café wall. "Where else would she go? What does Father think?"

"I haven't told him," Iqa said. "He'll worry. Danion, too. I thought I'd start with you."

"But you must tell him." Sasha leaned forward, her elbows touching Iqara's. "It's unfair not to, and anyway, his contacts are better than ours. He can find out where she went. Or were you covering up just now, and he's in worse condition than you led me to believe?"

"No. I told you. He's in wonderful shape for someone his age. Although you're right: I do try to spare him what I can. Not that he appreciates it." Iqa gave a rueful half-smile worthy of her brother and raised both palms to the sky. "I suppose I can't blame him. I hated it when he was the one overprotecting me. Bring Choli to eat dinner with us, and we'll tell him this afternoon."

Sasha nodded, her mind elsewhere. Reilu was becoming a serious nuisance; for a moment Sasha let herself imagine Danion's first wife being dragged off by a demon, like people in medieval tales who sold their souls.

The thought triggered her link with Danion, and she gasped.

"What?" Iqa said sharply.

"She's there," Sasha said. "On Kazratan. In the caves where the resistance movement lives. Oh, I could shake Danion. He's been hiding it from me."

"On Kazratan!" Iqa's tea splashed into her curry, and she said something rude in Tarkei. "That's dreadful. What is she doing there?"

Sasha touched the link again. How could you? You are putting yourself in danger—again—and keeping it secret?

I just found out, Danion said. I have been avoiding the caves, as you know.

She sensed his apology but would not let it mollify her. He had not planned to share the news with her; the link had already revealed that much.

I am sorry, Danion said. I should have told you at once. I didn't want to worry you with the news when you cannot help. And Reilu remains unaware of my presence.

Unlikely, Sasha said. She wormed her way into the consulate before your father sent her about her business, remember? You should assume she got whatever information she needed out of the government databases. If she's on Kazratan, she's there looking for you. With a gun.

I will be careful, Danion said. I did not come so far to lose you now.

Iqa snapped her fingers in front of Sasha's face. "You're talking to Danion?"

"I'm yelling at Danion," Sasha said. "For all the good it does me."

Iqa regarded her sympathetically. "What a family. Bring that daughter of yours to dinner, and we'll share the story with Father. Agreed?"

"Agreed," Sasha's head reeled with images of Danion and Reilu, together on Kazratan. What plot was her rival hatching now?

The air in the café became stifling. "I'm sorry," she told Iqa. "Meet me at the theater at five. I need to calm down."

"Of course." Iqa pressed a button to summon the wait robot. "Go. Lunch is my treat. See you at five."

"Stay here," Danion told Tamir. "You brought supplies?"

Tamir picked up the bag he had dropped during his headlong entrance and shook it. "Enough for a week, if we are careful. I thought by then the situation would be resolved."

"You did well." Danion nodded his approval and turned toward Vestris, who looked about to explode.

"What are you planning?" she asked as soon as she had his attention. "You aren't thinking of leaving Tamir and me in the cave while you go off and sacrifice yourself, are you? Because I won't do it."

Her intensity would have amused him if she hadn't struck so close to the truth. Danion sought words that would convince her without condescending to her. "You recently suffered a concussion. Tamir is sixteen." His mouth curved. "And I an old man, Nirrtu tells me. We can't expect to mount a frontal attack on armed troops."

"Nirrtu's older than you," Tamir said. That raised chin might have belonged on a Terran canine, but Danion could not object to his spirit.

"Not much," Vestris said. "He spent years in a rehabilitation camp. After the allied planets released him, I mean. For failing on Xantera. The police wanted to avoid an interplanetary incident; otherwise they would have killed him."

An interplanetary incident. But who would have reported the news?

More likely, the secret police had kept Tendak in reserve as a man susceptible to manipulation. When it came to conspiracies, it seldom served to underestimate the cunning of the Kazrati government.

"I did not realize that," Danion said. "Nirrtu would not have mentioned it, for fear of disclosing his true identity. He must have wondered whether I recognized him—as I would have done, if less time had passed, since I was the one who captured him on Xantera."

"He hates your guts," Vestris said. It was not a question. "You caused his suffering, his disgrace. That's how he'd see it. I'm amazed he hasn't murdered you already."

"I too," Danion said. "Perhaps he gloated at my ignorance. By the time I arrived, Nirrtu looked far different from the man I saw on Xantera. Whatever his fears, he must soon have realized that I had made no connection. He put on a good front."

An understatement. Nirrtu had lied through his teeth during their conversations about Sasha—pretending surprise at Danion's marriage, disbelief in her existence, concern for her safety, a willingness to assist in her rescue.

The secret police, if not Reilu, would have briefed Nirrtu on these details as part of his assignment.

Yet Danion had believed the act, whatever his reservations. That stung.

And if he had not? If he had seen through Nirrtu's deceit—recognized him, even?

Nothing. It would have changed nothing. By the time Danion learned the truth of Sasha's disappearance, she was here, on Kazratan, in government hands. He would have rescued her with or without Nirrtu's dubious assistance.

"But let's stick with the present," he told Vestris. "Despite the government's mistreatment of him, Nirrtu remains a loyal agent of the secret police?"

"Hard to say. He has worked with the resistance for a long time. Who knows where his true loyalties lie? But he files reports, and he played some part in the plot to bring Sasha here, or so I hear. He is not a friend of mine." Vestris picked up one of the pebbles that littered the floor, tossed it in the air, and caught it. "What are you going to do?"

"Prevent the uprising," Danion said. "It will be a bloodbath. That is its point, I assume—to justify the destruction of the resistance movement."

Tamir, staring at him out of wide dark eyes, said nothing.

"Agreed." Vestris rolled the stone back and forth in her palm. "How, though? As you say, we can't overpower them."

"I intend to use persuasion, not force," Danion said. "My appearance, if properly timed, should startle them. Perhaps long enough for some of them to stop and think."

"And if they don't?" Vestris asked. "At last count, you had not only Nirrtu to worry about but his lieutenant and your personal demon as well. Suppose they arrest you?"

"Then it will be up to you to get me out."

Tamir looked worried. Vestris, as he had expected, broke into laughter. So much for her concussion; she would pay it no heed, so long as he respected her skills.

And planning her part might keep her out of trouble long enough for him to do his job.

Choli let the warm water run over her head and down her back, easing the strain of tired muscles and washing away the sweat of a day in the studio. Of the many luxuries she had encountered since her arrival on Thuja's vessel, showers seemed to her the most magical. In her years on the streets, she had seldom seen water that didn't look as though it ought to be boiled before she drank it. Conditions in the caves were better, but austere and old-fashioned compared to life on Earth.

Sometimes she hated the opulence. It felt degenerate to enjoy such wealth when her own people remained locked in poverty. The girls who shared her classes, who complained if their touch pads didn't perform perfectly or their clothes matched someone else's, seemed like such spoiled brats she couldn't bear to be near them. They thought her peculiar, she knew. Some pitied her for her unfortunate past; others sneered at her. Choli ignored both.

So far, she had yet to meet anyone her own age who treated her as a person, but as Sasha reminded her (not often, because Sasha was kind), she had joined the school a short time ago. Choli acknowledged the truth of this.

It changed nothing. She liked Sasha—and Slava, who chucked her under the chin and called her little bird. Camille, too, whose devotion to improving her dancing seemed infinite. None of that stopped her from worrying over Danion and wishing he would return soon.

Choli turned off the water and let the warm air dry her, then slipped on fresh clothes before leaving the dressing area. Inside the locker room, she saw Sasha, talking to Danion's sister. Sasha's face was filling out, the lines of strain receding with the scars, the hair growing; it had reached her chin. It was easy to see why Danion thought his wife beautiful. She could have been ugly, and her vivid personality and exquisite movements would have drawn the eye.

Choli desperately wanted to become like Sasha. But if she succeeded, she suspected she would resemble Iqara, with her creamy skin and diamond ears and her own variation on Sasha's grace. That made Iqara Choli's chosen model; she studied her aunt every moment she could.

"There she is!" Iqara's outstretched arms welcomed Choli as though they were in truth family. "Greetings, niece."

Choli went toward her and received a flick on the ear. "You're coming to dinner with us," her aunt said. "Father is waiting. He says he needs more time to make your acquaintance, and he wants to hear about life in the ballet school."

A flash of energy sent shivers along Choli's nerves. She had weathered one meeting with Danion's father, but she wasn't sure she wanted to risk another.

"Iqa's teasing," Sasha said. "We need to tell him about something that affects Danion—who insists he should be coming home soon, by the way—but Father would like to meet you again, I'm sure."

Choli relaxed, letting her aunt steer her toward the locker-room door. Over her head, Iqara said, "I forgot to ask you. How are the rehearsals going? Has that Camille of yours whipped the company into shape yet?"

A giggle escaped Choli and was repressed. Not so Sasha, who laughed until Choli thought she might choke. "You have doubts?" Sasha managed at last. "Take a look."

They were passing the studio where the corps was practicing its entrance under Camille's gimlet eye. With an obvious effort, Sasha restored her self-control. "It wasn't as bad as we thought. They had been well trained at one time, but Tonio had become lax about making them attend class. As Camille told him in no uncertain terms. The rest was inevitable. Classical ballet demands constant practice: when they didn't get it, their technique suffered; once Camille forced them into the studio from dawn to dusk, they couldn't help but respond."

Sasha waved a hand at the studio window, where twenty-four young women in leotards stood in four rows of six, right legs extended to the side, right arms curved over their heads, in perfect symmetry. "As you see, it will be a memorable performance."

"Reilu would approve," Iqara said.

16. Renversé

WITH THE PREMIERE TWO weeks away, rehearsals moved from the company studios into the theater. The women of the corps, seeing for the first time the ramp down which Camille expected them to walk, balancing in arabesque penché at every other step, forgot their recently acquired serenity and howled into their dance bags. Sasha, who as the heroine escaped the hideous entrance, sympathized with them. Being prima had its rewards, and staying off that ramp counted high among them.

Bella, swinging one arched foot in the seat next to her, agreed. "Better them than me. How many of those things do they have to do?"

"At least thirty, I should think," Sasha said. They had become friends by now. "The ones in the front, that is. Those at the back get away with half-a-dozen or so."

Bella grinned. "Choreographed by a man, obviously."

"Obviously," Sasha said. "The screaming's normal, by the way. I've danced *Bayadère* a zillion times, and the shades fussed during every one. It's such a hideous part."

"Worse than Nikia?" Bella asked. "That snake variation of yours makes me lose sleep at night."

Sasha ran a hand through her hair. "Yes, but I don't have to hang around waiting for it. I'm either on stage or off." Whereas the shades stood motionless on the stage for twenty minutes at a time, only to burst into action for perhaps two or three minutes, then stand again. No wonder every corps she had danced with detested *Bayadère*.

Bella nodded. "Look at them, though. They've really improved."

While they talked, the corps had finished its howling and begun its descent. Its precision and balance were indeed remarkable; the women looked like dolls on a string.

"The credit goes to Camille, I suppose," Bella said. "That woman's a miracle worker."

Over her left shoulder, Sasha glanced at Tonio, sitting on her other side in the first row. "Happy?"

Her brother was staring at the stage. "I'd forgotten. I thought I remembered, and sometimes I wondered if I were exaggerating my memories—an old man's dreams of his youth, you know. Instead, I'd forgotten. Camille is unbelievable. Two and a half months, and she's turned that collection of would-be principals into a corps."

The corps finished its grand entrance. Camille clapped her hands, delight visible in her face. "You were brilliant, *mes filles*, brilliant. And now we do it again, *non*?"

The corps did not bother to protest. With slumped shoulders, the women filed out and regrouped at the top of the ramp. One by one, they began the descent again.

Tonio went on. "The last time anything like this hit the dance world was the year Baryshnikov defected. I can't wait. I'll be turning financiers away." Eyes bright, he faced his sister. "We'll put Xantera Ballet back on the map, right?"

He was such a child, but she loved him anyway. "Atop Mount Everest," Sasha said.

Danion walked through the tunnels at his usual unhurried pace. Behind the main cave where the motley army was supposed to meet, Vestris and Tamir positioned themselves, anticipating trouble.

Danion heard restless feet and hushed conversation. Not far now.

He stopped to make sure he had complete control over himself and to send reassuring (if misleading) thoughts to Sasha. As much as possible, he had concealed his intentions from her; she would be frantic if she knew the danger he faced. Only part of the bond lay under their conscious control, so he could not guarantee that his efforts would succeed, but they had up to this point. No doubt she would be furious when she found out, but he could handle that later. Assuming he had a later.

Danion focused on the opposite wall and took three deep breaths. The entrance to the main cave opened ahead. He stepped through.

No one noticed him. Perhaps forty of his students milled about the cave, checking weaponry and buckling belts for guns and ammunition. Piles of rocks sat in the corners; each student carried a bag slung over one shoulder. Not for the first time, Danion wondered what they thought they were doing.

At the front of the cave, three people stood apart from the crowd. Nirrtu, lined face intent, appeared deep in argument with Reilu. The old man's fists were clenched, and his face loomed so close to his opponent's that they could kiss. Not that Reilu looked as though she intended to kiss anyone: her marble face maintained its usual lack of expression. Neither Nirrtu's clenched fist nor his raised voice made the slightest impression on her. She might have been listening, although Danion, based on his long acquaintance with her, thought not; either way, she was not talking.

The third person, a heavyset man of about thirty-five with beefy cheeks and a sullen expression, watched them without interfering. He seemed familiar, although it took Danion a while to place him. D'Toth, Sasha's other guard, last seen lying in the street. Vestris had been right, and her partner had talked himself out of trouble.

"Danion! Is that really you?" The youthful voice rang through the cavern, and the forty-plus heads turned his way. Hands reached out to brush his sleeves as he walked toward the threesome, two of them staring in shock. Reilu, as usual, watched.

At the front of the cave, he turned.

"We thought you were dead," one young man said.

"So you decided to destroy yourselves?" Danion asked. "How touching. I think I prefer a different legacy."

The young man flushed dark brown. Half-a-dozen others hung their heads, and one or two edged toward the exit. Danion suppressed a ill-timed flash of amusement. His father could have hoped for no greater effect.

Alas, for every student he had abashed, three stood firm. What seemed to be a core group stared defiantly, their eyes not on him but on Nirrtu and D'Toth. He recognized none of them. Reilu sat on a large rock, swinging her foot and saying nothing.

"What are you doing?" Danion asked his students. He spoke without heat, trying to reach them through the haze of emotion that drove them.

A girl whom he remembered as an ardent idealist spoke, waving her half-assembled weapon. "We will show the government that it cannot trample on the simple people!" She had come from a fishing village, he recalled. It no longer existed. The police had declared it a nest of traitors and burned it, killing the vast majority of the inhabitants.

The students roared. The drooping heads rose, and those who had been edging away returned.

"Forty of you," Danion said. "Against the massed government forces. Can you leave no other example for the rest of the downtrodden than martyrs to emulate?"

"Enough," Nirrtu said. It was surprising he had let Danion talk as long as he had. "Seize him! Will you let his alien pacifism divert you from your purpose? Are you men or sheep?"

Cowed, not a soul protested as the ten or so that Danion had identified as the core surrounded him and bound his arms.

After a while, one or two students approached; the ten turned and clubbed them. The crowd drew in its collective breath.

"Traitors!" Nirrtu pointed at the unconscious students.

Startled by the sudden revelation of Nirrtu's true intentions, Danion assumed, about half the remaining students fled, leaving their weapons behind them. How they had thought they could stand against government troops when they could not even defend their leader escaped Danion, but he rejoiced in their safety—temporary as it might prove to be.

The rope, tight around his wrists, numbed his hands. Danion examined the twenty who remained. Those he had designated the core were, without exception, men—distinguished by their military bearing and the businesslike way they shouldered their weapons. Police agents, he guessed, brought into the caves by Nirrtu or D'Toth after he left.

The others he could call by name. He knew their stories, their strengths and their weaknesses. Idealists all, the woman from the fishing village among them. He could guess their grievance. His methods had been too slow for their taste; they had never understood that some goals are best approached sideways. The key to overcoming the Kazrati predilection for violence did not lie in greater violence.

Danion gazed into each implacable face, one after another, willing them to remember the months when he had cared for them, when they had listened to him. The woman from the fishing village refused to meet his eyes; she placed her weapon on the ground and walked away.

Nirrtu shot her, and she fell. The others Danion had known ran, scattering as the laser fire burned in the air. Only two escaped the cave. Danion, filled with remorse, prayed for the eight young bodies left on the floor. Perhaps if he had not come...

If you had not come, Sasha's voice said in his thoughts, they would have died in the streets, and the rest with them.

Fury lent its edge to her voice. What are you doing? How could you walk right into their hands?

Peace, *kaleita*. I saw no alternative, but I am not done yet.

She subsided. The scarlet glow that encased the bond made it clear she withdrew only so that her anger would not distract him. He would hear from her later. No matter. His wife's scolding would be a small price to pay if it meant he could go home at last.

Nirrtu stood in front of him, white head tipped back at the level of Danion's chin. Remembering how Sasha and Slava and Tonio had once noted the physical resemblance between Tendak and himself, Danion wondered how the man's true identity could have escaped him for so long. Looking at him was like looking into a mirror, a weird time-distorted reflection of himself many years from now. Vestris had spoken the truth: Nirrtu had suffered during his years in the camps.

No hint of sympathy touched the brown eyes so close to his, but he did see, right around the edges of the cornea, the line of contact lenses. One point for Sasha. He doubted it would mollify her.

"Hold him," Nirrtu said to two of the police agents. He glared at Danion. "I've wanted to do this for years." He drew back his right arm and punched Danion in the jaw.

As Danion fell back, propped up by the police agents, he heard Reilu sigh. "Why must I tolerate these cretins?" said the familiar glacial voice. "Not one of them has an ounce of imagination."

❋

Sasha had been standing at the barre when she realized what her husband was doing. The music, slow and flowing for pliés, was drawing her into its rhythm at the moment Danion's guilt reached her. With a gasp, she let go of the barre and dropped to the floor, arms wound about her head.

Slava crouched next to her. His hand touched her shoulder; she could hear his concerned tone through the babble in her mind. A word from Camille, and the music stopped. Sasha sat in the middle of a circle of feet. The babble outside matched the one in her thoughts.

"What is it, *ma belle*? Are you ill?" Camille's voice, clear and sharp, cut through the noise.

Before Sasha found an answer, Slava said, "She was fine a moment ago. Is that not so, my dove? It is that husband of hers, no doubt."

"Danion?" This voice was Tonio's. How many people were gathered round her? "Is he injured?"

Sasha pushed the noise away, talking to Danion in her head. Only when she knew what had happened did she look at the circle of worried faces, picking out those most likely to understand. Bella was rehearsing in a different studio. Tonio, Slava, Camille—no one else would know what she was talking about. "He's been arrested," she said.

The babble broke out anew. For a while, she ignored it as she struggled to calm herself enough to hear what was happening. She winced as Nirrtu struck his blow, setting off another chorus of concern.

"Hold on," she told Slava, although the quiver in her voice could not have reassured him.

After an immeasurable while, Danion's certainty, his calm, impressed itself upon her. It seemed extraordinary, until she realized that he had not, after all, walked into the trap without planning his escape.

That meant she had a task to perform. A relief. Sitting and waiting for events to unfold did not appeal to Sasha. Better to contribute something, however minor, to the plan. Otherwise, she might recall how often plans go wrong.

She forced her head up and her hands down. With the grace of a lifetime's training, she stood in the middle of her circle of well-wishers and addressed her brother. "I need to reach a starship. Can I do it directly, or do I have to go through the consulate?"

"He is free?" Slava asked. "Already?"

"No," Sasha said. "Not yet, but if his plan works, he will be soon."

Tonio had been watching her, astonishment clear on his mobile face. Now he jerked his head toward the door. "This way, Sasha. We'll try it first from my office." He waved a hand at the circle of dancers. "Back to work, the rest of you. You have only a couple of weeks till the performance!"

The dancers groaned and rolled their eyes—for effect, Sasha assumed, for they returned to their places even as they protested. As she followed her brother out the door, she heard Camille saying, "First position, demi-plié. Come, boys and girls, don't be late. Do you expect the pianist to wait for you?"

Fortunately, Nirrtu's strength did not equal his venom. Age and the camps had muted his punch. Danion tested his jaw as best he could with his arms tied behind his back;

it seemed unbroken. He grimaced for Nirrtu's benefit and hoped the prospect of interrogation and trial would defuse the man's urge to commit violence long enough for Vestris to intercede. If she intended to intercede. He had gambled a good deal on her assertions of loyalty.

To buy time, he talked. "Tendak," he said to Nirrtu, "a clever scheme. Had you planned this since Xantera?"

"I planned it." Reilu left her rock and clamped her fingers around the bruise on his jaw. Danion winced, although he would have repressed it if he could. It seemed unlikely that his first wife, having pursued him with such vigor, would settle for so small a payment.

Reilu fixed her gaze on him, cold but furious. "You never did give me credit, did you, my husband?"

Danion clenched his teeth against the pressure of her fingers, then forced them apart to answer her. "I did underestimate you."

"Yes," Reilu said. "You did. I contacted the Kazrati as soon as the allies released Tendak back to their custody. They refused to let me talk to him then, but once I convinced them that preserving him and acquiring your beloved human would let them wring whatever concessions they wanted out of your father—including your life, if that mattered to them—I had no trouble persuading them to cooperate. Tendak himself leaped at the idea. He hates you almost as much as I do, Danion."

Her fingers tightened, but this time he managed not to react. "Just think, husband—when the secret police dispose of you, that sweet little dancer of yours will suffer as you did. Worse, because she will experience every detail of what they do to you before you die. A fitting end for one of your quixotic nature. You and your joining." The green eyes narrowed until they resembled those of the vipers Sasha insisted infested the caves. "When I watch her grieve, my triumph will be complete."

"Will it?" Danion kept his tone one of polite curiosity. The anger she had sparked in him lay far in the past. She teetered on the edge of insanity; he could not pity her, but he regarded her as one would a scorpion, with wary fascination. "But what makes you think you will see it? I told her of your arrival, and she alerted my father. If you return to Tarkei or to any of its allies, you will be arrested."

He saw Reilu's eyes flash just before her hand cracked across his cheek. Warned, he did not flinch. "What made it worthwhile, Reilu?" he asked, in an effort to keep her distracted. Where were Vestris and Tamir? "Did it bring you revenge? That seems extreme, for a Tarkei. More a Kazrati motive. Did I injure you to the extent that I merit such treatment? Did Sasha?"

For once, her defenses fell. Her eyes blazed green fire. Nirrtu caught her wrist as she drew her arm back for the second time. "Enough," he said.

Reilu shook her hand free. "I say when it is enough," she shouted. "You owe me your life. Without me, you'd have rotted in those camps!"

Nirrtu stepped back, warding her off with his hands. "The sooner we take him to Headquarters, the less we need worry about losing him." He gave Reilu an assessing glance. "The sooner you can enjoy watching what happens to him."

Simmering, she stomped back to the rock. Danion turned to Nirrtu. "What was Jonthar's role in this? Or was he another victim?"

The lined face that resembled an older version of Danion's own studied him as if he were a laboratory specimen. Reilu might be swayed by her emotions, but Nirrtu knew what his captive was doing, and how much he would permit.

Although he might find Reilu more difficult to control than he expected: Danion counted on that.

"Why should I tell you?" Nirrtu asked.

Danion tried to appear impassive. "Why not? I am in your power. I cannot profit from the information; I wished only to learn the extent of your success in undermining my leadership."

Nirrtu treated Danion to the cynical smile he had so often produced in the days when they appeared to be friends. "Very well. I fooled you, and he fooled me. Claimed to work for me, then fell for your wife's big eyes and that waif look. The idiot decided vengeance was an ignoble motive, so I killed him. Jonthar always had a soft spot for women." His tone made it clear that this was not a compliment.

"And the police? Did they play a part in this too?"

"Of course," Nirrtu said. "As Reilu told you. The government saw a chance to wring concessions out of your father and put an end to the resistance movement. They were happy to profit from my hard work. But why should I share my prize with them? I don't care about this nonsensical pacifist movement of yours. I want to see you suffer for what you did to me. Given a chance, I would have tortured your wife in front of you. That didn't happen, but I can turn you over to the state. When I watch you die in torment, I'll be satisfied."

"Stop it." Reilu pushed Nirrtu aside. "Your vengeance would have gone nowhere without me, and even then you couldn't finish the job. You let her go. Well, I will not make that mistake. That woman has injured me for the last time. While the police are making you long for death, Danion, know that I will be taking care of her."

"You never answered my question," Danion said mildly. "Did we do you so much damage?"

Nirrtu scowled at him. Reilu stamped her foot. "How can you ask me that? You were mine." Her hands clenched with rage. "Our ancestors gave you to me. You had no right to reject me!"

Danion raised his eyebrows, not answering—striving to provoke her, to make her forget herself to the point where her fury would cause yet another delay. Vestris had betrayed him, but if Reilu created sufficient commotion, he might yet shake off his guards and escape into the tunnels, where he could hide until Tamir arrived or, if Tamir had also switched sides, until he found a way to free his hands from the rope. He had achieved his main goal—saving his students and preventing the uprising. Whatever happened next, he could go home. If he escaped from this cave.

Nirrtu put a hand on Reilu's arm. She shook him off, desperate after the years of deceit to cry her wrongs to the world. "You left me for her. And even when I got you back, you remained beyond my reach—thinking of her, grieving for her. You avoided me, although you were mine. For years, I blamed her. Then I realized that getting rid of her solved nothing. She was not the problem; you were. Since the day you threw me out for her sake, I have wanted you dead, Danion. And you will die, in agony." Her eyes gleamed—

irrational, obsessed, the years of extreme control stripping away, revealing the chaos beneath.

Danion, watching her, could not repress a shiver.

❀

Vestris glanced once more through the opening in the rock. A hand beckoned Tamir away from the crevice, back into the cave that lay behind this one. The boy came, dragging his feet. He kept looking over his shoulder, as though his failure to keep watch would cause Danion to disappear.

"Quick," Vestris whispered. "I know you don't trust me, but we have to work together if we're to save him."

Tamir picked up his pace. Vestris grabbed his arm and hauled him after her, lifting him half off his feet to minimize the noise. "We need a diversion," she said when she judged the distance from the opening sufficient to keep them from being overheard. "To get those police agents out of the way. I can take care of the rest."

Tamir stopped wriggling and concentrated. "How do I know you won't betray him?"

He was Kazrati. He would understand even though Danion did not. "I'm under blood oath," she said. "He saved my life. You know what that means."

"What do you want me to do?"

Good. He had accepted her argument. "Listen," Vestris said. "You have five minutes, no more. So far, Danion's managed to manipulate that demon woman into shouting at him, but he can't keep it up much longer. Nirrtu's losing patience, and so is D'Toth. We have to make our move."

She whispered in his ear. Tamir nodded and ran off before she had time to ask him if he could complete the task she'd set him. Vestris raced in the opposite direction, toward the main cave.

The man Danion had identified as D'Toth had remained silent so far. Now he placed a hand on Reilu's arm and drew her away from Danion. "Enough melodrama," he said, his tone more forceful than Nirrtu's. The voice of a man in charge. Reilu must have heard the note of command, or perhaps she had said what she wanted to say. Either way, she did not resist.

Danion braced himself. Without help from outside the cave, his chances of escape looked bleak. But his captors had made a fundamental mistake. They had bound his hands but not his feet. His best option was to drag his arms free and run. Even if they shot him and he died, he would deprive them of the opportunity to torture him.

And then, as Reilu would no doubt put it, Sasha would suffer and Reilu would win. A poor choice, but needs must. Danion sent his wife assurances of his love, tensed his muscles for flight, and permitted himself one moment of regret that he would not see another dawn.

A laser burst struck the feet of the guard to his right. The man yelped and jumped, clutching his singed foot in one hand. At a signal from Nirrtu, three guards raced toward the exit on the right. The guard with the injured foot limped to a rock and sat down, nursing his toes.

D'Toth snarled at him. The guard cringed and limped as quickly as he could after the other three.

A second laser blast shot across the cave, skimming the ear of a guard on Danion's left. It originated in a different section of the cave roof. D'Toth swore, and four more guards ran that way. Only the two who held Danion's arms remained.

His chance. Danion tore his arms free as two screams sounded behind him, one after another. Danion jerked his hands as hard as he could, trying to break the rope. It frayed, the edges rough against his sore wrists, but not enough for him to pull his hands loose.

He jerked again, harder. The rope still didn't break, but the knots loosened. He dragged one hand out, then the other. His wrists were on fire. He ignored them.

Reilu, then Nirrtu, fell in a burst of blue. Vestris, laser pistol steady as the expression in her eyes, stepped into the cave.

She trained the laser on D'Toth. "Don't move. Don't breathe. I'm out of practice, and I might not remember to hold my fire."

"My troops will return," D'Toth said, unruffled.

"Someday," Vestris said. "A person can get lost in these tunnels." She nodded at Danion. "Unless one has lived here for months."

"I wondered where he was," Danion said.

"An admirable deputy," Vestris said. "Slow, but thorough and dedicated."

D'Toth shuffled his feet, and her grip on the laser tightened. "I wouldn't count on relief, if I were you." Her tone suggested a casual conversation. "And believe me, you don't want them. You're about to become a hero. Why share the credit?"

D'Toth frowned. "Hero? You're mad. Our supervisor will have my head."

"Nonsense," she said to D'Toth. "Reilu is dead, and Danion is leaving. You have killed the traitor Tendak and are delivering his body to the police so that every citizen can learn the price of opposing the government."

"Huh?" D'Toth's confusion seemed to distract him from trying to escape. Although Vestris's unwavering grip on the laser gun no doubt provided another powerful incentive.

Vestris raised her eyes heavenward without tilting her head. "Do I have to explain everything, D'Toth?"

"I think you do." Danion suppressed an inappropriate desire to laugh, the result of his relief that the crisis was over, or nearly over. D'Toth was doing a good imitation of the village simpleton common in human folklore. He would have shared the image with Sasha if she weren't furious with him.

I see him, she said. The scarlet glare surrounding the bond muted into gold streaked with pink, although purple flashes of anxiety flickered at the edges. It looks like the fool will get the gold this time, too, if not the king's daughter (we hope).

Danion projected gratitude for her quick response, her understanding, her love. Soon, *kaleita*. I will join you soon.

It can't happen soon enough, she said. How he agreed with that sentiment!

Vestris pointed at Nirrtu's body and addressed D'Toth. "That man only pretended to serve the police. He resented being sent to the camps, so he played a double game. He didn't care about the government; he wanted vengeance against Danion. By the ghosts, D'Toth, he told you that much himself a few minutes ago. You can embroider it a bit, can't you? He lied about Danion's being dead, then took over the resistance movement and used it for his own ends, not the government's. When Danion returned and threatened his leadership, Tendak vaporized him. Then he shot Reilu. You killed the traitor as soon as you realized the extent of his betrayal. Without a leader, the movement will die." With one hand, she gestured at the caves, while the other kept the laser trained on D'Toth. "Got it?"

"And what's to stop you from showing up and contradicting me?" No longer confused, D'Toth had retreated to sulky.

"I don't want to return to the secret police," Vestris said. "Didn't you tell them I was dead?"

D'Toth glowered as he admitted this to his shoes.

"Good," Vestris said. Her former partner jerked his head. "Let them think it. That gives you a hold on me, because if they find out I'm alive, I won't be for long."

D'Toth managed an instant of grudging respect. "I need proof of Danion's death," he said.

Vestris circled behind Danion, examining him without lowering the gun. "The earring," she said after a moment. "I'm sorry, Danion. It's unique to you. They will believe you did not part with it willingly."

And he would not. Danion fingered the earring he had worn for sixty-eight years. Images flashed before his eyes, as people say happens when one is drowning: Sendar fastening it in his ear, freeing him from his marriage to Reilu and the demands of Tarkei tradition; Sasha caressing it, her fingers soft against the stone; Iqa touching it the day after he returned from the mountain, delighted to have her brother back after six years away; his father flicking it, accepting him at last. A lifetime of pictures, each one special.

He removed the garnet. Freedom exacts its price. He looked at the rough stone lying in his palm, glowing in the candlelight, then handed it to Vestris, who gave it to her partner.

"Lucky for you that Nirrtu grabbed it as a souvenir," she said. "Now get out of here. And don't get any clever ideas about coming after us. By the time you've delivered your burden, we'll be long gone."

D'Toth looked at her as though he had more to say. Vestris pointed the pistol at his chest, brushing the trigger with one finger. He slipped the earring into a pocket, bent, and picked up Tendak, also known as Nirrtu. With the old man's body slung over his shoulder, he stalked out of the caves.

Danion watched him go. Not until the last footstep had ceased to echo did Vestris holster the pistol. "Thank you," he said.

"Now we're even." Vestris beckoned. "Come on, Danion, time to leave. Before the police discover that you're alive after all. And watch your back from now on. They won't be happy when they find out."

Danion nodded. She was right. "Tamir?"

"Will stay with me." Halfway to the exit, she looked over her shoulder. "He'll meet us at the shuttle. He promised to collect your belongings and stow them for you. You'll have a chance to say goodbye."

His belongings. Most of them had no value, but he would be glad not to lose Sasha's shoes, more precious than ever as he journeyed toward his long-awaited reunion with their owner.

Vestris had moved into the passageway beyond. Danion ran to catch up with her. "You will take over the resistance movement, then?"

Vestris gave him her best Choli grin. "What else can a dead police agent do? That's why you can't have Tamir. I need one assistant I can count on. Look how the rest of them ran off and left you. What kind of help is that?"

Danion placed a hand on her shoulder as they walked quickly through the tunnels toward the abandoned houses that marked the first stage of his journey. "They were not trained to fight, nor should they be. That is not the answer. Nonetheless, thank you, Vestris. You have taken a great load of troubles from my back." To Sasha he said, Tell Thuja, *kaleita*. I am coming home.

I did, Sasha said. She's on her way.

17. Tour en l'Air

SASHA PUT DOWN THE pointe shoe that substituted for a vase and raised her arms in straight lines out from her shoulders, her face alight with joy. Slava ran to meet her and lifted her above his head. She stroked his cheeks.

"*Formidable!*" Camille called. "How you have captured Nikia's happiness at Solor's arrival."

Slava lowered her to the ground, then knelt at her feet. Sasha, her hands stretched toward him, danced around him, ending in arabesque. He turned her one way, then the other, before she leaned against him, her left leg extending to the side. "Little does she know, it's not for Solor but for Danion," she told her partner.

He tapped her chin. "Don't tell me he's finally left those miserable caves."

Sasha laughed, sending Camille into new transports. She darted in the other direction, Slava on her heels. Downstage, he caught her in time to support her through a series of turns.

"He's on his way out," she said, "after almost giving me a heart attack. Thuja has gone to collect him, but that's a formality. If necessary, he can fly home on his own."

Slava lifted her, her body in a straight line, and swept her against his shoulder. She wrapped her arms around his neck. When he released her, she skimmed in a circle around the back edges of the stage. He joined her on the other side.

Sasha smiled at him, stroking his hair for Nikia's sake. They turned together, one arm around each other's waist, free arms raised in matching poses. Sasha arched her back, and Slava pressed his face against her heart. When he raised his head, she glided off in a series of frothy bourrées interspersed with arabesques and grands jetés. When he caught up with her again, he raised her in another overhead lift.

"Will he get here in time for the opening?" Slava asked as he set her down. He knelt, arms around her waist, cheek pressed against her ribs, then walked away from her to stand behind the chalk circle representing the sacred flame, touched his heart, and pointed at the sky—his vow of eternal love.

Sasha as Nikia touched her heart in return, then skimmed across the floor again, arms out, the picture of happiness. She stopped at his side, shaking her head— Don't. Slava repeated the gesture—I insist—then put his arms around her.

As they circled the chalk on the floor, she answered the question. "It will be close. Thuja has to reach the Kazrati border, and she says she's two days away. Then it's a good five days to get here. But I hope he makes it. It won't be the same if he doesn't."

Slava ran a finger down her neck, lunged to the left, and pulled her into a half-sitting position on his bent leg.

"He'll make it, if he has to commandeer Thuja's ship and run it at top speed the whole way."

Sasha pressed her head against his chest. "You know, I expect he will."

The dancer playing the Head Fakir ran over and tapped Slava on the shoulder. When Sasha and Slava glanced up, the fakir gestured. Careful, the Brahmin is watching you.

They finished the scene to roars of applause from the corps, sitting in the front rows awaiting its turn.

The shuttle's sleek black form stood in the deserted clearing where Danion had left it. Tamir sat on a tree stump nearby, pulling pieces off one of Natari's rolled-up breads and stuffing them into his mouth. He did not look like a young man who had spent the better part of two hours leading Nirrtu's forces through tunnels in the rock.

Danion glanced at Vestris, who was shaking her head. "I see you eluded your pursuers," he said to Tamir.

The boy sprang up, his face open and eager. This was the Tamir Danion had come to cherish, the Tamir he would miss. With the thought, Danion realized that he might not see either of his young friends again. Or Kazratan.

Strange. He would miss Kazratan as well. Not the secrecy and the treachery. Not even the danger, although it had added spice to a life close to going stale. But the camaraderie, the intensity, the challenge—these he would definitely miss.

Tamir pulled the bread apart with an elaborate flourish. "They didn't have a chance. I took them straight (well, more or less straight) to that rickety old section you forbade us to enter in case the roof caved in. I bet they're still wandering around back there." The eyes Tamir fixed on Danion had a very non-Tarkei glitter. "Who knows if they'll ever escape?"

"Well done, Tamir," Vestris said with enthusiasm.

"Indeed," Danion said. "Thank you for your help." He inclined his head toward Vestris. "Both of you."

"You're displeased." Vestris, alert as usual, responded to the restraint in his voice. "You don't think we should leave them to be destroyed."

"A cave-in is not a pleasant way to die," Danion said. "It brings starvation or suffocation."

Tamir tore off another hunk of bread. "More pleasant than what they planned for you, Danion."

"They weren't innocents." Vestris assessed his reaction in a manner disconcertingly similar to Nirrtu's, as though Danion were a specimen she wished to study. "I knew most of them. None of them were forced into service. They joined out of conviction—or worse, because they thought they could turn it to their advantage."

"I am leaving," Danion said. "The movement is yours to direct. I do not tell you to spare these men. I suspect you're right: that they have injured many and, if free, will injure many more. My point is different: do not become what you abhor. Some people do not understand compassion. Violence is a means—sometimes a necessary means—to reach such people. But violence often becomes an end. If you lose your capacity for empathy, your opponents will win. To change Kazrati culture at its root, violence is not the means. Do you understand me?"

The concept was alien to Kazratan, a culture formed around its devotion to brute force, and especially to the secret police that had raised her. Outright rejection would not have surprised him; a quick acceptance would have aroused his suspicions.

Vestris produced neither. She regarded Danion, then Tamir, with a clear, steady gaze. "I'm not sure," she said at last. "I will think about it."

Danion's hand brushed Vestris's shoulder. "You will go far, my child. May you bask in Danar's rays."

"And you, Danion." Her face lit up in the expression that reminded him of Choli. "Tell your wife I forgive her for the rock to my skull."

"I will do that," Danion said. "Take care, Tamir. Serve Vestris well."

The boy set aside the bread long enough to hug his mentor. "Don't get caught, Danion. I hope we meet again one day."

Danion ruffled the boy's hair. "I would like that, Tamir."

Vestris and Tamir ran across the open area, taking shelter among the abandoned houses, ready to leave before Danion started the engines. At his command, the shuttle opened its door. Standing at the edge of the clearing, he raised a hand. His last sight of Kazratan was the two of them waving before darting into the tunnel that led back to the caves.

Rehearsals had ended for the day. Sasha invited herself to dinner at the Tarkei Consulate. Her in-laws required no excuse, but they leaped at the chance to hear every detail of Danion's departure. Iqara greeted her at the main door, hands outstretched, not even a semblance of Tarkei control in that vivid face. "Is it true?" she said before Sasha had finished explaining who she was to the guard on duty.

Iqa grabbed her sister's identity card out of the man's hand. "By the three suns, don't you recognize the prime minister's daughter? Be done!" The guard bestowed a repressive stare on her, but Iqa had turned her back. Sasha plucked her card out of her sister's restless fingers before Iqa had a chance to drop it and slipped it into her wallet. Iqa had made it halfway down the corridor, and Sasha hadn't answered her question yet.

Jenat, if more restrained, proved no less eager. "He has left?" the old man said as soon as his palms touched Sasha's. "He is safe?"

"Yes," Sasha said, getting the most important point out first.

"Yes, he has left?" Iqa asked. "Or yes, he is safe?"

Sasha queried the link. "Yes, he has left. He had a bit of trouble getting out, although nothing unusual. So far, at least, his escape plan seems to have worked. He says no one was looking for him personally—that is, he detected no unusual degree of security, just the usual need to control the border crossings."

She touched the link again, confirming. Iqa, apparently mistaking Sasha's concentration for worry, twisted her hands. Jenat stood rock-steady, concern radiating from every pore.

"And yes, he is safe," Sasha said as soon as she was certain she spoke the truth. Jenat swayed. Iqa grabbed one elbow and Sasha the other; together they helped him to the couch.

Iqa pulled a medical scanner from her pocket and pointed it at her father. "He'll do," she said after a moment. "It's relief." A professional hand touched her father's forehead. "Do you feel all right, father?"

Jenat brushed her hand away. "Stop your fussing, girl. I'm fine." He held out his own hand to Sasha. "Come, my child. Sit and tell me the whole. Where is Danion now?"

"He's crossed the border." In her peripheral vision Sasha watched Iqa circle the couch, checking the readings on the medical scanner from several angles, until she dropped the scanner back in its pocket and sank onto the nearest chair.

"He's in Allied space, waiting for Thuja." Sasha frowned, probing again. Danion did not seem to be waiting.

She returned her attention to the room to find two pairs of eyes fixed on her again. "He's safe, I promise. He's moving, he's far away, he's preoccupied, and I haven't seen him for months. It's not easy for me to reach him right at the moment."

The two heads nodded, although Sasha doubted they understood. Neither of them had experienced the joining, which at times was difficult enough for her to figure out. If it kept them from panicking (not that even Iqa would admit to panic), however, that was enough.

"He's traveling toward Thuja," she explained. "They're in communication, so they're planning to meet somewhere between Kazratan and Earth." A thought flew along the link, and Sasha smiled. "Danion promises to get here by opening night."

Jenat seemed to have recovered. "Let us eat dinner, then, and you can tell us the rest." He gave a great sigh and hauled himself to his feet, using the back of the couch as a lever. "I am most pleased by your news, my daughter." He glared at the couch. "If only they would not make these things so low."

Iqara raised her eyes to the ceiling. Sasha placed a hand under the old man's elbow. "It's very inconsiderate. As for the story, I think you'll enjoy it, now that it's over." But in the end, she sketched only the outlines, because Danion wanted to tell them about Reilu himself.

Danion reached Thuja's ship the next day. Once his shuttle had docked and he had released his friend's arms from his neck, he found himself in the unfamiliar position of having nothing to do. Thuja's daughter, despite her mother's scathing remarks, had no trouble piloting the ship in Allied space (although Danion hoped no vortices would present themselves), and he knew better than to impose himself on someone else's bridge. After wandering around the ship for an hour on a self-guided tour, he returned to the room assigned to him and settled himself on the floor.

His months in the caves had inured him to hardship; the ship seemed luxurious by comparison—not ornate or monumental, like Kazratan, but affluent in the discreet way that speaks of old money. The attention to detail that Danion had once taken for granted, as most citizens of the allied planets did, struck him with particular clarity. Thinking of the shoddiness of Kazrati construction, the dirt and the grime (except in the showplaces of the elite), he realized anew how far Kazratan had to come before it could meet the allied planets on their own terms. Perhaps the Kazratis' resentment was understandable, although like most resentment, it complicated the finding of solutions.

Sitting cross-legged on the floor, Danion counted how many months had passed since he had last been without company. The caves were always full of people; except for the day or so before Vestris regained consciousness, he had spent his entire time on Kazratan in the vicinity of others. Even when not in their presence, he could hear them.

In general, Kazrati did not place much value on solitude. The caves made it impossible, and unwise as well; there was, as the human cliché had it, safety in numbers. But Danion had spent much of his life alone, and so long as it did not threaten his bond with Sasha, he rather enjoyed it. This period of contemplation, secure in her mental presence, was a gift, allowing him to recover from a tension unacknowledged until it eased.

He rubbed the lobe of his left ear, where the earring had lain for so long. It felt as though a part of him were missing—so much experience tied up in a symbol.

What would Sasha say? She had always liked it—even when they met on the mountain, before he meant much to her at all.

He sensed her, rehearsing as usual. Only a week until *Bayadère* opened. The company would rehearse until the day the curtain rose, and beyond, as it had done with *Giselle.* Tonio and Camille, Sasha and Slava—the principals were in place. If he had already reached Earth, he could expect to see his wife only in passing.

Even so, he itched to reach his destination. Two years together, sixty-one apart, a day or two together, another three months apart—the time had long since passed for their separation to end.

He thought of Vestris and Tamir, of Nirrtu who was also Tendak, and of Reilu. Of the four, Reilu made the least sense to him. Tamir, loyal and dependable, eager to learn, looking for security after his parents' death; Vestris with her quick mind, her unwavering convictions hidden behind a mask of adaptability, waiting for a chance to break free; even Nirrtu, angry at what he perceived as injustice and vowing revenge on the man he held responsible—these he could comprehend.

But what drove his first wife he had never understood and did not now. She hated him for rejecting her; that much seemed clear. Hated Sasha, too, for succeeding where she, Reilu, had failed. But what caused her to value him so highly as a possession when she had no interest in him as a person—that he could not imagine.

Looking back, her death seemed inevitable, in the sense that as long as she lived she would have pursued her odd quest for ... what? Ownership? Revenge? But was it inevitable, or had some moment existed when he or another could have intervened, preventing tragedy?

Danion wished he knew.

❋

Sasha stood in a room of mirrors. On three sides her own reflection stared back at her, evaluating the fit and the style of the costume in which Nikia would suffer her fatal bite.

The mirror also revealed Bella, her arms swinging back and forth, up and down, as she checked the straps on the foundation of what would soon become an ivory tutu, striped with gold braid. As yet, it lacked its tulle skirt as well as its decorations.

"It's good," Bella said. "I can move freely. What do you think, Sasha?"

Sasha ran an experienced finger under the ivory ribbon. "Feels right. It won't do for it to fall off your shoulders, will it?"

"No. How's yours?"

The wardrobe mistress bustled up. A small, gray-haired woman with a tape measure slung around her neck and a pin cushion's worth of straight pins stuck into her blouse, she could have populated theater photographs from the nineteenth century to the twenty-fourth. "A good fit," she told Bella after repeating Sasha's test. "Try the other."

"I did," Bella said, removing the ivory satin and replacing it with her leotard. "I did that first. It's lovely, although there doesn't seem to be much of it."

"With your figure, why should you complain?" Sasha lifted a peacock fan, left over from an earlier costume fitting, and waved it in front of her face. The temperature in the dressing room had to stay high enough to warm the muscles of half-naked dancers, but today the radiators had outdone themselves. "Besides, it's not only the Rajah's prestige that leads to Solor's downfall."

Bella grabbed the fan away from her aunt. "Thank you for your support."

"How about yours, Sasha?" The wardrobe mistress held up a needle and thread.

"Ah." Sasha grimaced at the mirror. "It's too tight, especially across the shoulders. I have to do this." She bent sideways, one arm over her head. The sleeve of her costume separated from the back as she demonstrated.

"Yes, I see."

"And this." Sasha bent forward, right leg extended to the back until it became a continuation of the line made by the left, then brought the leg back to earth and pointed it in front, leaning her upper body in the opposite direction, her arms over her head.

"Excuse me," she said. The wardrobe mistress stepped aside, and Bella perched on a dressing table.

"And worse yet, this." Sasha balanced on her left foot, bending the left knee until her right thigh was no more than six inches from the floor, her upper body twisted and her arms stretched behind her. She turned, coming down on the right knee, left leg extended to the back, then sprang up into an arabesque on pointe. The other sleeve separated from its back piece at the same time as a small tearing sound came from her trouser legs.

"Dear me," the wardrobe mistress said. "Stand still, then. Let me see what I have to fix."

Sasha stood as requested, and the wardrobe mistress walked around her, muttering under her breath and periodically poking at the fabric. A seamstress came at her call, and the two of them went into a no-holds-barred discussion of the problem. Sasha tuned them out. Her job was to dance in the thing, theirs to ensure it held together while she did.

Her eyes met Bella's, and she smiled. Twelve and a half weeks of daily contact had worked wonders for their relationship, erasing the early hostility. As a result, creating it on stage had become difficult—a problem Tonio had not envisioned.

Today, however, Bella's brown eyes, so like her grandfather's, looked troubled.

"What?" Sasha asked. Bella turned her head, her cheeks flushed, and played with the peacock feathers of the fan.

Sasha retrieved it before her niece could destroy the wardrobe department's hard work. "Does the costume bother you that much? I could speak to Camille about it."

"It's not the costume."

Sasha waited. The wardrobe mistress and the seamstress continued twisting and poking; their intermittent muttering provided an odd background music.

"I wondered." Bella stopped. More waiting. Then she said in a rush, "I wondered if you loved Slava."

Sasha felt her eyes widen. "Of course. I've known him since we were kids and danced with him ... oh, that's not what you mean, is it?"

Bella, her cheeks red, shook her head.

Sasha fanned herself again, stalling for time. Bella and Slava—who would have guessed? Had Slava made a move, or did the interest come from Bella? And why on earth would Bella see her aunt as a potential rival? Tonio or Camille must have told her about Danion and the joining—or, if not them, Slava.

"Now do I say yes," she asked, keeping her tone light, "and guarantee that you play Gamzatti with conviction? Or do I tell the truth, so I don't have to check that basket every night and make sure you haven't put a real snake in there?"

"Don't tease, Sasha. I've worked hard on this; you don't need to manipulate me to get me to act."

"You have," Sasha said. "I apologize. It's disconcerting, that's all."

Bella's face froze. "What is?"

The wardrobe mistress and the seamstress finished their discussion. Together they stripped the costume from Sasha and carried it away for repairs.

She gave a sigh of thanks, grabbed her leotard, pulled it back on, and sat on a nearby bench. "Come here, so we can talk in comfort." She patted the place next to her, and after a moment's resistance Bella abandoned the dressing table and joined her.

"It's disconcerting to realize how much time has passed," Sasha said. "It's egocentric of me, I know, but I keep expecting people to remember me. Myself, I mean—not the legend of Sinclair and Zoshchenko. In this case, I assumed Tonio had told you. But why should he?"

"Told me what?"

Sasha tossed the closed fan onto the dressing table and watched it skid across the glass top. It rested at the base of the mirror. "First, let me answer your question. No, I am not in love with Slava. He's like a brother—not quite a brother but not a lover."

"It's acting, then? Because when you dance together, you look at him in *such* a way—"

Sasha burst out laughing. "Oh dear." Poor Bella looked distraught, and Sasha tried to stop herself, but the more she thought about it, the more absurd the situation became.

Bella edged away. Before she could get up and run, Sasha caught her wrist. "Bella, I'm sorry. I'm not laughing at you, I promise. If you love Slava and he loves you, you have my blessing."

Bella hurt looked like an older version of Choli—and not much older. Choli would not pout like that, whatever the circumstances. "Then what's so funny?"

"Me."

It didn't help, except that Bella's hurt gave way to the detached skepticism typically reserved for irrational members of one's own family. "You."

Sasha strove for self-control. Bella had a right to an explanation, and one not delivered by an aunt chortling like a hyena. "I could never love Slava, not in the way you mean. I'm laughing at myself because I assumed the whole company knew, and you don't, because it happened years before you were born."

Bella gave an exasperated sigh. "I'm trying to be patient, Sasha, but please get to the point. Why can't you love Slava? Does he prefer boys?"

She looked tragic enough to pass for Nikia, and Sasha hastened to reassure her. "Not for a minute. He's had girlfriends by the dozen, although not since we got here. When has he had the time? We're good friends and great partners, and we wanted to keep it that way. And I'm married. That's what I assumed Tonio had told you. I got married two years before I fell into the time vortex."

"How sad!" Bella's skepticism had morphed into sympathy. "I didn't realize you'd lost a husband."

Sasha shivered. Too close to the truth, that.

Danion reached out, caressing her cheek with her own white swan feather. I am not lost, *kaleita*. I will see you within the week.

His joy filled her with effervescent bubbles, and Sasha gurgled with laughter. "Thank you, but he assures me I have not lost him. He plans to be here by opening night."

Bella stood in front of her aunt, hands in the air. "I think I *will* murder you, Sasha, if you don't start making sense."

Across the link—blessedly close, glistening flame— Sasha sensed her husband's amusement. Gathering her resources, she pulled herself together and explained. "I am married to Danion of Tarkei, and I think of him when I dance with Slava. That's what you see. Slava responds for the sake of the performance, I guess, because he knows that my heart belongs to Danion and will for as long as I live. So if Slava was ever in love with me, I'm sure he's not now. And as for me, my husband is neither lost nor dead. He's coming home."

18. Assemblé

THE BLUE GLOBE ON the screen, clouds swirling around it, was familiar from a hundred pictures and a dozen previous trips. Danion, dressed in black velvet in preparation for Earth's chill, sat on Thuja's bridge and watched her daughter maneuver the ship into orbit, ready to land whenever the San Francisco Space Port Authority deigned to grant permission.

In the end, he had spent a considerable amount of time here. The day after his arrival, Thuja's daughter had asked him to help her improve her piloting. Danion, curious to see how much of his friend's lament over her helm officer was justified, agreed. Since then, he had spent most of his waking hours on the bridge.

Danion enjoyed the lessons: although he had spent much time teaching in the resistance movement, he had not had the opportunity to pass on his experience as a pilot to someone else. It awoke memories of studying with his mother eighty years ago—although then he had been the one struggling to master the intricacies of flying. The distraction also kept him from worrying about what might be happening on Kazratan and from chafing at his long-delayed reunion with Sasha.

Until today. So close to his destination, attempts to rein in his anticipation were about as effective as slapping a lid on a boiling pot. Danion touched the helm officer's arm, suggesting a correction, then drew back to watch her implement it. From long practice, he maintained his air of studied calm. Only the fingers digging into the armrests of his chair revealed to a careful onlooker his true state of mind.

At last, Thuja's craft landed, and Danion stepped down. On the other side of the barrier that separated arriving passengers from those who came to meet them, he saw a row of heads. His entire family had made the journey to the space port: his father and sister, Choli, Geoffrey, Tonio. Two heads in particular stood out: one blond and male; the other dark, its hair below chin-length. Sasha, poised on the tips of her toes, one hand on Slava's shoulder for balance, waved at him. Even as he watched, he saw the Russian grab her round the waist to keep her from darting toward him. Danion walked forward, his hands outstretched. Sasha, hopping with delight, caught them in hers and, heedless of the crowd around them, ran a finger down his face.

I am here, *kaleita*, he said.

Yes, my love, and none too soon.

Slava let go of her waist. "Here, she can cling to you now." With a grin, he smacked Danion lightly on the shoulder, said, "Welcome home," and vaulted the barrier.

Behind him, Danion heard the Russian greeting Thuja and imagined his friend hanging from Slava's neck. Danion lifted his wife over the barrier so that he could hold her more easily and flicked her ear. She caught his lobe in her hand, fingering the place where the earring had been. He waited for her comment, but whatever she might have said was lost in the onslaught of family crowding one another in their haste to greet him.

It was good to see the familiar faces, to know they cared enough to come and meet him. Good to be back on Earth, his mission finished, his wife in his arms. He touched ears or hands in turn, depending on the recipient. Jenat's thin face glowed. Choli bounced up and down, saying, "You kept your promise! I'm so glad."

Iqara, made more beautiful than ever by happiness, laughed when he flicked her ear and said, "*Now* I won't worry." Geoffrey, still irrepressible after almost a century, produced his Cheshire-cat grin and slapped his friend on the back.

Tonio shook his hand, welcomed him home, announced he had to run back to the theater, and was gone before Danion could say thank you. "Make sure that sister of mine doesn't miss the dress rehearsal tomorrow," he called on his way out.

Sasha turned her head long enough to make a face at his retreating back. "As though I would."

Slava came over, Thuja in tow. "*Bozhe moi*, look at them. Take her away, for goodness' sake. She has a bag somewhere. I'll drop everyone else off. Just stay out of the apartment; like it or not, you're entertaining an army."

Danion shook his hand. "Thank you, Slava."

"Yes, you're a trooper," his wife told her partner. Arm in arm, Danion and Sasha left the space port.

✻

The hotel—a bed and breakfast, really—stood atop a hill in Sausalito, its windows open to the Golden Gate. An hour or so after their arrival, Sasha, wearing nothing but a towel, sat on the floor and watched the dolphins at play. Far beyond the bridge, she saw the occasional whale spume. The sun shone, sunflower yellow in a clear blue sky, a rare San Francisco day.

Danion's fingers ruffled her hair, then closed around her wrist, pulling her up to stand beside him. She leaned against him, arms around his waist. The towel slipped under roving hands.

There was nothing she needed to say. He picked her up and carried her back to bed.

✻

Sasha woke and stretched, looking up into warm dark eyes. That Danion had returned safe and would stay seemed incredible, despite their glorious reunion. "What time is it?"

Danion glanced at the clock behind her shoulder. "8:43."

"Rats." She rubbed her face in her hands.

"You have missed Camille's class," Danion said.

Sasha pressed her palm against his cheek. "True, but not even Camille could fuss about that. Besides, after what I put them through the last ten days, I bet they're glad to see the back of me."

His eyes gleamed with mischief. "You did not wait with the patience of—what is his name?—Job?"

"I didn't wait with the patience of a horse at the starting gate." She stroked his eyebrow. "As Slava will no doubt tell you, I nearly wore the stage down prowling from corner to corner and in general made a complete pest of myself. In fact, it's a mark of his forbearance that he didn't tell you yesterday."

"I am sorry to hear that," Danion said, his solemn air at variance with his sparkling eyes.

"Not as sorry as they were," Sasha assured him. "The rats, however, were not for Camille but for Tonio's dress rehearsal, which starts in seventeen minutes."

Danion checked the clock again. "Fifteen."

Sasha waved her hands in the air. "Fifteen, fourteen, what does it matter? If I don't show up, Tonio will have a fit; you heard him yesterday. Will you come with me?"

"For a while," Danion said. "Then I must visit my father and find Choli."

Sasha rolled out of bed and ran for the bathroom. "She'll be at the theater. The school has canceled classes for the next two weeks, because half the students are in the performance. Choli has a walk-on in Act II. You'll find her sitting in the front row with the other girls."

Danion washed and donned his clothes with remarkable speed. "Very well, Sasha-*chan,* let us go. You do not require breakfast?"

"I do, but we can both eat at the theater. Goodness, are you finished already?" Sasha, dropping her skirt over her head, felt a lump in the pocket. "I almost forgot!" She pulled out a small box and handed it to her husband. "It's for you."

Danion, visibly puzzled, took it, turning it in his hand.

"Open it," she said. "Quick. We don't have much time."

Danion opened the box. Inside, against a bed of cotton wool, he saw a single garnet, a rough-edged stone with backing, almost an exact duplicate of the one he had surrendered to Vestris with such reluctance. Bereft of words, he stared at his wife.

Sasha took the stone from the box, rinsed the post under the tap, rubbed it with alcohol she produced from her toilet bag, and stood on tiptoe to fasten it to his ear. "Good. The hole didn't close up yet. I was afraid it might before you got home."

Words failed him. Sasha's vivid face crinkled in laughter. "Sendar sent it, when I called him and explained what had happened. I asked him to get me another stone, and he did. I knew you would miss it." She flicked his earlobe. "Me, too."

Danion caught her hand and raised it to his lips, more touched than he could say. Through the link he sent her his gratitude.

"You're most welcome," Sasha said. "I would have done much more than that to ensure that you came home safely." She looked around. "Is everything packed away? Then let's get out of here. Tonio's too old for explosions."

Choli was at the theater, as well as a surprising number of other people, many of them strangers. Danion held out both hands to his daughter, who left her seat in the front row and ran to greet him. Sasha, after a quick kiss on her brother's cheek, rushed off to change. Danion said hello to

Tonio, took Choli's hand in his, and sat next to her. Heads turned in the front row—checking him out.

"Tell me how you are," he asked Choli in Kazrati, listening with one ear as she launched into a long story of her life on Earth. It was September 27. Fourteen weeks had passed since Sasha's return home, four months since his fortuitous if unintentionally insulting comment about the Kazrati restaurant had turned his life upside down. Tomorrow evening, Sasha would perform in public for— excepting the one Kazrati broadcast—the first time in sixty years. The circle would be complete.

A pretty dancer in a striking if skimpy costume came over to talk to Tonio. She wore red silk, fine as gauze, a rich flame color that sparked highlights in her chestnut hair. The costume consisted of no more than a halter top, a straight skirt, and a transparent veil that fell from the small gold crown that topped her patrician head. She wore high-heeled gold sandals, not pointe shoes, as well as simple gold bracelets around her wrists and a gold necklace that figured, if Danion had not forgotten, in the plot. After his stay on Kazratan, the understated elegance was a relief.

Only one person in the ballet would dress like that, and anyway, he recognized her from the link. So when Tonio stood up to introduce her, Danion rose, extended his hand, and said, "Gamzatti, I presume. How do you do?"

Gamzatti, otherwise known as Bella, showed a child's delight at being recognized. "Well, thank you," she said, her tone surprisingly formal in contrast to the lively face. "How lovely to meet you. Sasha must be ecstatic."

"We're all ecstatic, love," Tonio said. "Maybe she'll stop driving us crazy now."

Danion gave them his half-smile. "She did mention that she had not contained her impatience well."

Bella made a choking noise, and Tonio's eyes rolled until it looked as if Danion might need to insert a spoon between his brother's teeth.

"That's one way to put it," Tonio said at last. "I couldn't decide whether Slava would strangle her first, or I would. Bella took it better than any of us, except Camille, who sat her down every so often and made her drink tea until she became bearable again."

"Such a violent family," Danion said, keeping his tone light. "My thanks to Camille, and to you, Miss Bella."

"I do get to throw her around the room," Bella noted. "It helped. Although I must say, you looked pretty wild-eyed with that knife sometimes, Sasha. I feared for my life."

Danion realized that his wife, clothed—to stretch the meaning of that term—in a white gauze costume even more revealing than Bella's, her hair ruthlessly confined under a crocheted silver hairnet, had come to sit at the edge of the orchestra pit. She threw him a squashed pastry. He caught it in one hand and examined it.

Sasha waved her own pastry at him. "It's safe. The only things that bite around here are the snake and Bella in a bad mood. Not a hint of meat anywhere. I even checked for butter."

Bella pretended to bite. Slava came over, grumbling about the food. Sasha ignored him for a while, then said, "I didn't have breakfast, Slava. Leave me alone." To Bella she added, "Listen to him fuss about my weight. You'd think I were an elephant. Do you get this treatment, too, or is it my bad luck?"

Tonio stood up. "Right, let's get started before Sasha and Slava quarrel. Come on, you two, I don't have time for sulks. Make up, so you can play your parts."

Sasha gave Slava a saccharine smile, and he responded in kind. She swallowed the pastry, jumped up, and put a hand on his arm. They walked off, laughing.

Bella, Danion noted with interest, watched them with narrowed eyes. "You are not in this scene, are you?" he asked her. "Do you wait in the wings, or sit here?"

"I perch," she said, borrowing a chair arm for the purpose. "For the sake of my costume, and not for long. It's warm today, but while the girls are dancing for the Rajah, I run off and start my pliés. Just in case. I don't have much dancing till the second act." She looked over her right shoulder at him. "But you know that, don't you? You've seen *Bayadère* before."

"Not the whole ballet," Danion said. "Only the grand pas de deux. I watched Sasha rehearse, though."

"But you weren't here," Bella said.

While he was considering how to answer this, Choli tugged at his arm, and he bent his head to listen. Through the corner of his eye, he saw Bella watching him, a puzzled expression on her face.

The orchestra filed in, tuned its instruments, and began the overture. Choli stopped talking to focus on the stage. It was the first time she'd been allowed to see the whole performance, she'd told him.

Bella said, "Sasha's an amazing dancer. Slava, too. Together, they're wonderful."

Danion examined her. He heard an odd note in her voice, reminding him of the anguished expression he had intercepted earlier. "They are. But you dance with him also, do you not?"

Bella flushed. "Yes."

She seemed as intent on the stage as Choli. Danion probed. "And you find him a good partner?"

Bella tapped her gold sandal against the carpet. "He's astonishing. Not like anyone else I've danced with. So responsive. It's as though he can predict where each move will end. But it's not the kind of rapport he has with Sasha."

"It wouldn't be," Danion said. "Her parents paired them twenty-three years ago, in their time. Sasha was eight, and Slava ten. They have danced together ever since. Each of them knows when the other will breathe, I think."

"And it doesn't make you jealous?"

"I am Tarkei," Danion said. Not much of an answer. Not even the whole truth. But years had passed since he thought that way.

Bella turned her head toward the stage, as if she could summon Slava the way a magician pulls a rabbit from a hat. "I'm sorry," she said at once. "I didn't mean to get personal. Forgive me." She had heard his gentle reproof.

"It is forgotten," Danion said. "And in fact, I was jealous for a while. But Slava, I think, was not jealous of me."

Bella swung her head in his direction, her brown eyes bright. For a moment, she looked like her grandfather's *Döppelganger*.

Danion squeezed the hand she stretched out to him. "I conquered it easily," he told her, "once I was sure of her feelings. You will do the same, I expect. The relationship between Sasha and Slava need not worry you."

On the stage, Solor had entered and dismissed his hunting party. Danion released Bella's hand. "If you will excuse me," he said. "I promised to visit my father." He bent to whisper in Choli's ear. "We will meet later, little bird."

She nodded. Danion slipped past Bella and left.

❉

Bella, watching him go, wondered what had possessed her to confide in Sasha's impassive husband.

Not so impassive, when she thought of it. She had expected coldness, but Danion was charming, not in the least intimidating, and quite unlike most Tarkei she had met. It made Sasha's affection for him easy to understand. Was that what had pulled the words out of her like beads on a string?

She pushed the problem aside. Soon Sasha would make her entrance. Since the day Bella had acknowledged, if only to herself, that Gramps's sister danced better than she, she had made it her life's work to watch her aunt's every performance. Not a gesture, not an angle, missed her eye. Sasha changed every day, her portrayal a matter of feeling that the details merely expressed, but in watching her, Bella saw how she could do the same. Each time she danced Gamzatti, she became stronger, surer.

Today she especially wanted to do her best. Only tomorrow was more important than today. Reporters filled half the theater; tickets for tomorrow were sold out, but future performances depended on the morning news broadcasts. If Xantera Ballet failed, it would not be through any action, or inaction, of Bella's; she had made that vow the day her aunt returned.

Today, moreover, Gramps had promised to sit through the entire rehearsal. By the time Act II ended, she wanted to show him that his company contained not one but two primas.

She did, too. Camille did not believe in the ancient saw about bad dress rehearsals making for good performances. In Camille's philosophy, practice made perfect, and only perfection in rehearsal guaranteed perfection in performance. For fourteen weeks, she had instilled this philosophy in her new company by every means available to her, and from overture to finale they made it clear that they had heard.

Bella, though, was her greatest triumph. The moment she came on stage, she made Tonio gasp, and by the end of Act II, Camille had to sit on her hands to prevent him from wringing them again.

At the end, she stood and clapped. That clear soprano carried even above the tempestuous applause from the crowd behind her. "Now, *mes filles et garçons*, we are ready. Tomorrow, you will show the world what ballet can be."

From corps to soloists, the dancers stood stunned.

The reviews hit the air before breakfast. Danion and Sasha, back in their apartment but taking advantage of Camille's unprecedented rescheduling of her eight-o'-clock class, woke to the impromptu alarm clock of Choli shrieking. "Sasha, Slava, Camille, wake up. You have to see this!"

Sasha groaned, rolled over, and grabbed her robe. Danion sat up, and she dropped a kiss on the top of his head. "It's the reviews. Do you want to hear them?"

He placed a hand on her waist. "Do you expect them to be less than spectacular?"

"Not really," Sasha said. "But I'm not a reporter. From Choli's pitch, I assume they're either fabulous or a disaster. I should ignore them, but I can't."

Danion reached for the clothes he had worn yesterday. "Then I will come and support you, in the unlikely event that every journalist in the galaxy has lost all common sense."

But of course, they had not. As Danion had predicted, the reviews were spectacular.

19. En Couronne

LATER THAT DAY, DANION sat in Sasha's dressing room. He felt as though he, not she, had dropped into a time warp. Except for the specifics of costumes and music, nothing had changed since that long-ago performance of *Giselle*. There was the same excited chatter in the corridors; the same rows of dancers wearing improbable combinations of lacy fabrics and wool legwarmers, going through the same exercises at the barre placed near the wings; the same smells of greasepaint and hot lights; and Sasha, dressed in the skimpy costume, making her preparations, oblivious as ever to the chaos around her.

"Curtain in five," the stagehand shouted, setting off, as he did every time, a kind of Brownian motion in the wings. Sasha, fully made up, left the dressing table.

"Dance well, *kaleita*." Danion stroked her cheek.

Sasha shook her head at him, as she always did. Her fingers caressed the garnet earring, restored to its usual place. "It's good that I'm not superstitious. I'd break a leg out of nerves. Couldn't you at least say, *Merde*?"

"It is a tradition," Danion said deadpan. "I do not wish to meddle with success."

Sasha laughed. "You're incorrigible." She ran out the door.

❋

Thanks to Camille's pointing finger, Danion found his way to a section reserved for friends, loosely defined, of the family. Tarkei diplomatic personnel occupied one entire row. Danion had worked with many of them, on one mission or another, and he took the time to greet those he recognized. Strangers held most of the remaining seats, although from the center of the row in front of the diplomats, three familiar faces stared, waiting for him to notice them.

Thuja—outrageous as ever in what looked like magenta silk pajamas and a hat with a three-foot plume, which had the stone-faced diplomat behind her clutching his brow—waved a long, skinny arm. Next to her sat Iqara, magnificent in ivory satin and plain gold jewelry (his sister knew from experience to dress in neutral colors when Thuja was around). Farther down the row he saw Jenat, and next to him Choli bounced in her seat, vivid and excited in a brand-new dress, a rich burgundy velvet that set off her dark coloring. She would stay for the first act, then run off to don her costume for her three-minute prance around the stage.

Tonio sat in the front row, hosting various important and wealthy-looking people whom he had probably targeted as future backers.

Danion surveyed the crowd, evaluating his options. On Iqara's right, a white head swam into view. Between the head and Jenat, he saw an empty seat. The owner of the white head was not waving, but the house lights gleamed in Geoffrey Anderson's eyes.

"Excuse me," he said to the person at the end of the row and picked his way through to sit between his father and his oldest friend.

✻

Geoff had not been at the consulate when Danion made his visit the day before. He seemed to be in a good mood now. "Have a seat, brother, and tell me what you've been up to since you got back. The parts you can, at least."

Before Danion could reply, his father flicked his ear. "Good to see you, boy. How's that wife of yours?"

Danion held out his hands, palms up. "Intent on her preparations, father, as always. She will join us after the performance. I am glad to see you also, and especially to see you well." It was true: Jenat appeared, if anything, livelier than before Danion's departure—revitalized by the return of his children. The discovery had been a relief; Sasha's concern had disturbed Danion more than he liked to admit.

Jenat's voice was dry but not unfriendly. "Your sister takes good care of me." He pretended to glare at Iqara. "Except when she's fussing me to death."

"Call it payback," Iqa said. "For the times you did the same to me."

Jenat bestowed an austere raised eyebrow on his daughter and returned to his conversation with his granddaughter, leaving Danion free to answer Geoff. He shook his friend's hand. "What have I been doing? I am sure I need not tell you. Renewing acquaintances. Bringing Father up-to-date on Kazratan. Readjusting to life on Earth. Did Father tell you that Reilu is dead?"

"Of course not. Nor Iqa, or she'd have let me know. How did it happen?"

Danion explained. They talked about the political situation, about Vestris and the resistance movement, about his escape and Vestris's part in it—ending with Reilu's death.

Demonstrating unusual restraint, Geoff listened without comment to the whole explanation, eyes fixed on his friend's face. At the end, he frowned at the heavy brocade curtain that veiled the stage. "I'd like to say I'm sorry, brother, but it would be a lie."

"I know," Danion said. "I too am relieved. Her obsession caused a great deal of harm. I wonder, though, whether we could have intervened sooner."

While Geoff was considering that point, Thuja leaned forward to comment. The movement dislodged her hat, and she grabbed for it. The diplomat behind her yelped as the plume caught him in the eye.

Thuja apologized, swiping his forehead with the plume as she turned. Being Tarkei, he accepted the apology with chill courtesy, but his long-suffering expression made it clear he was hoping the Pannthu would find another seat before she inflicted permanent damage. Whatever Thuja might have said was lost.

"An interesting question." Jenat rubbed his chin. "If unanswerable. I have informed Reilu's parents of her demise, my son. I will share the details with you tomorrow. Tonight I plan to appreciate the performances of my daughter and granddaughter." He leaned back and flicked Choli's ear. "Isn't that right, little bird? You will dance well for your grandfather?"

Danion sent Choli an amused glance, but the girl seemed quite serious when she said, "Absolutely, grandfather."

So his family had accepted her, and she them. That was good. "You will go far, little bird," he said. The house lights dimmed, the conductor made her bow, and the opening notes of the overture filled the theater.

From the rising of the curtain, Danion sensed the company responding to the presence of a live audience. Having grown up in a culture with no tradition of theatrical entertainment, Danion found it fascinating to see the synergy that developed between audience and dancers: each reacted to the other with a depth and complexity that no videotaped or even holographic performance could simulate. The older the work, the more likely it was to take that synergy for granted, and the more vital it became to a successful rendition. *Bayadère*, choreographed in the 1870s, was a perfect example. In the setting of this small, beautiful, and ancient theater, it came alive.

Solor had left the stage after bullying the Head Fakir, one of the temple residents, to deliver a message to Nikia. Eight priests and as many temple dancers replaced him. A whole group of junior fakirs, like their head semi-clad in rags and dirt, crawled across the floor before demonstrating that they had been picked for their jumping ability by leaping back and forth across the pretend eternal flame, legs opening and closing like scissors. *Bayadère*'s originators had had no qualms about introducing extraneous characters: the stage was littered with them. Thuja wondered audibly where Nikia was supposed to dance; Jenat glared at her, Iqara shushed her, and the beleaguered diplomat behind her hissed. Danion did not interfere.

The temple dancers were in motion now. The fakirs had subsided behind the eternal flame to await their next outbreak, and the priests were lined up against the wings looking stolid. The High Brahmin, an older dancer Danion did not recognize, stood at the center of the circle of women. He had an arrogance a Tarkei might envy and seemed surprisingly comfortable with the elaborate mime his role required. Mime was so very nineteenth-century; choreographers had abandoned it long ago. Xantera Ballet was one of the few companies that still performed the classical repertoire, so it was difficult to imagine anyone comfortable with it, but perhaps the Brahmin had danced with Tonio before. Danion could not say; he had avoided the ballet during his wife's long absence.

The temple dancers shimmered off to stand in front of the priests, leaving center stage clear. The Brahmin stepped forward, hands raised over his right shoulder as though he were supporting a jug of water. Nikia's symbol, meaning, in this instance, "Fetch Nikia." A priest peeled away from the pack and walked to the bottom of the steps that marked the entrance to the temple. At the top, the curtains parted, and Sasha stood there, dressed in the skimpy costume, her face obscured by a white gauze veil. Placing each foot with elaborate care, she descended the steps.

The audience clapped. Thuja gasped. The diplomat hissed again. A delayed reaction to the plume, perhaps, since otherwise the reaction was unfair. Thuja would not be the first person overwhelmed by the grace of a ballerina's walk.

Scene I progressed along its inevitable course. Having reached the foot of the steps, Sasha stood in first position, hands touching her shoulders. The Brahmin, seeing Nikia for the first time, drew back in shock, then stepped forward to lift the veil from her face. He mimed again, and she moved into her opening dance. Danion watched her in pure pleasure; the audience could have howled like banshee, and he would not have noticed.

The Brahmin declared himself and was rejected; the fakir delivered his message; the stage cleared. The fakir reported his success to Solor, who went into hiding. Midnight arrived with astonishing speed. Sasha, water jug over her shoulder, slipped out the temple curtains and began her second solo. Looking for Solor, she traveled from one side of the stage to the other, her body stretched in yearning. As she was about to retreat, shoulders drooping, he emerged from the wings and clapped twice, their prearranged signal. Sasha placed the water jug on the ground and turned, her arms spread wide, her face alight with joy. No wonder Bella had wondered if it made Danion jealous.

It's for you, her voice said through the link. Slava was holding her above his head, gazing at her as she stroked his cheek.

I know, Danion told her. It would take too long to explain, and he did not want to upset her performance, which was wonderful, by introducing guilt over Bella's understandable qualms. So he repeated the assurance. I know, *kaleita*.

It worked. This meeting of Nikia and Solor is one of the loveliest pas de deux in ballet—light and frothy and, for anyone who has ever been in love, instantly recognizable. Danion let the bubble of happiness rise within him, feeling the long reign of grief loose its wintry grip. He could not have watched it at any point during Sasha's absence; the pain would have been unbearable, yet now it brought home as few other events could have the extent of his good fortune. Tarkei to the last, he did not weep or laugh, but he let the feelings flow, making no attempt to force them into one mold or another. All were appropriate, and his time with Sasha had taught him to value each one.

The Brahmin became visible, peeking through the temple curtains. The Head Fakir, standing watch, noticed long before Nikia and Solor, caught up in each other. At last, he captured their attention and hustled them out of danger before the Brahmin could act. The Brahmin emerged, stormed about the stage, and, hand clenched over the eternal flame, vowed to kill Solor. The curtain fell—end of Scene I.

Scene II began without intermission. The set piece Bella had dismissed as the girls dancing for the Rajah showed off the effects of Camille's training on the corps; otherwise, it did little to advance the plot. Danion waited for Gamzatti to appear, which she soon did. The audience clapped again. Someone in front of him whispered to the person next to her, "My goodness, what did they do to Isabella Sinclair? Last time I saw her she had about as much expression as the backdrop." His father quirked an eyebrow in his direction, and Danion responded in kind.

With queenly grace and tilted head, and far more expression than the backdrop, Bella as Gamzatti accepted the Rajah's declaration that he planned to marry her to Solor. Servant in tow, she stalked from the stage, and Solor arrived in her stead. Where Gamzatti had accepted her father's announcement, Solor backed away, horrified to discover that marriage to a princess lay in his future. Danion watched with a mixture of curiosity and distaste as the story, so like his own marriage to Reilu in some respects, played out. He had recognized the parallels before, but never so clearly as now. Beside him, Jenat shifted uncomfortably in his seat. In Danion's life, Jenat had played the Rajah's role.

Danion glanced at him. The old grudge made no sense after so many years. He touched Jenat's hand, forgiving him, and was pleased when his father relaxed.

Gamzatti returned, now shrouded as Sasha had been, and the Rajah was the one to lift the veil. Bella did indeed look gorgeous, and Slava was taken with her, even as he resisted. He kept shooting sidelong glances at her and, when given her hand by the Rajah, escorted her with a flourish to the side of the stage.

Danion, who had escaped such temptations regarding Reilu, had limited interest in Solor's troubles. Bella's portrayal of Gamzatti, however, fascinated him. Not having seen her dance before, he had only Sasha's word, and that of the people in front of him, that this represented an artistic breakthrough for her. It made no difference to him, anyway. What drew him was her ability to capture and project a personality so uncannily like Reilu's that at times he wondered whether Sasha had shared his first wife's story with her niece.

No, Sasha said. It comes from Bella. We talked about Gamzatti, and I did notice the resemblance. But the idea was to provoke Bella into thinking, so I went out of my way *not* to mention that I knew a person like that.

Remarkable, Danion said. Watching her, I almost begin to understand what drove Reilu.

Oh, do you? And do you understand Solor's attraction to her as well? Sasha asked. He could hear the teasing in her voice.

Not that, he said, except at the most superficial level. She is quite beautiful.

She is, isn't she? Sasha's voice now held a note of pride.

His wife disappeared to prepare for her next entrance. Danion turned his attention back to Bella, assessing her performance. What did he see that reminded him so strongly of Reilu's obsession? Gamzatti's acceptance of the marriage seemed comprehensible enough; in the days when people considered affection less important than economics as a basis for marriage, she would not be the first girl grateful to discover that her father had picked a handsome young warrior for her husband.

Sasha made her entrance and performed her dance of blessing—supported not by Slava, hiding behind a pillar, but by a member of the corps unfamiliar to Danion. A strong member of the corps, since he had to balance Sasha on his chest while she sprinkled lilies over Gamzatti's bowed head to signal the temple's approval of the union. Somewhat premature, as it turned out: the temple did not approve. The Brahmin, unaware of Gamzatti eavesdropping and hoping to destroy his own rival, told the Rajah of Solor's love for Nikia and discovered, to his horror, that the Rajah wanted to sacrifice Nikia, not Solor.

Danion returned to musing about Gamzatti's motives. Having accepted the marriage, she must have experienced shock when she discovered that her chosen husband loved someone else. Reilu had not had that excuse. Not at first. Although it was true that, despite a litany of complaints, she had not tried to prevent his joining the priesthood. Only after he returned with Sasha had she taken up arms. So perhaps there was a similarity.

With Nikia in the palace, the temptation to buy her off must have been almost irresistible. Unfortunately for Nikia's survival, if not for her ethics, she refused to relinquish Solor, no matter how many necklaces and bracelets Gamzatti thrust at her. "He loves me," she said in mime, sending the princess into further paroxysms of fury. Gamzatti dragged Nikia around the stage when not pushing jewelry at her. When Nikia tried to leave, the princess barred her way, until Nikia picked up a dagger one of Solor's soldiers had forgotten and went after her tormentor. Gamzatti's servant intervened at the last moment, and Nikia ran distraught from the room.

Bella conveyed this melodrama with understated clarity—the elegance and the appeal, the shock and anger and grief, and, most impressive of all, a restraint that peeled away in moments of solitude or extreme emotion, only to be donned again like a mask when the presence of others required it. But what struck Danion from the beginning was Gamzatti's underlying ruthlessness, her lack of empathy not only for Nikia—somewhat understandable—but for

Solor, equally the victim of her determination. And her father's, he supposed.

Reilu, like Gamzatti, could not accept a world that refused to accommodate her expectations. She could not adjust to a changing reality. Through the seven decades that she had burdened Danion's existence, she had striven constantly to turn back the clock, to force those around her into the rigid patterns of life as she defined it—as she had forced her surroundings, her possessions, into strict symmetrical forms. To her, flexibility was synonymous with chaos. If she had to trample everyone around her in pursuit of order, then trample she would.

In a flash, he recognized that Reilu's rigidity and lack of empathy, which he had long identified as her most fundamental character traits, explained both the tragedy of her life and his immediate subconscious antipathy for her. That was why he had refused to touch her; years before he could name those qualities in her, he had recognized and rejected them. In that, his reaction had been simpler than Solor's.

Gamzatti stood, one pointed foot crossed behind the other, her face set. With savage grace, she extended her left arm level with her shoulder, hand pointed toward the absent Nikia. Her other hand, clenched into a fist, came over her head and down past her waist. It quivered with fury. "I will kill her"—that was what Sasha had said the gesture meant.

And indeed, Bella looked exactly like Reilu at the moment he walked into that cave on Kazratan. Danion bowed his head in silent appreciation. The audience was cheering as the curtain fell.

❀

He did not share his insights with his father. They would increase the old man's guilt, and what purpose would that serve? Instead, he helped Jenat out of the row and strolled among the crowd, discussing neutral topics and half-listening to Thuja's bubbling commentary on the ballet. Geoffrey egged her on with an occasional remark, although he did more listening than talking.

Thuja's playful suggestions as to the precise methods Camille had used to instill discipline in the corps and emotion in Bella grew more absurd each time Jenat countered them with logical disdain. The Pannthu had spent more time following Xantera Ballet in the last six decades than Danion had, he saw. She must be enjoying herself if her usual nervousness around his father could give way to such delight in tweaking Jenat's composure.

Still, it was not something that required a response from Jenat's son. Just as well, since Danion did not feel capable of responding. Bella's uncanny reproduction of Reilu's monomania had shaken him more than he had expected, and much more than he wanted to admit to his father or Thuja.

Only Iqa grasped his state of mind. Danion and his sister had always been close. She slipped a hand through his arm, leaving Thuja and Jenat in happy argument ahead. "Eerie, isn't it?"

"Very." Danion squeezed her hand. "She's dead, you know."

"I didn't," Iqa said, "until I heard you mention it to Geoffrey. What happened?"

Danion told the story again. It already seemed remote—another life, another world—but something he had not yet acknowledged must have communicated itself to Iqa's quick and sympathetic ear. It had escaped Geoff, and even himself, but that was one of the traits that set Iqa apart.

"You're sad." She sounded surprised. Danion looked down at her. She still sounded surprised when she said, "And so am I. How odd, after the dreadful things she did. I didn't expect to rejoice, but to grieve?"

In the back of his mind, Danion heard Sasha's gentle questioning. Bella's nuanced portrayal alive in his thoughts, he sifted through his reactions. "Yes," he told Iqa, "I am sad. It was such a waste. It took courage, that scheme of hers—courage and organization and intelligence. So much talent spent on a vain search for revenge. She could have done whatever she wanted, and she chose that. And why? Because some ancient tradition had declared me her possession, and she refused to be thwarted. Even if she had succeeded in destroying me, she would have lost."

The lights flashed, calling them back to the performance. Ahead of them, Thuja turned Jenat as skillfully as she turned her starship. Geoff followed. Danion, Iqa's hand clasping his arm, let them pass before falling in behind them. Sasha's fingers brushed his ear through the link.

"Yes," Iqa said. "I understand."

The second act was less harrowing, and even Jenat admitted that the character dances were impressive. The Golden

Idol, rigorously coached by Slava, leaped high enough to wring gasps from the audience, one leg bent under him while the other flew straight out to the side. The Water Carrier flitted about the stage, chased by two would-be samplers of her wares. Each time she had to balance her jar on her head and bourrée front or back, her eyes showed her nervousness, and each time she completed the movement successfully and landed in fourth, she produced a relieved grin so genuine that the audience smiled with her. Only at the end, when she lifted the jar from her head and danced away, beckoning to her followers, did they realize her anxiety was not feigned: that jar could have crashed to the floor at any moment.

The stage filled with people: young women holding parrots or fans, young men dressed as Mughal soldiers. Even the children from the school had parts; Choli strutted with the others escorting Solor. Danion admitted to a certain fatherly pride; she looked charming and danced well for someone with such limited training, at least as well as the rest of the escort. After a few turns about the stage, everyone retreated to the back as a group of nomadic horsemen dashed in. The horsemen leaped and shouted like Cossacks (a style the audience appeared to appreciate)—not too plausible, perhaps, for an elite Indian betrothal ceremony but exciting to watch. Danion relaxed into his chair, enjoying the spectacle.

"Stand still, Bella!" Sasha pushed one last hairpin into place, kissed her niece on the cheek, and dabbed powder on the spot her lips had brushed. "There, you're set. Break a leg. Break two. Half the galaxy is watching, and by the time you finish those fouettés, they'll have decided you're the greatest ballerina in the universe. Right, Camille?"

Camille reached out a hand and brushed a stray wisp of hair into place. "She is a Sinclair. It is her destiny."

"Goodness, listen to you." Sasha applied powder to her own forehead. "You sound like Jenat on a bad day."

Camille shook her head at her frivolous prima, then bestowed an austere smile on said prima's niece. "But I admit, my Bella, that you have more than exceeded my expectations. Next we will tackle *Don Quixote*, I think. Mercedes will be an excellent stretch for you. Ah no, that man with the blue light, what is he doing? We do not need the blue until the next act." Camille darted off, leaving Sasha and Bella staring after her.

"*Don Q*," Sasha said. "Well, that will be fun. Have you ever danced it?"

Bella shook her head.

"You'll love it," Sasha told her. "Mercedes gets to slink around the stage and seduce a bullfighter with a roving eye, and in our production she usually doubles as the street girl in the first act. Very flashy."

Slava came up behind them and snaked his arm around Bella's waist. "Sasha loves dancing Kitri. That's what she really means." He tapped Sasha's nose, and she swished her shawl in response. "She's right, though. It's my favorite ballet, too."

He kissed Bella's ear. "You'll do wonderfully, love."

Sasha raised the powder puff as if it were a bouquet. "Solor and Gamzatti pairing up, I see. Well, good for you."

Slava grinned. "Don't worry. I'll yearn convincingly for the audience."

"I don't doubt it," Sasha said. "I do, or so they say." She patted Bella's shoulder. "If I had the lilies, I'd shower them over your head."

Bella smiled. "Thank you, Sasha. Whoops, there's our cue."

Slava's arm tightened around her waist, and together they ran onto the stage.

Pyrotechnics—thus Tonio had once described this pas de deux to Sasha—and it was. Gamzatti's solo required one big movement after another, making it enjoyable to watch without demanding a great emotional investment from the performer. The ivory tutu set off Bella's peachy coloring, emphasizing her natural regality and her excellent legs. The audience kept its eyes fixed on the stage, only the occasional in-drawn breath or head shake marking one or another particularly dramatic moment.

Danion agreed that no one could fail to enjoy Slava's momentous leaps or the sight of Bella kicking one foot high in the air, only to turn on pointe and repeat the sequence. And the fouettés—he counted twenty-four—brought the house down as they always did. Even here, though, Bella showed that she had exceeded Tonio's expectations by injecting character into her technical feats. Queenly and self-confident, her Gamzatti was also possessive and demanding: each time Solor threatened to slip away into memories of Nikia, she called him back, literally wrapping her bent leg around him on one occasion. Solor yearned, but Gamzatti acted, refusing to yield her claim on him. Again, Danion was reminded of Reilu as she had appeared during the years after Sasha's disappearance, when he was consumed in grief and guilt.

The pas de deux ended, and Solor and Gamzatti, with her father, the Rajah, took their places at a table that the soldiers had set up at the right side of the stage. Sasha, a complete contrast to Gamzatti in soft, filmy charcoal-gray harem trousers, a pale blue shawl wrapped around her, walked in from upstage left, preoccupied with her internal torment. As she passed the ring of bystanders, she looked up, saw Gamzatti with her hand in Solor's, and tossed the shawl aside. Beneath it she wore a black velvet bodice that left her waist bare. A translucent black veil fell past her hips.

At the farthest point from Gamzatti and Solor, she crossed her right leg behind the left and arched away from the couple at the table. From the tips of her fingers to the pointed toes, anguish limned her body. She repeated the pose in the other direction, then again to the right before bending forward in arabesque penché, the step that the shades would repeat throughout their long entrance. Thus marked by death, she moved into her dance.

Danion sent Tonio and Camille a silent nod of respect. From the beginning, they had recognized the difference between their ballerinas and made the most of it. Urged by Camille, Bella had had the style and the talent to create a Gamzatti beautiful enough, compelling enough, that one could understand Solor's vacillation, but she had neither the depth nor the subtlety Nikia required. Sasha, whose steps demanded at least as much in the way of balance and skill (she went from the floor to full pointe at least three times in this one variation), made her technique look as effortless as breathing. Instead of the complex steps one saw the arms curved in despair, the feet hammering their fury into the floor, the wide eyes that signaled the biting snake, the droop of her shoulders as, eyes on Solor, she threw away the antidote that would have saved her life. When she collapsed, half the audience made audible Solor's silent shriek of remorse.

The curtain closed on his broken form.

※

The house lights came up again. The others stood, leaving only his father. "Do you wish to walk some more?" Jenat asked.

Danion, struggling with an emotion he had thought long conquered, turned his head to find unexpected sympathy in his father's eyes. He controlled his voice. "Iqa will wait for you, I'm sure."

"She left with Thuja and Geoffrey," his father said. "But you misunderstood me. I have had sufficient exercise."

Danion wished he would go, but he refused to say anything so rude. The rows behind and in front were clear; he and Jenat sat alone amid a sea of coats and Thuja's three-foot plume. The diplomat had persuaded her to remove it.

"Very striking, this dance," Jenat said in a conversational tone. "I admire the human facility for emotional expression. Tarkei could benefit from it, I think. In moderation."

Danion stared at his father. Of the statements Jenat might have made, his son found this one the most difficult to swallow. "Untruths? At your age?"

Jenat shrugged a shoulder. "Why not, at my age? I have nothing to protect these days. But it is not entirely a lie. I have not sought emotional expression in my own life, that's true. At the time I did not see it, but I reacted to your mother's death by withdrawing into myself. I felt responsible, and therefore guilty." He waved a hand at the lowered curtain. "As that young man did."

"I too," Danion said. "You knew that. Toward both Reilu and Sasha. I thought rationality had won out long ago, but I was wrong."

"I wondered if there was more to it than you admitted," Jenat said. "Whether that was why you allowed Reilu to stay for so long. If that was why you went to Kazratan."

Danion considered the question—glad, after all, that his father had chosen to stay. With how many people could he have this conversation? "To punish myself?"

Jenat flicked his ear and nodded. "That was the question."

"Perhaps. The first part, anyway." He touched the electronic program set into the arm rest and watched it blink through page after page. "I had not intended to travel to Kazratan. I agreed in the hope of uncovering whatever game you were playing."

Jenat's dark eyes twinkled like a Christmas elf. Sasha's image, of course.

Sasha herself touched his thoughts. *Is that why you let her stay? But how could the time vortex have been your fault? You had less responsibility than Solor!*

I knew that, *kaleita*, he told her. In my head, but not, as you would say, in my heart. The guilt marked how much you meant to me. I didn't want to think you could be torn from me through an act of random violence.

Through the link, Sasha blew him a kiss. I forgive you.

My Altanai, Danion told her.

To his father he said, "I did you an injustice, though, regarding Kazratan. I recognized that as soon as I received confirmation of Sasha's return. You had heard the news?"

"Rumors, although some came from trustworthy sources," Jenat said. "How annoyed Reilu must have been."

"That the crash did not kill them—yes, I expect so." Danion touched his father's arm. The rows around them were filling as the intermission ended. "But it served her purpose either way. She had switched her hatred to me, and it was my destruction she sought. Sasha became her instrument."

"An evil woman," Jenat said. "I am pleased that she did not succeed."

There seemed to be no answer to that.

Solor, mad with grief, gave in to the Head Fakir's urging and puffed at the jar of opium the other man had brought. The fakir left, and Solor fell asleep. Against a gauzy backdrop, Nikia appeared, clad in her white tutu. It still did not look like anything a self-respecting ghost would wear, but it suited her. Linked to her, Danion sensed her satisfaction. The costume felt right, and that was enough.

She disappeared. The backdrop lifted. Solor sought her but could not find her. He left the stage. At the top of the ramp, the first shade appeared. She leaned forward, one leg extended high behind her, the other bent. Returning to the upright, she pointed her front foot, arms in a circle around her head, and bent her upper body backward. Three steps down the ramp, and the second shade joined her. They bent forward and back, and a third shade emerged.

Even Thuja fell silent. The diplomat ceased to hiss, although the Pannthu had resumed her hat. Around the theater, no one coughed, no one whispered, no one moved. One after another, the shades descended in a symmetry so perfect it seemed unearthly—not mechanical but inhuman. Each bent back replicated the one before it; every leg matched the others in height. Ten, twenty, thirty times the dancers performed the same step, every repetition identical. Danion marveled at their skill, thinking of the corps he had seen in his wife's thoughts a few months past. Camille had earned her reputation.

There was a fourth act, Sasha had told him, in which the temple collapsed as the gods wreaked vengeance on those who had killed Nikia and forced Solor and Gamzatti into marriage. This company did not perform it, preferring to end the ballet with Nikia's forgiveness. Under the circumstances, Danion was glad. He had suffered enough from others' need for vengeance.

The corps dancers finished their long entrance and shimmied off to stand in two lines along the edge of the stage, pointed feet crossed behind their standing ankles, circled arms resting on their tutus, eyes discreetly lowered like the Victorian maidens they represented. Slava entered at the far right corner of the stage and began a series of leaps that circled the entire open space and brought roars of applause from the audience. He was no longer, Danion noticed, moderating his jumps.

Having failed to find his dead love, Slava as Solor came to a halt downstage, right arm curved above his head, eyes gazing into his palm. His left foot pointed behind him. He knelt, right leg extended. From the wings, Sasha walked on pointe across the floor. Slava moved his arm forward as she reached him, and she balanced in arabesque, matching his pose. She let go, bent her knee, and bourréed around her kneeling partner.

Compared to this, the broadcast on Kazratan had merely hinted at their skill. Free of injury, restored to their company, invigorated by the live audience, Sasha and Slava soared. Slava tossed Sasha over his head as though she had no weight and leaped after her as though he had none either.

He's in love, Sasha said through the link. With Bella. Poised on one toe, she leaned yearningly toward Slava as he promenaded her around, holding her hand over her head. Danion saw his own picture in her mind. In her thoughts, she blew him a kiss.

Slava stopped. Sasha released his hand and balanced on the toes of her left foot, right leg extended to the side. The audience produced a gentle collective sigh. With exquisite slowness, she brought the leg down before accepting Slava's outstretched hand. The audience clapped. Facing her partner, she jumped and began the sequence again.

Danion smiled. A true smile, obscured by the darkness. They were home. The circle closed, and with it the devastation the vortex had wrought in his world.

Ballet Terms Used in the Tarkei Chronicles

Adagio: A dance calling for slow, sustained movement.

Alignment: The positioning of the body—shoulders in line with hips, ankles, and feet—that exemplifies the upright stance characteristic of dancers. Correct alignment is essential to balance and prevents injury.

Arabesque: A position in which one leg is extended to the back while the dancer balances on the other. The arrangement of arms and legs determines the type of arabesque (first, second, etc.). Normally the head remains upright in arabesque; if the dancer tips the entire upper body forward, it is called penché (suspended).

Assemblé: A jump from one foot to two, in which the legs come together (assemble) in the air.

Attitude: Similar to arabesque, but with bent knee. Attitude can be performed to the front and, more rarely, to the side as well as to the back.

Ballonné: A step or jump in which the working foot shoots out, then returns to the standing ankle. Can be performed in any direction.

Bourrée: On pointe, a series of small traveling steps. Often the feet stay so close together that they seem to shimmer across the floor.

Cambré: A bend of the upper body, forward or backward or to either side.

Chassé: Similar to a two-step, where one foot leads and the other closes behind (chases) the first.

Échappé: A small jump from a closed position, usually fifth, in which the feet "escape" to land in second or fourth position.

En couronne: A port de bras in which the arms rise to create a circle framing the head, like a crown; also known as fifth position of the arms.

First (second, fourth, fifth) position: The basic starting and ending placements of the feet. First—heels together, toes to the side; second—same as first with a separation of 12–18 inches between the heels; fourth—one foot about 12 inches in front of the other, heels aligned to opposing arch (open) or toes (closed); fifth—feet together, heels aligned to opposing toes. Third position is a modified fifth used by beginning dancers, not professionals. Each foot position has an associated arm position, but the different national traditions vary.

Fondu: A step in which the working foot is placed at the ankle of the standing foot as both knees "melt" into plié, usually followed by developpé, in which both legs extend.

Fouetté: A turn in which the working leg remains stationary while the standing leg and body move. Often used as shorthand for fouetté rond de jambe en tournant, in which the working leg is whipped from front to side or side to back, depending on the national tradition; as the dancer turns, she brings the working foot into the knee, then extends it again to finish, as she started, in plié on one foot.

Frappé: A movement in which the foot shoots out from its base at the opposite ankle, striking the floor on the way to full point. It can be performed with foot flexed or straight. In a double frappé, the foot is stretched and beats both sides of the supporting ankle before striking the floor.

Grand allegro: A fast-moving dance calling for big movements, especially big jumps.

Grand jeté: A big jump in which the legs (ideally) form a straight line in the air.

Pas de chat: A big jump in which both legs are pulled up to the knee as quickly as possible, then returned to the ground. If one leg is bent while the other extends to the front or side, it is called an Italian pas de chat or grand pas de chat.

Pas de deux: Any dance involving two people, typically a man and a woman. A grand pas de deux is a formal version of this, in which both dance together, usually in adagio, then each dances separately, then they come together again for the finale—often the high point of a ballet. When it propels the action of the story, it may be called pas d'action.

Passé: A movement in which the working foot is pulled up the standing leg to the knee, then (usually) "passed" down the leg to close on the opposite side. Both legs are strongly turned out. A position often used in turns.

Penché: See arabesque.

Petit battement: A small, quick, beating movement of the foot at the opposite ankle, front to back or back to front.

Piqué: A stabbing movement of the foot into the floor, often the entry to an arabesque. It can also initiate a pirouette (piqué en tournant or piqué turn).

Pirouette: Any turn.

Plié: A knee bend. Used as a basic warm-up exercise, as well as to initiate and to end every jump and turn.

Pointe: The act of balancing on the tips of the toes. Although dancers use reinforced shoes (pointe shoes, more casually referred to as toe shoes) to sustain balance on pointe, the position is attained and held through a combination of strong feet and perfect alignment. The shoes are merely an aid. One can spring onto pointe in a single movement, but good technique requires the dancer to return to the floor by standing on the ball of the foot before lowering the heel (known as "rolling through" the foot), ending in plié.

Port de bras: Any movement sequence involving the arms, including cambré.

Promenade: A sequence of steps in which the dancer, by making small adjustments to the position of the supporting foot, circles while in pose (most often, arabesque or attitude). Often performed as part of an adagio, especially in pas de deux, when the man walks in a circle, turning the woman on pointe.

Relevé: Rising to stand on the balls of the feet or, if one is wearing the appropriate shoes, on pointe.

Renversé: A step in which the working leg makes a 180-degree turn, either front to back or back to front, while the body remains still.

Révérence: A curtsey, in which the placement of the arms often reflects the character portrayed, particularly in the Russian tradition. Also the last section of class, in which slow movements usher in the cool-down period.

Sissone: A jump from two feet landing on one.

Standing leg: The leg that remains stationary while a movement is performed. Also called the supporting leg.

Temps de flèche: The "arrow" step, a jump involving two kicks to the front, usually with straight legs.

Tombé: A step that ends lower than the step preceding it, into plié from a normal standing position or into either plié or heels flat on the floor from relevé.

Tour en l'air: A big jump, most often performed by men, in which the dancer turns 360 degrees—once, twice, or three times—in the air before landing in fifth position plié.

Turnout: The dancer's ability to rotate the legs from the hip socket. Ideally, the feet form a straight line. If the dancer can rotate 180 degrees in this way without training, (s)he is said to have "natural turnout."

Working limb: The leg or arm that performs a movement.

Acknowledgments

ONCE UPON A TIME, I decided to write down a story that had occupied my thoughts for years. One scene led to another, and soon I had a quarter of a novel. It grew and evolved, and as it did, thanks to comments from my friend Wendilee Heath O'Brien, it turned into a book. So large a book, in fact, that I ended up splitting it in two. *Desert Flower* is the first half, and *Kingdom of the Shades* the second.

Thanks go also to Jon Sherman and Sharon Friedler, who have made it possible for me to indulge my love of ballet by permitting me to take Jon's class for twenty-five years, as well as to Catherine Thomas Nobles and Colleen Kelley, who read and commented on both novels before publication. And to the great classical ballerinas Nina (Nino) Ananiashvili and Alessandra Ferri, whose exquisite artistry and phenomenal technique became my inspiration for Sasha. When I started work on this story, they were at the height of their careers; they have since retired from most active performances, although they continue to dance on special occasions.

Although I finished the first draft of these novels in the late 1990s, it took much longer for me to feel confident writing fiction. Helped by comments from my fellow-members of Five Directions Press—Ariadne Apostolou, Courtney J. Hall, and Diana Holquist—I published three other novels before deciding that this story had grown up enough to face the world. I thank them for their many contributions along the way—and, as always, my husband for his love and support.

And for those who may have read *The Not Exactly Scarlet Pimpernel,* the idea of two characters in mental communication had its origins here. I adapted it for the later novel after convincing myself that the Tarkei Chronicles might never see the light of day. But times have changed, and here they are.

May you enjoy Sasha and Danion's world as much as I enjoyed bringing it to life. They have been and remain dear to my heart.

The Author

AS A CHILD, C. P. Lesley thought everyone told themselves stories to help themselves fall asleep. It never occurred to her that anyone would pay her for them, and for a long time, she was right—no one would. But after years of producing horrible prose, reading books about novel writing, and pestering hapless fellow-writers and friends to read her drafts, some of the advice stuck, and she finished *The Not Exactly Scarlet Pimpernel.*

In addition to *Desert Flower,* the first part of Sasha and Danion's story, she has published *The Golden Lynx* and *The Winged Horse*—books 1 and 2 of Legends of the Five Directions, a series set during the childhood of Ivan the Terrible. She is currently working on Legends 3, *The Swan Princess.* Find out more about her and her books at www. cplesley.com.

When not thinking up new ways to torture her characters, she edits other people's manuscripts, reads voraciously, maintains her website and blog, and takes classes in classical ballet. She also hosts New Books in Historical Fiction, a channel in the New Books Network (http://newbooksinhistoricalfiction.com).

THE GOLDEN LYNX (EXCERPT)
C. P. LESLEY

Kasimov, Sha'ban 940 A.H. / February 1534

THE LYNX FOUND NASAN just before the ambush. She glimpsed its tufted ears through the tangled branches of the birch tree, then lost sight of it when her brother launched his attack. Alerted by his joyous shriek, she jumped sideways and stuck out a foot, sending him somersaulting over the blizzard-kissed ground. She pelted him with snowballs, taunting him. "You forgot again, silly. How can you take me by surprise if you yell like that?"

He lurched to his feet, grumbling, and she laughed. Girei tried, but too often he forgot to save his war cries for battle.

He soon recovered. Most of the snowballs bounced off Nasan's quilted overcoat or hit the birch trees that bounded the clearing they had chosen as their private playground. But a few better-aimed missiles sent icy shivers across her cheeks, reddened by the cold. One smacked her on the forehead, knocking her hat to one side.

She pushed the sheepskin cap into place and aimed another snowball at Girei, who yelped when it broke over his neck. While he scooped ice from inside his coat, she leaped in celebration, bending her legs almost double behind her and shouting, "Hurrah!"

Her moment of exultation cost her. Girei darted toward her, grabbed her round the waist, and tossed her into a drift. The impact jarred loose an entire branch's load, covering her in snow. "Yow," she said. "I'm going to get you for that."

Girei grinned. "You didn't hear me coming, though."

She shook her head, giggling. "No, I didn't. Truce?"

He nodded. Nasan kept a wary eye on him as she wriggled free of her drift. A few months ago, he couldn't have picked her up that way. But these days he seemed to grow taller with each passing minute; for him manhood lay just around the corner. Sha'ban led into Ramadan, and the ending of the fast marked his fifteenth birthday. Within weeks, he would ride off to join the army with their father and older brother. He couldn't wait to go.

Leaving her with their mother and the women. Wives, aunts, cousins, half-sisters, servants: a bevy of females determined to mold Nasan into a replica of themselves—preoccupied with her place among the hierarchy of her eventual husband's pretty playthings. At sixteen, Nasan knew better than to resist marriage and motherhood. Women existed for no other purpose. But while she slept, the grandmother spirits whispered their promise: life offered so much more.

A pair of fingers snapped before her face. "Are you dreaming?" Girei asked. "Possessed? Wake up."

She rubbed her gloved fist against his forehead, where the unruly hair refused to accept the confinement of his hat. "A nightmare, more like. You off to the army, and I to supervise the kitchens. Is that justice?"

"Oh, sister," he said, "if only you could join me."

How she would miss him. No one else understood her as well.

But she could not hold onto him forever. Already a faint mustache showed on his upper lip; his face increasingly resembled the portraits of their ancestor Genghis Khan. Genghis lay hidden in the eastern steppe, long buried in a sacred precinct marked only by the spirit banners where his soul perched between flights, but his illustrious lineage survived in the rulers of Khankirmän, which the Russians called Kasimov. Girei had grown up compact and muscular, short and sturdy like his father, with dark hair and black eyes. His quilted winter trousers and overcoat, the sable hat pulled low over his forehead, only heightened his resemblance to the Mongol warriors of old.

To slip past her mother, Nasan had borrowed clothes from Girei's servant. For these few stolen hours, she reveled in the liberty the garments gave her. She didn't want to be a boy, but she loved the freedom to move, to choose, and to explore that boys took for granted.

Embarrassed by the thought, she brushed snow off her jacket. Pointless to long for the days—only two years past—when she and Girei had raced their ponies across the steppe, ululating their joy into the wind that ruffled the feather grass. The image of Ana appeared before her: an older version of Nasan—slim but indomitable, black hair hidden beneath a cap, dark eyes flashing with annoyance at her daughter's independent ways. "Princesses stay in the palace," her mother's remembered voice said in a tone that brooked no disagreement.

Nasan would pay for her disobedience when she got home. But sunshine had beckoned from outside her window, Girei's departure drew ever closer, and the winter woods lured her with mystery and silence. A scolding seemed a small price for a morning's release from duty.

A flurry of snowballs snapped her back to the present. "Truce over," Girei cried. He bombarded Nasan with what remained of his hoard, then ran for his pony, vaulting into the saddle. "Bet you can't catch me."

Traitor! Snow covered her from nose to hips. Set on revenge, she shook herself off and leaped for her horse's back. Girei had a good head start, but she rode better than he did. Her sure-footed steppe pony dashed along the flattened snow that formed the road—the frozen Oka River on one side, unbroken forest on the other. The horses galloped nose to tail when a dozen men burst from among the trees and grabbed the Tatars' reins.

Russians.

No doubt about that. Many Tatars had European features, but none looked like the leader of this group. A platinum-haired giant, he towered over his men.

Too late, Nasan remembered her mother's warning that more lurked in the woods than screech owls and lynxes.

A man with brown hair and rotting teeth dragged her off her pony as if she weighed no more than the last snowball she'd tossed at Girei. His grip on her waist stopped her breath.

But Nasan had spent much of her childhood wrestling her way into boys' games. Small as she was, she had learned a few tricks. She drummed her heels against her captor's shins until, swearing, he released her and grabbed his leg.

As she pulled away, she felt hard fingers clamp down on her shoulder. Another soldier materialized in front of her. Although shorter than his comrade, he made up for it in girth, and the slap he dealt her hurt. The man she'd kicked clenched his fists. She cowered, hoping to prevent a beating.

Her plan worked. The man grabbed her above the elbow. With both arms secured, Nasan faked acquiescence. Nothing to do but pray that the grandmothers would show her an exit. Pray and watch: the more she learned about their captors, the better her chances of saving herself and her brother.

Meanwhile, Girei fought the two men who held him, excoriating them as the offspring of rabid dogs and whores. The soldiers stood, stolid as the trees around them, immune to insults delivered in a foreign tongue. After a while, the leader walked over, tipped back Girei's head, and looked at him. "Bulat's son, I vow. Boy's the spitting image of him."

He said the words in Russian. Nasan puzzled them out, one by one, wishing she had paid more attention to the language. She had learned Arabic and Persian, but her Russian came from eavesdropping on her brothers' lessons. Custom required her to marry a Muslim; she didn't need Russian. Everyone said so.

But she had a Russian servant. She could have ordered Tanya to teach her.

Too late for regrets. Today she would manage as best she could. But tomorrow she would insist on learning Russian. Tomorrow, after she freed herself and Girei.

The leader examined Nasan as he had her brother. Determined not to show fear, she stared into his frosty eyes and tugged at the unyielding arms that held her. Branches encased in ice refracted the sun's glare in sparkling patterns and cast shadows that shifted with each passing breeze. Bleached by the effect of sunshine on snow, the Russian looked like an ice man. His brows met in the center, like the tufts of a screech owl. A scar, pale with age, bracketed tight, cruel lips.

"Not so clear with this one," he said. "We can't afford a mistake." He tipped his head, considering. Sunshine danced across his face, highlighting an eyebrow, his hooked nose, the whorls of his ear. The hollows of his cheeks remained in shadow, dark as the empty sockets of a skull.

Why had he captured them? He wore the armor of a nobleman, not the rags of a thief. And he could not hope to profit from robbery or murder. Even in these troubled times, the khans of Kasimov protected their own.

The man waved his free hand. "We want to punish Bulat, not expand the blood feud."

She gasped. *Blood feud?*

Three months ago, a Russian had killed one of Nasan's cousins in a drunken brawl. The victim's brothers slew the killer and left his companions unscathed—as honor required. Even Russians understood the code of the steppe: a life for a life, and there the matter ended.

Not this Russian, though. Where the Tatars perceived justice, this man saw vendetta.

The blood drained from her face, leaving her light-headed. This Russian meant death.

They had to get away. On their own, because no one would search for them at this early hour. Ana had ordered them not to leave the palace. Ana did not expect defiance.

But how could Nasan have guessed Russians were hiding in the woods today? She had rubbed the spirit dolls' lips with grease and asked for their blessing, as she did every morning. No hint of regret or warning had crossed her mind.

She must not have listened carefully. Remorse burned her throat.

Ice Man studied her, more monster than man. Nasan shuddered. He liked that, she saw—that he inspired fear. He held her chin a moment longer, then turned back to Girei.

Plans darted through her brain, never settling. In her book of epic tales every heroine, sooner or later, stood alone against the foe. She could not submit. She would not.

The ancestors were testing her. Here, when she least expected it. Spirits often prodded and teased, forcing growth as farmers force a plant. But they helped, too, if asked.

Grandmothers, show me the way!

Her mind cleared, as if an outside force had swept uncertainty from her head. She saw what she must do, laid out before her in miniatures like the ones that adorned her book. Princess Chichek drawing her bow, her arrow whistling toward the target. Princess Saljan, wielding her saber against six hundred soldiers.

The two men gripped her arms. Obedient to the images in her head, she went limp. Her collapse caught her captors off-guard. Using a move she'd learned from her older brother, Nasan kicked the man on her right in the groin and dragged her arm away from him as he doubled over.

The man on her left stumbled. She fell backward, dragging him with her and using his greater weight against him, then twisted away and ran into the forest, shouting, "To me, Girei, to me!" To help him free himself, she dragged a pair of rocks from beneath the snow and hurled one at each of his captors. They staggered.

"The horses!" Girei raced toward her.

Nasan spun on the balls of her feet. Frightened animals surrounded her, bucking and weaving, upset by her shouting. Their hooves trampled the snow. She yelled louder and waved her arms, smacking a few on the rump to increase their frenzy. They spread into an incomplete circle, knocking into one another and their owners.

She hesitated. Horses she understood. Even these horses: the Russians bought theirs from the Tatars. But these beasts had not learned her voice or her smell. Did she have the skills to capture and mount one, let alone keep her seat if she did?

Girei shouted her name in warning. Feet crashing through shrubbery pushed her into a decision. Better to risk a throw from a panicked horse than whatever the Russians planned for her. Amid floundering men and distracted beasts, Nasan vaulted into the nearest saddle. The animal reared. She clung to its mane with both hands and whispered into its ear.

Mashallah, the horse had spent its babyhood among her people. The familiar sounds of Tatar calmed it. It stopped bucking. She patted its neck in encouragement.

A quick glance over her shoulder revealed Girei heading her way—still on foot, but close enough that she watched him reach for a dangling rein. He raised an arm, and with a wave of acknowledgment she sent the gelding hurtling toward the river road, sure Girei was right behind her. In the pandemonium they'd left behind, she doubted anyone would see which direction they took.

At the edge of the trees, she pulled up. No sounds of pursuit disturbed the wintry scene. Exultant, she punched the air. Success, despite the odds! She had overcome the fears of a frightened animal, then ridden it to safety. A few more yards, and she and Girei would find their ponies. They would free the horses they rode and head for home.

Her horse skittered, its hooves slipping on the packed snow, its ears pricked. Swiftly she leaned over its neck, murmuring soothing words and offering a carrot from her pocket. Silence surrounded her.

Then the truth hit home, and she pulled herself upright in the saddle. Her eyes fixed on the woods, and she held her breath, listening for the smallest noise.

No one had followed her—including Girei.

What happened? He was inches from escaping!

The forest remained silent: no horses, no people. She waited, reluctant to breathe in case the Russians heard her, but Girei did not appear. Closer to the palace stood their ponies, digging grass from beneath the packed snow and chewing it. She nudged the captured Russian gelding with her knees, walking it toward the ponies. Her otherworldly calm vanished, leaving her cramped and lost, horrified that her clever plan had saved herself but not her brother.

What to do? Help waited at home, but by the time she rode there, found someone, and persuaded that person to stop scolding her long enough to hear about Girei's predicament, assistance would arrive too late. She had to stay and free him.

But it would be stupid to go back into the woods without sending word. Even more reckless than sneaking out in the first place.

The steppe ponies grazed a few feet away. Nasan slid off the Russian horse, tying it to a tree a safe distance from the road. Girei would need it later. She tiptoed through the snow, then darted at her brother's gelding, slapped its flank with one hand, and grabbed her mare's mane with the other.

Girei's horse ran for its stable without looking back. Nasan exhaled and gentled her mare. When the pony arrived riderless, someone would investigate. Meanwhile, Girei depended on her.

She considered the two horses that remained. If she left them in plain sight, the Russians might find them— and her. But if she hid them, her family would not know where to look. And if she chased them off, she and Girei would have no way to reach home before their enemy recaptured them.

She decided to compromise. "Stay, Sorkhokhtani," she whispered in the mare's ear. Then she checked to see that the trees hid the gelding and slipped back into the woods.

FIVE DIRECTIONS PRESS

THIS BOOK WAS TYPESET using Athelas, a body font inspired by British literary classics, with headings in Cochin Italic, a display font produced in 1913 by Georges Peignot based on the eighteenth-century engravings of Nicolas Cochin— here intended to evoke both the classical formality of ballet and Tarkei script. The desert flower type ornaments come from Poetica Supplemental Ornaments.